So Much Pretty

Cara Hoffman grew up in an economically depressed town in upstate New York. She dropped out of high school, bought a one-way ticket to London with her savings, and spent the next three years working under-the-table jobs in Europe and the Middle East.

In the 1990s, Hoffman returned to the United States, became a mother, and began working as an investigative reporter at a daily newspaper. She covered New York State's rural and Rust Belt communities for over a decade, reporting on environmental politics, county legislatures, and crime. In 2000 she received a New York State Foundation for the Arts Fellowship for her writing on the aesthetics of violence and its impact on children.

Hoffman lives in Manhattan with her son and works as a tutor at the Lower Eastside Girls Club. This is her first novel.

Praise for *So Much Pretty*

'Intelligent and gripping stuff.'

Financial Times

'This beautiful, stealthy novel creeps up on the mesmerized reader, subtly drawing new strands into itself until what begins as the suspenseful story of a rural American murder grows into a dark, disquieting and urgently fascinating examination of the violence and concealment practiced by a whole society ... Hoffman never surrenders the compassion, insightfulness and humor that make her a masterful navigator of the human heart. This is an impassioned, intelligent and important work of art.'

Chris Cleave, author of *The Other Hand*

'[A] fearless first novel ... For all the passion in this intense narrative, Hoffman writes with a restraint that makes poetry of pain. She also shows a mastery of her craft by developing the story over 17 years and narrating it from multiple perspectives. While each has a different take on the horrific events that no one saw coming, the people who live in this insular place remain willfully blind to their own contributions to the deeper causes that made this tragedy almost inevitable.'

New York Times Book Review

'A dark but powerful debut ... Hoffman maps the atmosphere of paranoia that descends on the formerly tranquil town as she moves deftly between its inhabitants.'

The New Yorker

'A mixture of *The Lovely Bones* and *The Girl with the Dragon Tattoo*...
Hoffman's narrative oscillates between various characters, carefully building suspense, depth, and new insight with every chapter.
Let's hope we will be seeing more of this talented new writer.'

Booklist

'A spectacular debut: This beautifully constructed mystery, with its engaging characters and intriguing premise, has everything a reader wants.'

Globe and Mail

'In this remarkable debut, Hoffman addresses serious injustices in present-day America.... This searing novel will linger long in the reader's memory.'

Publishers Weekly, starred review

'The way investigative reporter Hoffman navigates the line between what is spoken and unspoken, and portrays a community's desire to address any crisis but the one next door make *So Much Pretty* a staggering read.'

Huffington Post

'*So Much Pretty* delivers a skillful, psychologically acute tale of how violence affects a small town ... To say more about Hoffman's constantly surprising story is to reveal too much, but the payoff is more than worth the slow-building suspense.'

Los Angeles Times

'Dark, atmospheric tale of murder in a small-town world.'

Stylist

'[Hoffman's] insight into the psychology of violence is eye-opening and cleverly wrapped in this chilling novel.'

The Bookbag.co.uk

So Much Pretty

CARA HOFFMAN

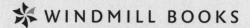
WINDMILL BOOKS

Published by Windmill Books 2012

2 4 6 8 10 9 7 5 3

Published in arrangement with the original Publisher,
Simon & Schuster, Inc. New York

First published in Great Britain in 2012 by Century

Windmill Books
The Random House Group Limited
20 Vauxhall Bridge Road, London SW1V 2SA

Addresses for companies within The Random House Group Limited can be found at:
www.randomhouse.co.uk/offices.htm

The Random House Group Limited Reg. No. 954009

www.randomhouse.co.uk

A CIP catalogue record for this book
is available from the British Library

ISBN 9780099558484

The Random House Group Limited supports The Forest Stewardship Council
(FSC®), the leading international forest certification organisation. Our books
carrying the FSC label are printed on FSC® certified paper. FSC is the only
forest certification scheme endorsed by the leading environmental organisations,
including Greenpeace. Our paper procurement policy can be found at:
www.randomhouse.co.uk/environment

Printed and bound in Great Britain by
Clays Ltd, St Ives plc

For Noah

So Much Pretty

Prologue

THEY ARE LOOKING for someone with blond or dark brown or black hair.

Someone with blue or maybe brown or green eyes. She could be five foot six or five-eight. Her hair could also be red, could be an unnatural color like pink or white.

It is likely she weighs between 110 and 140 pounds and may have a scar or bruise on her throat.

She would be working somewhere unseen. Working as a waitress or secretary or laborer. She could be a student. There is a strong possibility she would have a nontraditional job. That she's transient, works agriculture or construction or second shift.

She has physical strength and is articulate. Could be speaking English or Spanish or French. Could be in New York or Illinois or Tennessee. Canada or Mexico. Places where it rains all day or places where the grass has burnt to yellow. Could be among hollows between road and field, trails where the creek bed has dried. Could be anywhere.

She could be hitchhiking or taking public transportation, could be walking. She could be named Jamie, or Catherine, or Liz. Alexandra, Annie, Maria. Any name at all.

She may be aloof. She may be sensitive and drawn to helping people.

She is on her own and likely broke, and might be reliant on those she doesn't know.

Searches peaked in the spring and summer months, and they are looking for her still.

As we are well aware, it is easy for a woman who fits this description to just disappear.

Claire

ALL THREE OF us walked in our sleep.

Later, when I would think about what happened, I would tell myself she was sleepwalking. Acting out a nightmare. Sleepwalking ran in our family. Dreaming while walking. Dreaming while talking. I know this is not an answer. The real answer is too simple.

Did she have health problems? Was she low–birth weight? Did she have headaches? Self-destructive behavior? Sudden changes in grades or friends? No.

Alice was a remarkably consistent soul. Healthy and athletic like her father. At home wherever she was. Happy at school and happy with all the things outside of school. Gymnastics and trapeze. And later, swimming, building, archery, shooting.

Her focus was so joyful, so intense. Like her happiness, when she was little, about swimming in the river, about building the cardboard forest or the paper Taj Mahal. Once she made a mobile of hundreds of origami frogs, locusts, paper dolls, and butterflies.

She was never bored. Had the same friends at sixteen as she'd had at four. Her teachers talked about how she was a "leader." It was a word they used often, and this is certainly part of the problem. "A Leader." But they also talked about how she was sensitive to other children, always so caring.

I am not trying to justify a thing. I am not trying to make excuses for my daughter. I am describing it as it was.

Before April 14, the words "I am Alice Piper's mother" meant very little to anyone but me. Now those words are a riddle, a koan. A thing I have to understand even though nothing will change, even though the phrase "nothing will change" is something we fought against our entire lives.

The years in which we raised her were marked by diminishing returns for our diminishing expectations. But it hadn't always been that way.

Things were different in the city. We moved because of Constant's uncle. Because of Gene's dreams about land and air and autonomy. But also because of me. Because of traffic and noise and sewer smells and the seventy hours a week I worked at the city's Comprehensive Free Clinic for the Uninsured on First Avenue.

Prior to moving upstate, Gene and I lived on Saint Mark's and First Avenue. Then later in a two-bedroom apartment on First and Seventh, with Constant and Michelle Mann, who were also done with their residencies and, like Gene and I, planned on working for Doctors Without Borders. We moved to First and Seventh because of the rooftop, so Gene could have space to plant. In those days everyone but Gene was exhausted—sometimes punch-drunk on three hours of sleep a night, nodding off on the subway coming home from Lenox Hill or staggering bleary-eyed in clogs and scrubs from Beth Israel or CFC. We all felt like the walking dead, knew we were in bad shape, envying Gene, especially later, when he was home all day with the baby. In the end, moving to Haeden was all we wanted.

When we drove out to the house and barn through that wet and green countryside, we were excited. We would finally have a place of our own. The apparent beauty and possibility of it all was overwhelming, something we had tried and failed to build for ourselves the last six years in New York.

Even the double-wides and sloping farmhouses with their black POW and American flags seemed oddly majestic with so much land around them, the tiniest trailers close to creeks or ponds.

As we drove in, I was thinking about Michelle when we worked in the clinic together, saying the responsibility of every intelligent person is to pay attention to the obvious. How had we missed the obvious benefit of all this land? A whole house and acreage for the cost of one room on the Lower East Side. I was thinking how, the second we got out of the car and brought our boxes inside and wrote Uncle Ross his rent check, this whole thing would start. In those days I could not wait for it to start.

Alice was two then, and we walked inside and put our boxes down and sat on the kitchen floor, nervous and tired from the drive, eating some blueberries we had bought on the way. She had just woken up and her face was placid and her hair was tangled and she leaned against me eating blueberries, her body warm and gentle from sleep. Then evening came in from the fields and lit the place with sound and stars. Peepers called up from the river, and crickets played below the windows in the grass. It was the first time Alice had heard crickets, and we went out on the porch together, Gene and I, watched her listen, quiet and alert and hunkered down, her whole body taking in the sound. Her blue-stained lips parted and her eyes shining.

It was Alice's happiness, her joy in those moments, that allowed me to stay even years after, when paying attention to the obvious became a horror.

And for a long time we did not regret our singular vision. Our attempt to strip the irony from the slogans we'd come to live by. Phrases that buoyed us and embarrassed us at the same time. "Demand the Impossible," "Beneath the Paving Stones, the Beach," anarchist sentiments we first took up in the city as a joke, then ultimately to comfort one another, to remind ourselves that we were different from our cohorts. Those words seemed—with all the incessant construction, and the destruction of the natural world, and Gene becoming fixated on "living the solution" and bringing down corporate agribusiness—more poignant at that time than when real revolutionaries scrawled them on the Paris streets in 1968. We might not have been burning cars and shutting down a city, but we were living in the sterile and violent future they had imagined, and we were certainly committed to destroying one culture by cultivating another.

This sensibility was one more way we were sleepwalking, dreaming. We did not stick with our plan. Though all four of us had passed the initial screening process for Doctors Without Borders, only one of us left on assignment. Gene and I were graced with Alice; Constant became plagued by an American concept of freedom, liquidity, mobility. These changes did not seem pivotal at the time, seemed instead the best possible outcome, exciting, a release. And how could we not admit that what we had been looking for by joining Doctors Without Borders was a release. Absolution from the lifestyle our postresidency careers seemed to necessitate, a lifestyle that was making the four of us—and not our colleagues—sick.

Those early years in Haeden were restful. Literally. Luxurious eight- and ten-hour nights. Waking up to quiet and birds instead of traffic. No six A.M. meetings at the clinic. Each season with its own particular beauty.

Bright, quiet winters snowed in and baking bread together, sitting around the woodstove, each of us silently reading. Summers resonant with the hum and staggered harmony of insects. The meadow in front of our house growing tall and strange from the warm rain. Swimming in the river and tending our vegetable garden. Alice could talk pretty well when we moved, and she loved the sounds, imitated them. Never herself, she was a frog, a mermaid, a bird. Radiant fall spent roasting and canning peppers with the smell of wood smoke on the cool air. And spring: Alice's favorite time in the world, when everything comes back to life and it's warm, with patches of snow, and we would wear shorts and big rubber boots and celebrate the first snowbells and crocuses. The air was lush and still cold and smelled like mud. Alice loved to run along the mowed path all the way to the river. In those early summers she was no taller than the goldenrod, just a head above the jack-in-the-pulpit that flanked the trails between the barn and woods. She loved to climb in the exposed roots of trees along the pebbled riverbank and collect stones and dried skeletons of crayfish. She was fearless.

We expected after a few years our friends would come, build, plant. Once Constant had made the money he wanted, once Michelle had finished her assignment, we would get back to the land, we would live and drink and work by the ideals we'd always had. Mutual Aid, No Boredom.

We expected, when Alice was bigger, we'd have enough money to have a real farm and for me to go back to some kind of practice. But these things never happened, and paying attention to the darker aspects of the obvious became a bad way to live if we wanted to stay happy and make friends.

Sleep had won out at last. We moved through our days in Haeden in a somnolent kind of daze, blithe when our senses called for panic, blind to our deepest fear, even as it lay, naked among the tall weeds, waiting.

Flynn

WHEN I GOT to the woods, they had not yet moved her. I ducked under a makeshift barricade—a carpenter's horse painted orange—so I could get closer, and I stood looking at the taped-off gully until a form became clear in what had previously looked like a pile of discarded clothes. A hand revealed itself to be connected to a pale mottled arm reaching forward, a twist of denim and pink. And then the tangle of blond hair, which wisped across white lips, one open eye and skin like skim milk shining through the mud, reflecting back the blue and red strobe from the cop cars.

Dino was looking up the road away from the woods, talking on his radio, and Giles walked past me unwinding a roll of yellow tape. His face was red. No one else was there yet. I had run down from the office when I heard it on the scanner.

I had my notebook out already and didn't realize I had walked around to the other side of the ditch and crouched beside the body until I glanced up and took in the woods and road from another angle. Saw what she might have seen in the last moments she lay there, had she been alive. New red leaves and blue buds. Scrub grass, gravel, generations of wet and blackened leaves, something pale green and flowerless about to uncurl. I rested my gaze on these things for a moment before standing to take in the situation at hand.

"Is it White?" I asked Dino. I saw the pink sweatshirt, dirt-covered legs beneath the miniskirt and long wide bare feet, chipped toenails lacquered with the last fading ghost of clear glitter nail polish.

"Is this Wendy White?" I knew immediately that she had not been there as long as she'd been missing. Hollow-cheeked as she was, she'd clearly arrived a few hours before us at most. The smell of filth and staleness, not decomposition, hung in the air. A wave of nausea descended upon me and raised sweat across my back, up my neck. Giles walked by again, now wearing rubber gloves and a dust mask. This was not the way they did it back in Cleveland.

"Still haven't gotten ahold of him," Dino told Giles.

"Try again. Maybe he's up at the dairy."

I wrote the date and time across the narrow page. It was April 3, 2009. I walked back over to stand next to Dino and didn't say another word to him. I had nothing to ask him that I couldn't already see.

Later, I would have difficulty driving past Tern Woods without holding my breath. I would see the marker for the "woods," a little wedge of remaining forest, not half the size of a city block, and forget to inhale.

Wendy White is a name people know the same way they know the name Haeden—both have entered into the national vocabulary as catalysts, a particular kind of tragic iconography. I was interviewed a few times about the White case and about April 14. I tried to put it in a broader social context, but somehow I was unable to ever really make things clear. I talked about national statistics on rape, on abduction, on rural poverty, on adolescent violence, but then the show would air and it would be me talking about April 14, or worse, me talking about me.

The first and last "TV reenactment" I was interviewed for was during the early days of the search for Alice Piper. A studio interview for which I was asked to wear contact lenses.

"You arrived at the same time as the police," the interviewer asked by way of statement.

"Yes."

"Five months had gone by since anyone had seen Wendy White," he said, softly emphasizing the word "months." His face was tense, telegraphing the response I was supposed to give. A brief holding-forth through silence in which I could suddenly smell his cologne. Then he said, "It must have been a horrifying scene."

He was only out of character for a moment; he raised his eyebrows and gave a nearly imperceptible nod. I had a sudden sense that his next question might be about whether it was hard for me to stand in the woods in high heels. Whether my boyfriend had to come pick me up after I puked or peed my pants. I knew I wasn't a source, wasn't telling him any story—I was part of the story.

Then he said, "Were you frightened?"

I remember the feeling of wanting to stand up and walk out. I remember the heat of the fill light and thinking, *I will never do this again.* And the vague sense of paralysis that prevented me from leaving but unfortunately didn't prevent me from rolling my eyes and making an impatient "wrap this up" gesture, which was not the kind of press I needed, considering my "situation."

In the footage I am wearing pale pink lipstick and a black turtleneck. The interview lasted eight minutes, but they had to do several takes because they said I squinted. I smirked. Kept shrugging.

When I watched it, I couldn't get further than my answer before turning it off, disgusted with my own face, ashamed I had ever agreed to talk about it again.

"Well," I exhale, shake my head slightly. "I don't get what you mean."

"Let me ask you this . . ." the interviewer begins. He would ask me what I was really brought there to answer. What made me a subject instead of a peer.

"Why?" he would ask. "Why did you write what you wrote after Wendy White was found?"

I want to put this event in context. If you just want to read about April 14, you can go buy one of those paperbacks they sell in the checkout line at Wal-Mart. But if you want to know what really happened, you need to know where it happened. And you need to know why. You need to know who Wendy White was and that I made some mistakes. I didn't intend to become part of this story.

I took this job when I was twenty-four. White was nineteen the night she walked out of work at the Alibi and never came back. I am not trying to avoid my responsibility, say that I was too young to see the things I saw. I'm just making sure the details are straight.

Prior to taking the job, I was writing for an independent in Cleveland, and I had a pretty good little scene going on. I lived on Schiller Street, where there were still a lot of family duplexes and old houses and where the abandoned mills and meatpacking plants were being converted into studios or bright, high-ceilinged offices for start-ups that had moved into the neighborhood. My apartment was a tall efficient box of exposed brick and leaded-glass windows that buzzed when trucks drove past, cool in the summer and cold in the winter, with a fire escape overlooking garbage cans. There was a renaissance of strangeness going on in the neighborhood. Sculptors, painters, art students, and busi-nesspeople rented space alongside old Jewish and Slavic and black families, several generations living in the same sprawling houses divided up into apartments. Grandparents on the porches and wiseass scruffy kids on the sidewalk. It was a neighborhood in the process of being converted and would soon morph into a business and tourist district. At the time I didn't like it, the gentrification, but a few weeks after moving to Haeden, I longed for the life of my old neighborhood badly, especially the sounds; traffic, parties, kids on the street. The utter silence of my new home woke me up at night.

I stayed in Haeden at first because I was committed to writing my big-picture story. And because I wanted the word "editor" on my résumé. But I did not stay there comfortably.

Haeden was the whitest place I had ever been. And it was a

specific kind of whiteness, a blankness I'd never experienced. Apart from the musicians, who played at the Rooster and the Alibi, and the guy who made stump sculptures of bears and eagles, and the ladies who knitted afghans or painted landscapes on rusty saws, there wasn't much of a scene.

Before I took the job, the *Free Press* was run by a guy named Stephen Cooper. He had been the paper's editor, reporter, and photographer for thirty years. Everyone called him "Scoop." Nice nickname, if not exactly accurate. A weekly paper in a one-paper town rarely gets the chance to break news, and the major competitor usually has the word "swapsheet" or "pennysaver" in its masthead. Still, his was one of the few important professions left in town: chief of police, head of public works, town judge, volunteer fire chief, and Scoop. A tight affiliation of people who kept the place from becoming just a point on Route 34 you'd miss if you closed your eyes for eight seconds while driving by. My job was to write all the content for the paper, making it folksy and general enough so that it could be reprinted in five other local papers if the need arose. *Free Press* was owned by *Weekly Circular.* My paycheck came from Syracuse, New York, and was not signed but was stamped by a name I was unfamiliar with. Despite the fact that I had clearly replaced Scoop, he liked to act as though he were my boss. He had after all interviewed me for the position.

Scoop smelled. Fried onions or peppermint or sweat. He wore yellow suspenders and a flannel shirt nearly every day, like a uniform. In winter he wore long underwear under the flannel, and in summer he just rolled up the sleeves. He was tall and very thin and had an unruly salt-and-pepper beard to which crumbs stuck; he would let it grow up his face to just beneath his eyes before finally shaving. Scoop would come around the office once a week or so to see how things were going. And things were going dull and well before the White thing happened.

For the most part, Scoop was a good guy and a decent writer.

He left Haeden for J-school in the sixties, then came back and took over the paper from some other old guy who was retiring. That was the longest Scoop had been away from home. Upon his return, he moved into the house in which his grandfather was born. Also the house in which his father and he and his brothers were born. He married the girl he'd dated in high school: a smart, round woman who taught third grade. All this background is just a way of saying Scoop wasn't a guy from whom I was taking reporting advice.

A couple days after White disappeared, Scoop took me target shooting, a local pleasure for which I had no aptitude. Then he took me to the VFW for beer, gave me a can of pepper spray to keep in my pocket, and told me to keep an eye on the White case. I was not happy about the impromptu meeting. I had my own story ideas and hadn't thought much about White. I had assumed she ran away because she was bored, something I felt I might do at any minute. I had to keep reminding myself that Haeden being boring was actually part of the reason I was there. The perceived tranquillity, the silence, the old family homes, the meth labs and poverty and giant swaths of corn-infested, shit-covered nowhere, lives intersecting and connecting through pure habit. The meanings of things having been shaken loose half a century ago.

I understood that this was Haeden: Apart from the lake and the river and the little chunks of forest, the town itself had evolved into a strip of highway that doubled as the village's main road. This was lined with a strange mix of houses, old brick buildings, and a little farther out, chains and big box stores: Home Depot, Subway, Wal-Mart. The edge of Tern Woods was a parking lot, a wide black expanse of asphalt with a grid of yellow lines covering what had once been the fullness of a forest. The lot was often empty, and during the hours when people were shopping, it was barely half full.

Haeden was supposed to be farming country. I thought maybe

I'd see sheep and cows wandering around on the hillsides, but this was no country I could reconcile with my imagination. And this became the main focus of my reporting—the disparity between what things were called and what they actually were. In a million ways, this little town was getting fucked over just like the low-income neighborhoods in Cleveland—environmental problems, food prices, bad mental-health services, disproportionate numbers of returning veterans, poverty, obesity—but unlike in Cleveland, these people were isolated, scattered throughout the county roads where the sound of a rifle report or a tractor motor was more common than a neighbor's voice.

When I first took the job, Scoop said I would need to get off the main roads to see some of the big farms. Which I was very happy to do. He told me I should drive out to see the Haytes dairy and gave me directions. Told me that the Haytes and three other farms were what constituted the real local economy, unlike what he called the franchises, by which he really meant multinationals.

I was waiting for the rain to stop before I scouted for farms. It seemed to rain constantly in central New York, and I had yet to get used to it. The sky was often a solid white-gray color for days at a time. The first sunny day that came along, I set out on County Road 227 in the direction of fucking nowhere with the windows down and the Pretenders playing on the radio. Haytes Road was five miles in that direction, and I found it easily, as the dairy could be seen from miles away, atop the low green hillside, from the winding road below.

Part of the road had washed away and collapsed into a ditch filled with mud and stones and grasses. The air was lush and humid. I stuck to the middle of the road, where it crisscrossed the gentle incline. As I got closer to the dairy, gravel gave way to a new, shiny black asphalt drive as wide as a highway, leading all the way to the central complex, the slate-and-silver-colored pole barns separated by narrower roads and footpaths comprising the enormity of the Haytes empire. From the top of the hill, you could see the entire farm. It took up what would have been four or five city blocks. You could also smell it.

Three metal buildings like storage units or warehouses, as big as football fields, were butted up to one another, windowless and silent. There were two massive lagoons of liquefied manure, millions of gallons stored in dark blue two-story open tanks flanking the operation. A chemical smell hung over the surrounding area, not like cow manure but something else, something rancid and chlorinated. It was nauseating, and even up on the hill, it made your eyes burn. Driving back through the valley and past the buildings, the smell was worse, but oddly, there were no flies. I heard no insects or birds at all. And the land around the warehouses was all poured concrete that appeared smooth and almost polished. The low grasses near the various pole barns and modern concrete structures were yellow and powdery white. I stopped the car and looked up at the buildings and contemplated the vast scale of the manure tanks.

Scoop had told me this was the oldest farm in the county, here before the town was even built. Owned by the Haytes brothers. I realized, standing there, that I didn't know what a farm was.

And driving along the dirt roads back to town, I realized I didn't know what the countryside was, either. Mile after mile of lost places. Old wind-and-rain-battered houses, the windows empty of shades or curtains and sometimes glass. You could look right into these houses, right through them. Piles of garbage and furniture stacked up to the ceiling were visible in the upstairs of one rickety colonial, the porch crumbling, filled with empty paint cans, rusting tools, tarps, and canvases. It was like the owners or tenants had just disappeared, or might have died there and no one had happened along to find out. Farther down the road, five weathered school buses were up on blocks outside a barn with a caved-in roof, the paint faded to white and peeling from the sides. There must have been a school bus auction at one time, because I'd seen buses on property closer to town that looked like they had been converted into trailer homes, and old Ross had a school bus on his land, too. There also must have been a fire sale on American flags and prisoner of war paraphernalia.

Beyond the buses and some silent stretches of corn and soybean fields was an overgrown rectangular weed yard filled with junked tractors, lawn mowers, and agricultural equipment, some of it antiquated; a hand-painted sign on weathered plywood in front of the wreckage read TRACTORS WANTED DEAD OR ALIVE. The wide frame of a sprayer was tangled in a bale of chicken wire; the broken and twisted necks of hay balers, threshers, and metal objects that couldn't be identified were scattered and forgotten, nothing but rust exoskeletons of their former selves. Broken machinery as far as the hills.

Beyond the farm-equipment boneyard sat a quasi-neighborhood of double-wide trailers, all slate green and dank gray-white, sidled up to their driveways close to the road. The yards held satellite dishes of various sizes, one nearly as big as the metal swing set that stood unoccupied beside the septic tank. Some yards sported tall white flagpoles flying American and black POW flags. Others were replete with painted white tractor tires, makeshift flower beds in which marigolds grew. One of the trailers had Christmas decorations laid flat in its crabgrass yard. Jesus and Rudolph, wide-eyed and partly covered with mud. Two feet of white picket fence, made of wood-textured plastic, stuck out of the ground on either side of the cinderblock stairs. A wreath hung on the dented metal door. No one played or worked outside. And apart from the occasional silhouette of a human form in front of a television, no one was visible inside the trailers that day.

Farther down the road were vinyl-sided ranch houses with attached garages. Then a variety of smaller restored farmhouses, and enormous vinyl-sided mansions with oversize Palladian windows, and newly dug ponds. Closer to town, a square white

Greek revival stood blind at the end of a winding drive, overlooking a meadow of phlox and chicory. Long driveways housed tarp-covered boats on trailers parked off to the side under open carports.

I drove back to my apartment that day knowing where I really lived, and knowing I'd never be able to write about it for a tiny local. I was excited. I figured I'd be able to pitch this ghost-town U.S.A. story pretty widely. Wendy had yet to disappear. Piper had yet to become a household name. And I was definitely frightened in a way I had never felt on Schiller Street. The valley below Haytes Road seemed to me a dangerous place to live.

Gene

SHE WAS WEARING black-and-white-striped tights and a large paper bag into which she'd cut holes for her arms and head and drawn a picture of a tree in green Magic Marker. She was folded at the knees, hanging from a low bar connected to yards of heavy rope, which was attached to the ceiling of the barn. Her hair hung down, almost brushed the floor. Her face was flushed with the blood running to her head. She smiled, and her tiny white teeth formed a frown. Beneath her was a pile of straw, around which several pairs of socks with sewn-on button eyes lay, staring up at the vast and empty space.

"Are you getting hungry?" Gene asked her. He was still standing in the wide square doorway. "There's food in the house when you get done hanging. Uncle Ross is coming over for dinner. And I think he's bringing someone you want to see."

"Then we'll need another trapeze," Alice said. She smiled and stretched her arms out at her sides, then extended them forward and curled up to hold the bar with her hands.

"I could not agree more," Gene said. "One trapeze is hardly enough."

She pulled herself into a sitting position, then grabbed the sides of the rope so she could perch in her stiff and crumpled bag. Her hair was so blond it was almost white. Her eyes were an icy translucent blue. Her skin was pale, but her cheeks were rosy from playing and hanging. The light dust of freckles that covered her cheeks and nose was invisible.

She was a strong four-year-old and had the aquiline features of her father. Had his muscles in miniature, his flexibility, his distant dreamy face. He wondered sometimes if her skeleton looked like his.

He watched her swing. Watched her think as she looked up into the rafters. Her lips moved as she said something to herself he couldn't hear.

"Well, legs," Gene said, "I know you're a tree today, but you might get hungry nevertheless. And there are some people who want to see you."

Alice smiled wide at him but didn't move. She was always hesitant to leave the barn, and he had to convince her.

"Somebody special, maybe," Gene said.

"Someone like Theo?"

Gene nodded at her. She stood on the trapeze and began pumping her knees to swing, looking up at the ceiling. Gene looked, too.

Swallows glided, diving in arcs inside the barn. They flew with her. Their ragged nests, dark in the corners at the loft's beam, like the straw bales below that she landed on from the trapeze. The place smelled wonderful. Like hay and rotten apples, grease and the faint musty odor of mold. She could swing very high because the rope was so long. She closed and opened her eyes quickly while she swung, he knew, to get a strobe effect from the sunlight shining through the slats.

Gene saw how she got lost in it, made herself dizzy, played at being upside down with her head raised to the ceiling, somehow claiming the entire space, claiming every direction, a seamless radius around herself.

"Jesus!" he said. "You are one brave girl. Ready to jump?" He held out his arms, clapped his hands. Then counted with every upswing. "One . . . two . . . three. HUP!"

Alice leaped from the trapeze, her legs bent and braced to land, her arms outstretched toward her father. The bag made a loud hollow crumpling sound as he caught her, and they both laughed. She had her mother's dimple on the left cheek. Her eyes shone, curved into little arcs, her blond eyebrows and eyelashes visible only when she was this close to him. Her body was strong and delicate in his arms, and he felt like he'd caught something wild.

He kissed her on the cheek and hoisted her to his shoulders, carried her out and along the long mowed path to the little farmhouse. Ross's truck was parked in the driveway, and the doors were open. They could hear the old MC5 album, Claire's favorite, playing on the five-dollar thrift-store turntable—a kid's toy, really—the tiny speaker thumping and threatening to blow out.

Ross Miller was drinking from a brown bottle with a white label, sitting at the table with his five-year-old nephew Theo. Ross wore what Claire called his Libertarian Avenger Uniform: plain white T-shirt, Wrangler jeans, his VFW baseball cap with a little American flag pinned upside down across the front, and square BluBlocker sunglasses that wrapped around the sides of his head. He was a skinny man but strong and poised, with big straight white teeth. Nodded when he talked. Squinted and looked out of the corners of his eyes. He was known for long pained pauses in conversation in which he appeared to be considering whether or not it was worthwhile to go on speaking.

Ross was not related to the Pipers. He owned the house where Gene and Claire and Alice lived. He owned the barn and the fields and woods that lay between the Pipers' house and the ramshackle compound he called home—a metal pole barn, a black and gray yurt built on an assortment of salvaged concrete blocks, and two gutted school buses, the one in which he slept retrofitted with an unfinished roof of partially shingled copper flashing and a chimney for the pellet stove.

The boy, Theo, was a tall lanky towhead one year older than Alice. His parents lived in Haeden but taught classics at the university in a neighboring town. Their commute and workload and social schedule often resulted in the boy spending several days a week with his Uncle Ross. During the two years that Gene and Claire had rented Ross's house, the children had become inseparable. There in the kitchen, Theo was fully engrossed in playing with two large rectangular magnets, making one repel the other across the table.

The fact was, the adults had become inseparable in many ways, too. For Gene and Claire, moving to Haeden instead of somewhere else upstate was simply a matter of who knew whom. In this case the whom was Ross, and the who was Gene's best friend, Constant Souriani, who had introduced them. Constant was related to Ross by marriage and had visited Haeden often—first when his Aunt Hediya married the man and, later, on weekend trips after he moved to the States to attend NYU.

The house had been a dream for Gene and Claire, but apart from their friendship with Ross and their daughter's love of Theo, the reality of living in a town this small was something they were only just beginning to feel. There were few people their age there. Young families were becoming less common than the middle-aged and older couples hanging on to the remains of land and buildings that had been willed to them. Not too many people moved to Haeden, and it was obvious that the Pipers' newness would be new for as long as they lived there. Despite what Constant had told them about friendly small-town life, people did not warm up quickly to "outsiders."

It seemed the place was closed to the idea of a wider world. So resistant that people would continue to use words like "farm," "forest," and "town" long after the words no longer fit the reality of the landscape. Haeden was being collectively dreamed by its inhabitants, Gene thought. And in a way, it was a beautiful thing. He and Claire wanted to be part of that collective dreaming, the most recent reinvention of getting back to the land. And they had every intention of making it work.

Gene and Claire hadn't moved here blind; they might be idealistic, but they had studied the demographics. Unless one of them went back to practice, chances of finding a job weren't great. The largest employers in Haeden were not in Haeden at all. They were a big box store in the next town and a university a couple of towns beyond that. They had also understood that Haeden's transformation from a self-contained farming village to a service-industry bedroom community on the margins of Appalachia was something that could be felt but was not discussed. A secret shame among friends. Gene and Claire believed all that could be changed. With the right influx of energy. With the right attitude.

Some days the idea of change made Gene almost manic. What surrounded them was intoxicating—so much space, so much opportunity—he felt that with enough time, they would make it their own.

In the summer of 1995, sitting parked in the silver Mazda outside the odd, slightly sloping yellow farmhouse with the car windows rolled down and tears of relief in her eyes, Claire had breathed in the smell of grass and a sweet smell of things gone to seed, and Gene had watched as she surveyed the old clapboard and dormer windows, the overgrown clematis winding up the white pillars and out along the clogged gutter, thick with black decaying leaves. They could not believe their good fortune.

Back in the baby seat, Alice slept surrounded by boxes and backpacks. Everything they owned fit in the two-door.

Sensing Claire's slight pinch of guilt at having this new home and leaving her patients at the clinic behind, Gene leaned over and kissed her. "We're going to be way more useful here than anywhere we've ever lived," he said. "We're fucking DIY, baby, and we're going to get things done."

He looked at Claire now, sitting on the counter in bare feet and a long denim skirt, wearing a white tank top screen-printed with the words CFC 5K RUN. Claire had strong ropy arms and legs, veins and tendons showing in her feet, in her forearms and hands. He loved the way she carried her otherwise voluptuous body with an unconscious tomboyish grace.

The kitchen smelled like cumin. Pots hung from the ceiling on hooks. A wall of square shelves served as a pantry and dish cupboard. One of Alice's little wooden chairs was pushed up next to a pot containing a young avocado tree, its lower branches spread out along the floor, circling the chair. Blocks and wooden animals sat in the dirt at the base of the plant, as well as a notebook, crayons, and binoculars.

Claire looked up and smiled at Gene and Alice, stopped talking to Ross in midsentence. "Oh, good!" she said. "We were *waiting* for the tree. C'mere, tree." She picked the girl up and hugged her tight. The bag crumpled and tore a little at Alice's shoulder. Claire looked at her daughter's rosy face, kissed her. Alice was sweaty, but she still had an otherworldly baby smell: milk, grass, rain on pavement, carnation. Claire put her nose on the girl's hair and closed her eyes. "Did you see who was here?" she asked quietly into the top of Alice's head. Ross sometimes made the girl nervous; Claire could always make her feel relaxed, give Alice strength by simply holding her or speaking one quiet sentence in her warm tenor voice.

Alice nodded. Put her forehead on her mother's chest, wrapped her legs around her waist. "It's Theophile!" Claire said, smiling, and the dimple in her cheek revealed itself, then disappeared. Alice's eyes brightened, and Claire put her down.

Theo, who had been waiting, jumped off his chair. "He gave me the magnets," the boy said, following Alice into the living room. Gene grabbed a Saranac from the refrigerator and stood before his wife for a minute.

"What are you grinning at?" Claire asked him.

He shook his head, touched her waist gently to feel the smooth skin beneath her shirt. "Ross, you need another?" he asked.

"Nah, not right now," Ross said. "I was just telling Claire about these assholes at the VFW who don't believe we're starving the Iraqis to death with these fucking sanctions so we can occupy that region for the next millennium. Christ, what the Christ do you take out a country's infrastructure for? They're not stupid. Why the fuck else do you do it?"

"Wait," Gene said. "I think you told me about this."

"Nah. That was last Sunday, same assholes. We're just sheep, man. Especially those bastards at the VFW. You'd think we'd have some idea about what's going on."

"'We'?" Gene asked.

"Yeah. We, goddammit. Did you get up in this country today and drink a cup of coffee?" Ross paused, squinted, and pushed up his sunglasses. "*We* fucking live here, man. I don't just mean the true believers." He nodded to himself, and his eyebrows became visible for a moment above the heavy frames of his glasses. "*We! Me and you and all of us that came here to do the right thing!*"

"You were born here," Gene said.

"Well, I *stayed* here because of the good folks, not 'cause of some assholes who were happy to go off to Vietnam and then happy to see their kids go off to Iraq."

"Plus, you had all that good weed back then," Claire said, winking at him.

"That's another story," Ross said, laughing. "And don't think that story's unrelated, 'cause it isn't! Everything's connected, is my point."

The sun was starting to get lower in the sky. On the turntable, the Motor City 5 scratched out a tinny driving refrain, and Claire smiled broadly. "You know this band, Ross?"

"Can't say I do." He stretched his legs out and folded his hands on top of his cap. "But they're pissed about something."

She laughed. "We're going to have to do something about your musical education. This is the album that got me through residency."

The low ambient hum of insects came to their ears between the thump of the chorus: *Call me animal, that's my name, call me animal, I'm not ashamed.* Gene admired Claire's lips as she softly sang along.

Ross and Claire had slipped into silent reveries of their soldier days. This happened sometimes, and Gene would observe them, blanked out but somehow tied to each other, safe and gone. And still wearing the flag, the badges and scrubs from fights no one even knew had taken place. Fights no one here would believe happened, or care too much about if they did.

Gene sat with their distance and their proximity. Far away now from Vietnam and far away from the secondhand poverty and violence that made Claire what Claire was. Not quite underground, and maybe never able to live at the surface. A mother, whispering in her kitchen; his wife, his oldest friend, mentally leafing through a vespertime hymnal of the Motor City 5 while Ross talked about war. He'd seen it before: MC5 or the Clash or the Ramones used to drown out the din of silence in her head when the image of teenage girls sitting in waiting rooms with their caseworkers got to be too much. He remembered her, drunk and dancing to "Know Your Rights" on the jukebox at the International on First Avenue after work. Remembered her looking up at him, tight-lipped, eyes shining, resilient, proud of her work. Until she had become pregnant with Alice, he had never once seen her cry.

He looked at Ross and Claire and took in the expansive, silent damage they radiated, the way they could occupy the world by drawing a private one around them, like Alice in the barn with her head thrown back, blinking. He loved them, but he did not feel what they felt. Was haunted by no past or place. The mystery of Gene had always been how he could slip into the present and disappear.

Alice

IN THE LIVING room the city's roads were the zigzag lines on the old Persian rug that Constant's aunt had left in the house when she left Ross. Shoe boxes, cereal boxes, blocks, and butcher paper were spread across the floor and scaled, in a precarious masking-taped pyramid, up the lower part of one wall. The cars on this city's roads ran on magnet power.

The city's newspaper occupied a whole shoe box. A white pipe-cleaner sign stuck up from the roof reading SHORT & SWEET. Inside, a wooden Peg sat in a dollhouse chair in front of a cube on which an open eye-shadow case had become a laptop computer. Peg was a fairy and a reporter who had lost her power to fly yesterday afternoon and could only get it back if she wrote a story about what happened to the forest. She had gold glitter glued to her round head, blue sequin eyes, and she wore a green tie made of embroidery thread.

Alice clicked the eye-shadow case closed and made Peg walk outside the *Short & Sweet* and get on top of the magnet car, which Theo drove by pushing the other magnet behind it, all the way into the woods: green and orange cardboard pine trees glued to butcher paper, on which other pine trees were drawn with a crayon and marker. The car stopped at the edge of the woods, and Peg got out. Theo's band of plastic praying mantises, frogs, and snakes were waiting there for her.

"She would never have been able to meet them if you didn't bring the magnets," Alice said to Theo. He nodded at her gravely. They couldn't believe it when Peg lost her power to fly. It was because of the dust in that one stream of light just when the sun was setting Friday night. It was sinister dust! They tried in vain to restore her power, and finally, Theo came up with the heroic plan to get her a magnet car. It was hundreds of miles from Peg's newspaper to the woods. And there was no public transportation, because they didn't have any animal-cracker boxes.

The insects and frogs gathered in a circle around Peg. The largest frog hopped through the low forest brush. He towered over her. But she wasn't afraid at all. She knew they would help her through the forest.

The frog stared at Peg, and finally in a low chirp, he said, "We have something to show you."

Flynn

WHEN WHITE DISAPPEARED in the fall of 2008, there was a lot of praying going on. A lot of people talking about praying, telling one another they were praying. We ran a full-page ad for months, featuring a picture of Wendy and calls for the community to pray. I prayed for Wendy myself while covering a town board meeting and bowed my head again for her when asked to do so before a high school football game. It was easy to get caught up in the idea that it might work. When White disappeared, stupidity became a form of politeness. Failure to feign stupidity would engender indignation and reproach, as if it should be clear to everyone that silence must be instituted in order to make it all just go away.

The White investigation was defined by how it did not unfold. It was a story about a name added to a federal list, about horrified parents and organizing community members and the repetition of the phrase "we are pursuing all avenues." When she was found less than a mile from her apartment, it would have become a story about grieving and a funeral and the topic of off-the-record speculation, had I not been there to put it in context.

People liked to say it was a drifter who killed her, someone passing through. There's only two thousand people *in* this town, and they've all been here for-fucking-ever. So naturally, no one from here did it, or someone would come forward. Get it? Someone's brother or mother or father or friend. A tight-knit little town like this one, someone would have known what was going on.

I always think of one thing when people start talking about the town's heyday or start quoting the PR that the town board attempted in the aftermath of April 14. I always think of these pictures I found in the paper's archive: four black-and-white shots of an incredibly well-attended Klan march in 1941 through the Haeden town square. While clearly large enough to include most of the residents' grandfathers and great-uncles, it was thought, as the cutlines read, to have been attended entirely by people from "a nearby city."

As I sat at the bar in the VFW with Scoop that day, after failing to hit even one Mountain Dew can with whatever kind of bullets went in the handgun I didn't really want to fire, he told me that everyone was staring at me and that a reporter should be inconspicuous. He talked so slowly I could barely stand it.

"If you're going to cover this case, you need to get rid of those crappy glasses," he said. He took a sip of his beer and seemed to be lost in thought. "And stop wearing those polyester shirts." Paused again. Then: "You know, you should stop wearing those polyester shirts, period. A grown-up doesn't wear stuff like that to work." He also expressed skepticism that even people in Cleveland dressed the way I did.

Scoop wasn't just talking about my clothes. In this land that time forgot that was the VFW, there was nothing untoward about a guy in his sixties making ten or twelve specific comments on a person's physical appearance. His critique of my clothes was just the beginning, and I suspected it was a way to talk about my size. I am a small woman. I buy my clothes and shoes in children's departments, often the boys' department, because I'm not into floral prints and velvet dresses. When that doesn't work out, I make my own clothes. I easily fit into things I wore in fifth and sixth grade and have altered these vintage items. Scoop was obviously concerned that I looked like a kid. His other editorial advice that afternoon included "It wouldn't kill you to put on some makeup." "You've got such nice silky long hair, maybe you should use a clip to hold it instead of a pencil." And then eventually, the one I was waiting for, the great fishing question that would intimate that my line has some kind of miscegenation uncommon in these parts: "Black hair and blue eyes, that's a little rare, isn't it?" I was waiting for the comments on my smooth complexion to follow, but I got something even better: He said I looked like I thought I was a hotshot. People around here, he said, didn't trust people from cities who wore Malcolm X glasses and thought they were hotshots. "You will never," he said, "be able to get the cops to talk to you unless you clean up a bit."

"Yeah, just a minute," I said. "I'll get the crumbs out of my beard. Oh yeah, hang on, my bald spot is getting a little flaky, too. Oh! And I fucking forgot to floss again. Can you believe that? How's that? Is that any better? How do I look now?"

"I'm just saying," he said, grinning, "you're doing more than covering the Friends of the Library bake sale now. You should dress for it." He handed me a brown paper bag he'd carried in from the car. I took it and peered in. "Now, that there's called a blouse," he said. I looked at the tag. At least he'd had the presence of mind to buy an extra small. He said, "If you put it on, it will make the glasses bearable."

I smiled. "Your shooting," he said, "is a different story altogether. I don't know what in hell could fix that."

Scoop was right about the cops. They didn't talk about White. And this is one more reason why I wrote what I wrote once she was found.

Captain Dino didn't seem to be looking very hard for White's abductors. He didn't seem to have much paperwork on the White case at all. And the medical examiner, who hadn't shown up at the scene, was not, it turned out, required to have a medical degree. He was elected (along with the town judge) by popular vote every two years.

Dino and I met at the Rooster pretty often in those days. Usually just before happy hour. But he had little to say. He was a big thick guy with a large pockmarked nose and small green eyes. Had a shock of mercury-colored hair, a well-trimmed mustache, and impeccably clean dentures. Dino went running every day with a couple other guys from the PD. They would all wave to me as they went by the newspaper office, and I would look to see if there was a new guy. Preferably someone under forty who didn't look like a beefed-up queer. Someone smart and unmarried who thought he might be protecting the citizens and liked to drink. But Haeden was too small for even the most clichéd cop/reporter romance.

Dino wasn't a stupid man, and most of the time I didn't mind dealing with him. I watched him watch people. I knew his look of knowing things. Our jobs were not dissimilar. In many ways he was a quicker, meaner version of Scoop, and there was something appealing about that at first.

Dino had a lot of off-the-record theories for me but, unfortunately, no clue what could have happened to White. Nothing. No leads on anyone local.

His aloofness didn't stop me from trying to get more information. I spent most of my time hanging around the police station having off-the-record arguments and wasting whole afternoons at public records sitting at the long oak table, looking up things that were so tangential to the case that I wondered if I was trying to avoid what was right in front of me. Trying to distract myself from a growing paranoia that White's murderer was someone I was sitting next to at the bar on Thursday nights, that Dino had no intention of calling him in.

I began watching people, wondering who knew what and wasn't talking.

I watched men loitering on Main Street outside the Alibi or Sal's, or down at the Rooster, with their worn tanned faces and paint-covered clothes. I listened when they talked about contracting jobs or music festivals. A lot of them dated high school girls or undergraduates from colleges nearby. I watched other men driving nice cars, stopping by Sal's to pick up pizza on Friday nights, or ducking into the Savers Club to buy a gallon of milk, their ties off and top buttons unbuttoned. Salesmen, managers, teachers, and the occasional professor. In a region as poor as this, these were the people who were considered upper-class, successful, the intellectual and cultural elite.

From what I'd observed, the single women in town were generally waitresses or babysitters or just students biding their time before graduating and getting real jobs. There were, in fact, very few women in Haeden. So it wasn't unusual for a thirty- or forty-year-old guy to be going out with a nineteen-year-old he remembered first "noticing" when she was ten or twelve. I could see that kind of thing playing out with Wendy White, and some nights right after she went missing, I thought I could see changes on certain people's faces when the subject of White was brought up: information silently transmitted and destroyed. At first it all seemed too obvious, like I was so far outside the culture, I couldn't trust my judgment. But after a month, I was pretty sure she hadn't just run away, and I became obsessed with what could have happened to her. The place was so fucking tiny, so accessible, I thought. I was sure I could personally find her. Certain I could do it all myself.

I remember this period of time in fragments. I remember sitting in my little living room, drinking coffee at three in the morning, watching news from the Iraq war on CNN with the sound off, the Humvees and footage through crosshairs, and the shit about waterboarding, guys in blacked-out goggles and orange jumpsuits sitting in the sun behind razor wire. The light from the TV would reflect off the ashtrays and half-empty cereal bowls filled with cigarette butts.

And I would listen to the interviews I'd recorded with White's parents and with her brother and sister-in-law while the war played out in a pantomime of looped footage. I was trying to find something I might have missed that would bring it all together. I am sure this did me no good. The late hour and the war and the exhaustion and the restrained panic of White's parents' voices.

The switch from coffee to Labatts somewhere around four A.M. so I could sleep for a few hours. Those were the little details that would make the next day in the newsroom exhaustingly surreal. The obsessive reading and rereading of a situation I was unable to crack in time to have made any difference at all.

My friends from *City Paper* in Cleveland would call sometimes after they got back from the bar. I was usually up and wired on coffee, sitting amid stamped and redacted copies from county records, watching the mute television while they told me about shit going on in my old beat, or asked if I'd covered any dairy parades lately. One night when they were waiting for election returns, they called from the office and just sang "Come baaaaaaaaackkkkk" drunkenly for several minutes. "Come on baaaaaaaaaackkkkk, girl, come baaaacckkkkk, it's too loooooooong."

None of them thought much of the White case.

They wouldn't. The situation with White was not at all uncommon. People disappear and then reappear as corpses. That's how you get your chops. You see a dead person, and it sets you apart whether you like it or not. Then the getting over it; the fact that on occasion it constitutes something positive for you professionally.

The White case was not like other accidents or exhumations. Not like seeing the remains of some kid who had decided he was a failure and went drowning. Not like that at all. This is shitty to say, but there's not much pathos involved in a case like that. Think about it: Little So-and-so the Fourth drowns himself Tuesday night after receiving his midterm grades in the school of civil engineering. The body goes back to Westchester, and a lounge in the library or a nature path gets named after him, and a bunch of other blue-blood kids remember him fondly. Sorry. There's about one story a year like that. Poor Billy Fuckup, Jr., in his Gap khakis, the pressure of going to classes all day really *got* to him. If I were a better person, I would have felt badly having seen things like that.

White's body did not have such a wholesome end, wasn't a victim of drunkenness or impulse or perfectionism. And White's body was not so fully intact when Brenda Hodge caught sight of it on her way to work. Thought she saw someone crawling out of a ditch near the wooded edge of the Savers Club parking lot.

White's body, as it turned out, was put to use for months before being found.

Gene

"Hup!"

Alice extended one leg out straight from her body, her toes pointed, and Gene watched her, standing close in case she fell. He called again for her to change positions. "Hup!"

She bent and put her hand where her foot had been. The homemade balance beam stood two and a half feet off the ground and was nearly as high as she was tall. She lifted her leg straight up, slightly curved behind her.

"Hup!"

She bent and put her other hand down on the beam.

"Hup!"

She gave a slight bounce in her hips to spring up into a handstand on the beam, arched her back, and faced forward, smiling at Gene. Her body was strong and small.

"Want to try to walk on your hands?" he asked.

"Sideways?"

"Yes. Front ways if I hold your legs."

"No, no. Don't hold my legs."

"Okay, then, sideways, please. Hup!"

She lifted her hands slightly and was able to remain straight while taking the first tiny steps on her palms. He could see that she was not gripping the beam but, rather, feeling the way her hands must move and stay stiff, feeling the way there were points on her palms that could balance her whole body. She got braver and extended her reach farther down. Then he watched as she miscalculated where her hand should go and she missed, her body tensed, and she gave a little gasp as her head came down, about to hit the beam.

He grabbed her ankle and pulled her up quickly, upside down, raising her feet high above his head. Her face hung suspended before his. Her eyes were wide, and she opened her mouth in surprise. He could see the ridges on the roof of her mouth and the bone-white buds where her molars were beginning to come in. She giggled nervously, and he kissed her on the nose.

"Wow, Daddy. I almost fell."

"We better get you some butterfly wings so that never happens again," he said. He raised her up and down a few times. Then said, "Hup!"

She bent at the waist and grabbed his wrist, he let go of her ankle, and she hung straight down from his arm. He slowly lowered her until she was standing on the ground. "Want to do it again?" she asked.

"Yep." He smiled. "Hup!"

Alice grabbed the beam and flipped upside down to hang by her legs, then pulled herself up to a sitting position.

"Hup!"

She stood, her hands out to the sides. "Pretend these are my butterfly wings," she told Gene.

"Which?" he joked with her, pointing at her little hands. "The butterfly wings?"

"Yes." She wiggled her fingers. "Zzzzzzzzzzzzz."

"All right, good. Now you won't have to get caught. You won't get caught, and you'll do it all by yourself."

EVIDENCE *P47906*

4/16/09 8:45 A.M.

Sgt. Anthony Giles

My Favorite Place
By Alice Piper
Grade 2
Mrs. Major
September 15, 2000

My favorite place in town is Rabbit Run Road. This is a good name. There are rabbits on it sometimes and they like to run. Rabbit Run Road winds along downhill and you can see the river from it. When I get my new bike I am going to ride down Rabbit Run Road to school. It's my favorite place in the whole town and I like how it is connected by roads like this one that have flowers and pine trees beside them.

My other favorite place is the barn behind our house which has birds in it (swallows). It has a trapeze and a rope and a loft. My father, Gene, painted the barn and now there are big tulips on it. You can learn how to be in a circus there. You can learn how to be an escape artist or you can read up in the loft or you can eat there if you don't feel like going inside for dinner.

I would invite everyone to live there, especially my whole class. The river meets up with all other rivers and then goes into the ocean. We could find sunken ships like the ship called the *Sea Venture* which sunk in Bermuda in 1608.

Pirates are very good people because they let everyone

be a pirate. Mermaids attacked people in mythology. Some mermaids were 160 feet tall. In real life they were just manatees but not big. Pirates need to be on the lookout for Selkies which are people who turn into seals.

I love to swim with my parents and Theo and the river might be one of their favorite places too (mermaids). We could talk to them and put them in the circus. But it is a really bad thing to keep an animal in a cage or make them do tricks. They don't understand it. Bears and lions don't know what a circus is. So they shouldn't be there. People think mermaids were sirens in Greek mythology with their beautiful voices, but sirens were birds, not fish. A siren is not a beautiful sound now. Mermaids have beautiful voices. But it is doubtful that we would be attacked by mermaids because apart from manatees they aren't real. No one has ever ever really seen them. They only hear people talk about them. So you can't prove they ever happened.

Wendy

PEOPLE HAD ALWAYS described her as "fair," "big-boned," "a classic country girl." They remembered her mother at that age, remembered her aunts. They talked about her smile. How it revealed her to be a polite, well-loved girl.

People noticed and remarked that she had an easy relationship with traditions. Commented on how she liked cooking with her mother and grandmother. Wendy was someone who appealed to parents and teachers because she kept her thoughts to herself. Was not shy but had those rarer qualities: composure, common sense. Wendy always tried to play the hand she was dealt.

She wasn't bothered by her family's tight budget, accepted it as part of what made them who they were, gave them their sense of humor. She helped out and she made do. Wendy liked babysitting for her brother. She did filing and invoicing for her father's drywall business. Her sister-in-law cut her hair for free every month or so into a blunt shoulder-length bob.

If she found this life boring, if it hurt or embarrassed her, she didn't say so to her family. By comparison to many families around they were well off, and it would just be wrong to talk about it. Sometimes, though, she looked very, very tired. Sometimes she felt she had fallen asleep inside herself while she was wide awake working.

Being outside kept her happy. She went snowmobiling with her dad in winter, and in the summer she swam across the lake with the girls from swim team. She was a big girl and fit, and she loved to swim.

People called Wendy friendly. And practical. They praised her for not moving away from home until she knew what she might want to do. Said she liked home. And it was pretty much true. She loved her brother and sister-in-law and couldn't imagine not seeing them or not seeing her nieces.

But there were other reasons Wendy decided to stay in Haeden. Working in the office it wasn't hard for her to see when the money was coming in and where it was going. She'd been writing the monthly checks for White Walls loan payments since she was fifteen and setting them out for her father to sign. Making dinner in the weeks leading up to the holidays so her mom could work the Christmas-crunch time at Wal-Mart. Wendy understood the delicate balance of the system and her family's part as people who were from Haeden. People who worked. And were patient. Did not take handouts, did not take student loans, did not run up credit cards or miss payments. Did not make a move until they knew right where they were going and had a solid thing like her dad's business.

Wendy recognized the obliviousness of her friends, how they couldn't seem to see the difference between each other's houses, how they would eat a whole box of cereal at another kid's house after school, not even because they were hungry, not even stopping to think where it fit in that family's budget. And she hated it. Hated being the only one who saw it. Silently doing the math and making the petty point in her mind again, but never out loud.

It was because of her father that the Whites were not poor, and her father was one bad back or slip on a ladder away from having to reconfigure the balance of the whole family. She didn't want to be self-righteous. And she didn't want to draw attention to their situation. But it was senior year, and people were applying for school. And that changed some things. Made her feel things.

Every day she had to hear from friends who couldn't wait to graduate and get out of this "hellhole."

"But there's nothing quite like a hellhole to raise kids in," she joked.

And her friends laughed. All their parents said they had stayed there because of how safe Haeden was and how everyone knew each other. Yet that was what kids hated about it. Wendy wasn't going anywhere soon and she knew it, but it wasn't a big deal like the other girls made it out to be. It was stupid to make a fuss about something you had so little choice in. She thought it was funny that people wanted to be from somewhere big or dangerous. She could shrug off a couple of years at home and save money if she had to. Sometimes that made her feel tougher and smarter than her friends. Her dad always told her that was what built character.

"Anything I want to do, I can do right here," Wendy had told Jenny Hollis, walking home after swim. She felt good saying it. She was fucking sick and tired of Jenny talking about SUNY Geneseo and how great the campus was, and what she bought for her dorm room, and how "intense" it was going be when she was finally bilingual and a physical therapist. Wendy was sick of Jenny, too, her bright red hair and round pale face and double chin. She looked like an eight-year-old boy. And talked like she was always earnest or astonished. Like she was giving a pep talk—worse, like she was giving a pep talk and was also feeling kind of sorry for herself at the same time, keeping her chin up even though people had let her down.

Jenny reminded Wendy of dogs she'd seen in obedience class who always looked out of the corners of their eyes at their masters, like they wanted to do something bad and the only reason they didn't was because they had a choke collar on. Jenny wasn't free or out of a hellhole because she was going to school. Jenny was spoiled. She thought her blob of features was pretty the way only rich girls could. Expensive shirt and no one notices you have weird-looking tits. Two years of braces and no one remembers that your real teeth were more crooked than the trailer trash you won't even talk to. It was gross. Wendy was freer and happier hanging out in her dad's shop than Jenny would be trying to make people like her for her personality instead of the clothes she wore. Wendy wouldn't miss this walk home at all.

"Yeah, but don't you want to see the *world* a little?" Jenny asked. This also annoyed Wendy—when people talked about "the world" as if Haeden were another planet. Wendy stared at Jenny and knew the girl couldn't read her expression, knew that she didn't think Wendy was pissed or that she had her own ideas. Jenny was starring in a play about Jenny in her own head.

"Haeden is actually a part of the world, you know," Wendy said.

"Uh . . . not really?" Jenny said. "I mean technically? But—"

"It's not that big a deal to leave the place you're from anymore," Wendy told her. "Everybody does that. It's more unusual to stay in your hometown—especially if it's been your family's hometown for a hundred years."

Jenny looked at her pityingly. Wendy knew that the Hollises had lived in Haeden for 150 years, and so did everyone else, because of Hollis Road. And they had no problem coming and going. Of course they didn't. Wendy suddenly felt like she might laugh out loud because smart, earnest Jenny didn't realize the conversation they were having was about money.

At times like these, Wendy liked her family more than ever. But there was no way to say so without seeming uncool or poor or insecure. And then when she got home, she kind of couldn't stand them again.

It wasn't just Jenny or her parents or nieces who were wearing on her. She was beginning to talk back to people in her head and answer their questions in a funny way to herself. She knew her mother noticed. One time at dinner, her nieces and sister-in-law, Beth Ann, were visiting and being so loud, and her mother looked up at her with such a funny smile that Wendy thought she could read her mind. That they were making the same silent jokes. Maybe her mom and all her aunts had always done this. Maybe she was only just starting to catch up to them.

Sometimes, out walking on Sunday with the girls and Beth Ann, Wendy had the urge to throw all her things in the river. All her things—her purse, her schoolbooks, her stupid jewelry, her shoes—she wanted to stand there at the bridge and drop everything, watch it go by in the current until she was free, not free of Haeden but of some person Haeden expected her to be and that she hadn't been strong enough to resist.

Things got better in the fall when people left for college. Wendy missed them at first, even Jenny, but most of her girlfriends went to schools nearby, and she could visit them if she wasn't working on the weekends. She didn't like the dorms, which seemed trashy, and the hallways were too narrow. The campuses all looked the same: concrete buildings, mazes of parking lots and walkways. She liked it better when her friends visited home and stayed at her place, and they would go shopping, stay up late watching movies or drive into Elmville to go dancing. And it felt like her town now. She knew everyone, not only her friends' parents and her parents' friends—she knew all the working people. Liked the working people. Her friends only knew each other.

There were some boys from her class who had taken jobs in Haeden or Elmville, or lived at home helping their fathers out while they figured out what they wanted to do. But the girls didn't. The girls always left.

A lot of guys who stayed had plans to build nearby. Two of the boys she went to school with were going to "live off the grid" on some land left by somebody's grandfather. They said soon everyone would be living off the grid. This made her dad laugh out loud every time she told him about it. They were making a straw-bale house, said they would put up a windmill. Her father said it was all just making a big deal out of the way things used to be back before construction got easier. The only people who could afford the houses were rich people, he said. That's the joke! Next rich people will want to live in a cave. They're already paying four dollars a half gallon for unpasteurized milk!

Some boys from her class went to Iraq or Afghanistan. Her dad said more people from rural places like Haeden were fighting in the war than people from cities. Said it was always like that for farm boys and working boys. And he told her don't ever date those boys when they come back. On slow days, she and her dad would sit in the office and talk, tell stories about her nieces, and think about what the future would be like. She would read over the specs he got for projects and try to picture what the houses he was working on would look like when they were finished.

She loved hanging out with her dad. When she was little, she used to sit in the shop and eat saltines and draw houses. He taught her how to plot out the interiors. She was pretty great at drawing houses inside and out, and at doing the finances.

They also gossiped. Talked about how people lived, how folks knew everybody's business and still liked each other, pretended they didn't know all about each other's private lives, or forgot about them, or gave them the benefit of the doubt. Slow days were a mixed blessing. She worried about her dad's business, but she liked having him around.

Eventually, he had enough time to do all his own invoicing, and she took a waitressing job at the Alibi on Main Street, a block from the dollar store, half a block from the Rooster, to earn more money. She got an apartment a few miles from her parents' house on Town Line Road, near the little woods and the Savers Club. And over break, when her friends were home from college, they helped her move in, had a housewarming. The place was beautiful.

The Alibi was busy during happy hour. When the men got off work from the Home Depot and the contractors and painters came in to eat dinner, they sat at the polished wooden bar on red stools, drinking PBRs and looking up at the TV, or they crowded into booths. On Thursdays a band of three skinny guys in Carhart pants and flannel shirts played old-time music. Banjo and bass and fiddle. They sang "Cotton Eyed Joe" in unison, sitting in a circle with their heads raised toward heaven and their eyes squinting. People gave her their orders and chatted. She knew nearly everyone by name. And they all knew her.

The men in their late twenties and thirties talked to her about old teachers they had in common, and whether they could buy her a drink, asked if her brother was ever going to buy that land. They were responsible, like her dad, and didn't yet have a wife and kid like her brother. There were one or two of them she would think about later, like Dale Haytes, who graduated when she was a sophomore. She wondered what he was doing. Dale was twenty-two now and came into the bar quite a lot. Dale and his uncle, who was actually just a little older than him, and a bunch of men from the dairy. He always had his little brother with him, too, which Wendy thought was sweet. Bruce was a stocky quiet boy who played JV football and had really clear skin. He reminded Wendy of herself sometimes, like he was thinking a lot but happy to watch instead of talk. Dale would be the kind of boyfriend her parents would love. They had a lot in common even though he was older and his family had money. They both made the best of what was around them, respected their families. They both had been so dedicated to their teams in school. And there was something about the way people could almost dismiss Dale, kind of overlook him, the way Wendy had been overlooked. She remembered him from when she was a sophomore and he was playing ball. Didn't remember if he'd had a girlfriend. She could imagine someone calling him plain. Could see there were things he was thinking about but didn't say.

In the slow time after prepping and before she had to serve, Wendy smoked menthols with the cook and the dishwasher, sitting on the rail of the back deck overlooking a narrow creek.

They talked about movies, and Chad, the cook, talked about other places he'd worked and how busy things were or what kind of food they had. The dishwasher, Bill, talked about using the whipped cream to do whip-its.

"Nah, man. That shit is no good for you, and it wears off way too soon," Chad told him.

"It's fucking great!" Bill said. "I saw a flock of birds, like those bluebirds from Snow White, flying right at me and straight through my head, I could feel their wings, and then it was over like right then and you're good to go. You can buy it at the store." He sang, waving the can back and forth, "You can put it on ice cream. I'd say it's pretty practical."

Wendy laughed. She liked the way Bill talked. How he didn't care what anybody thought about him. He was someone she could go out with maybe, too. Not care. Do whip-its. Ask him to teach her how to skateboard. So what if he was thirty?

"Oh my God!" Wendy said. "My nieces love Snow White, but they can't pronounce it. All they talk about is Thnow White and Thindawella." She didn't know why it made her laugh so hard right then. Maybe she was just happy. "I'm Thindawella!" she said again as she exhaled and flicked her cigarette off the porch.

"You *are* Cinderella," Bill said, grinning at her.

"Yeah?" she said, laughing and holding her foot out. She was wearing red plastic gardening clogs from the Agway. He leaned forward and curled his arm around her waist, looked up into her pretty face, and Wendy thought for a second he might kiss her. Then Chad said, "Order up."

With running from the kitchen to the tables, missing meals at her parents', and then the walk to her apartment every day, Wendy began to get fit, even more fit than when she was a swimmer and still had some kind of softness about her. She could feel it. Her arms getting stronger and leaner from lifting trays. She began to look rosier. Baby fat began to shrink and show the line of her jaw, her cheekbone, the definition of her calf. She started to worry less about her hair and let it grow, wearing it up in a clip. She felt free. Like she could be in Haeden and shake off the silly pretensions of being *from* Haeden, the habits of talking about who owned what land, where you vacationed or who your grampa remembered, and the almost required speech about how you just loved the pretty pretty views, even when you didn't notice them or had never seen anything else to compare.

Wendy was a late bloomer, stepping elegantly, surprisingly, into the beauty of her youth. She still went to her sister-in-law's salon, but mostly for manicures and highlights. She wore dark pink lipstick and a little mascara. And she was tender in that way, that soft, angular, seamless way she was supposed to be. The way she had wanted to be all along.

She thought now that she looked like this, maybe people would see her. Be able to read her face better. Stop calling her "polite" and "friendly" and asking "Aren't you a White?," which always made her want to burst out laughing in their faces. Or "Aren't you Danny White's little girl?," which she thought was hilarious back before she dropped the weight. People must have felt sorry for her, but she never felt sorry for herself. Must have felt sorry and assumed she was dumb or shy or naive or that she couldn't possibly think anything bad about thin, rich, friendly people. Couldn't have her own thoughts about things. But now they'd be able to see her. The less makeup she wore, the thinner she got; people would just assume she was getting smarter, too. Wouldn't think she'd been smart all along, wouldn't realize that she'd been pretty all along, either. And she had to admit, she liked being noticed. She liked the freedom that came with it. Being the pretty girl. The girl people looked at like they were getting an unexpected present.

One day, after she poured a beer for her dad's friend who owned the dollar store out on 227, she put his change on the bar and he said, "Well, thanks, Miss America."

Wendy smiled at him. Noticed that he and his friends were all looking right at her.

"Don't you love blondes, though?" said the man sitting next to him. It was Doc Green. He was a large-animal vet, worked for the dairy. Came and talked at her school one time.

"*Oh,* yeah," her dad's friend said. Then he winked at her and left a dollar fifty where his beer had been.

Flynn

THE TRUTH IS, after they found the body, after I put out the paper, I didn't want to go back to work. I didn't want to see anyone. I didn't want to know anyone. I didn't even want to go to my apartment. I thought of leaving town that day.

I watched men who had no business doing anything other than writing traffic tickets, working the crosswalk, or wrangling drunks handle the series of intimate procedures involved in packing and shipping a body that had once belonged to their friend's daughter or their kids' babysitter.

The night they found White's body, I wanted to be alone. Because this complete quiet had settled over everything. Like a radio that had been playing for so long you don't even notice it had suddenly been shut off. Noise didn't fix the problem; it only became more obvious when people spoke. Their words hung in the air. As if all peripheral thought, all the ambient observations, the things I would picture or think of saying, were wiped out.

This silence feels like calm. But really, it is a point beyond rage.

Nobody could do a thing about Wendy White. No one could do anything to her or for her ever again. And nothing that might be done to the people who put her where she was would change that. All your passions and ideals and understandings about justice and humanity, all your autopilot notions and senses and "beliefs," are just things your brain lets you entertain so you will have somewhere to focus your grief.

The silence lets you know it's already had the answers for a million years. Answers comprising not words or sounds but smells you were unaware you recognized, gestures shared by animals.

When I went home after putting the paper to bed, I stood in the bathroom for a long time, looking in the mirror with the water running in the sink, just to hear something. But the quiet soon drowned it out. My face and hair covered my skull, and my round wet eyes stared back at themselves. In the quiet, I was yards and yards of skin, autonomic responses, little hairs and pores.

How disposable is a woman's life? How expected. How unsurprising. How normal. How many times a week, a month, a year does this happen?

I wanted to be alone. But I could not have been alone in thinking those things that night. And in fact I didn't end up spending the night alone at all.

Wendy White told me a story with her body, one that I already knew. One that, until that moment, I had been unable to relay. And I wrote it all down. I told it to Alice.

I still don't know if I am sorry. I only know that when I think about it now, I see that moment at the edge of Tern Woods like the opening of the tinderbox. And for better or worse, I know White's death was not in vain.

EVIDENCE *P47907*

4/16/09 8:40 A.M.

Sgt. Anthony Giles

Hibernation
By Alice Piper
Grade 5
Mr. Kennedy
September 23, 2003

When people think of hibernation they picture bears in caves, wearing stocking caps and slippers, or moles or badgers or hedgehogs or porcupines, asleep huddled together for warmth. People don't think of insects because insects do not live long and there aren't many images in stories or in textbooks of them sleeping.

This essay (and accompanying diagrams) will give an explanation about one of the most interesting topics I have come across in many many years of liking science. I had to go to the library at the University of Elmville to find all of this out . . . BUT (drumroll please):

Insects hibernate! Usually as larva. Cricket and grasshopper eggs freeze for the winter before hatching in the spring. Ants hibernate. Wasps, beetles, and some species of butterflies also hibernate as adults (see diagram A3 for geographic information on varied species of grasshopper).

Hibernation for insects is called diapause. It does not just occur in winter but in any time when the insect has to survive "predictable, unfavorable conditions such as cold weather, drought, or starvation" (see drawing 7.) Diapause is a resting state similar to what occurs in seeds when they are in the ground but have no water. It can also be described as: "the suppression of questing activity." Once it is dormant, special stimuli are required to release the insect from its sleep, not unlike a kiss on Rose Red (see diagrams A8–A12 and drawing 8).

While environmental factors cause and stop diapause, changes in the environment and unpredictable weather patterns (global warming!!!) can have an adverse effect on insects by releasing them from hibernation too early. Some scientists think this is causing extinction of some insects. At particular risk of extinction are the following species of butterfly: Mourning Cloak, Comma, Question Mark, and American Snout (see diagram B2, timeline 1).

Bees and butterflies are important for our whole ecosystem (see diagram B3), so it is important they not be disturbed while sleeping (see drawing 4). So . . . shhhhh-hhhhhh!

Stokes, Donald. (1993) Stokes Butterfly Book: *The Complete Guide to Butterfly Gardening, Identification and Behavior.*

C.A., Masaki, S. (1986) *Seasonal Adaptations of Insects.* Oxford University Press.

Flynn

I HAD NO TROUBLE getting information about Alice Piper. Even though she was a kid, a teenager, when it happened, she had already had a very public life in Haeden. I'd written several profiles on her, met her about a month after I started at the paper in 2003 because she got first place in the middle-school "verbal advantage" contest. After that, she went on to beat all the other brainiac nerds in the eastern U.S. I interviewed her back then, and we ran a feature.

She was a long-legged skinny kid at the time, with wavy blond-white hair. A very small girl. Just baby-looking. She had these tiny freckles and big blue eyes, translucent eyes. She was really just a sweet kid. Had an incredibly alert mind. I liked Alice. I knew how it was to be the littlest kid in class. It can make you pay extra attention to the details.

Later that year she won a county-wide science contest funded by the poultry industry, for designing a parachute and landing device for a raw egg. She built it out of foam and wire and the plastic things that hold six-packs together. She could launch the egg, and with this thing she built, it would land without breaking nine out of ten times. Very cool thing for a child to be able to do.

By the time she started high school, we were running stories about her or her projects twice a year. She was top of her class, she was captain of the swim team, volunteered as a hospital aide. Few parents could ask for more in a kid. But she wasn't the typical "good student." You always saw her doing things around town, kind of weird things, like trying to draw the world's longest hopscotch game in chalk on Main Street. There was no interference with traffic, but Dino put a stop to it after four or five blocks.

She and her friends also played a game they called Bigger Better.

Alice and this tall skinny boy I used to think was her brother and another girl named Megan would come by the newspaper office sometimes after school with random objects and ask if I would trade them something bigger or better. They did this all through town, these sweet, bored, nerdy kids. They would start out with a rubber ball or a paper clip around three o'clock and end up with a used microwave or a cracked and moss-covered lawn ornament by the time they had to go home, then start it all again the next day. The best they did was start out with a spool of thread and end up with a dented apartment-sized washer/dryer that actually worked. I offered them fifty bucks, but they let it go for a bag of Hershey's Kisses. Bigger Better would be the resonant theme for Alice throughout the time she lived in Haeden. She was an achiever.

It's true that I was the one who made decisions to cover this kid, but anyone would have. She was incredible—and not a rich kid, no private lessons or things like that. Just, you know, herself. Her dad worked part-time for Soil and Water, and I often got maps and information from him. Her mom worked from home on occasion, proofing medical textbooks. I loved writing about her until I hated it.

Unlike the White case, the Piper case produced mountains of official information, and nothing the police gave me was redacted. *Nothing.* They would just hand stuff over like I was their buddy, names, addresses, and phone numbers still visible. Not a line of black marker. Illegal shit, too. Like names and addresses of juveniles. This was unusual, as I hadn't been able to get even the blotter from Dino when I first got to town. He said the paper never needed the blotter before, and there was nothing to report. "You think people want to read gossip about their neighbors being in a domestic?" he'd asked. "Or about somebody's uncle touching 'em where they shouldn't? People don't want to read that kind of stuff about their neighbors; that's not real crime, it's just sad. Plus, that shit gets around before the paper comes out, so I don't know why you'd need the blotter."

During the Piper investigation, I would walk into the little police station and ask to see documents, and the secretary would hand them over, whole depositions and interviews. I thought I'd gotten lucky and tried to hide it from Dino, but although he wouldn't say anything for attribution other than the usual "we are pursuing all avenues," he would give me anything I asked for. Even things I didn't ask for. He thought he had uncovered a conspiracy. That belief is the one thing he and Alice Piper had in common. Belief that they were seeing evidence of a cell. There were times when I suspected Dino truly thought he was going to tie it all back to Al Qaeda or Earth First.

People don't know much about the details, and consequently, a lot of details were simply made up. The event happened two weeks after White's body was found, not the next day, which has become the common urban legend. It wasn't like that.

Reporters from everywhere descended on the town. They were using the nut graphs from my original stories, filing their pieces from the Alibi or the Rooster, stopping in to the *Free Press* to talk. To try to get me on record. I knew I had primary-source stuff they didn't, and a better understanding of the locals and the cops, despite Dino's feelings about what I'd written. And I knew they wanted to fuck me over in the national press too. I had to stay on top of the story. For a lot of reasons.

What I had seen and what I had researched were not working out well for me in those months before my twenty-ninth birthday. I'd put up with five years of living in Haeden, writing about high school football games and town board meetings so I could use my downtime to gather information about state and federal environmental policies. So I could see how it all worked, find out where things were quietly buried. I had not expected to get drawn into any real town news at all. I spent my time between forensics and file photos. And if I went a day without writing, I would start to feel physically ill.

The *Free Press* had pictures of Alice on file from the time she was in seventh grade, which everyone wanted later. We sold prints of the one you've seen. It was taken the summer before it all happened. In it she's smiling, tan and freckled and hair short and choppy and bleached from the sun. She has this loving look on her face, standing in front of the butterfly house she designed for the elementary school. Butterfly was her event, and the swim team sponsored the project for the little kids. In the picture her shoulders are strong and defined, her body an athlete's body, her eyes bright, ice blue, a dimple on her left cheek. She is looking straight at the camera. I read somewhere that someone had enlarged and reproduced it, that it became a staple of college-town poster shops, a decorative motif for the walls of many young women's rooms.

Claire

CLAIRE WATCHED AS the dark green Lexus pulled up to the curb in front of the Rooster and Theo stepped out, then reached back into the car for something that he put in his pocket. He stood a minute and waved as the car merged back onto Route 34, then he headed into the bar.

"They just drop him off like that?" Harley asked. "Why do they never stay?"

"Too good for us," Ross said, but he only half meant it. He was proud of his sister the professor, and he liked being with the boy. Plus, he knew she didn't like the old-time music, and it would only offend people if she hung around rolling her eyes. Theo walked through the dim bar toward the back booth where they sat. Claire watched him smile when he saw Ross. He was wearing the same shirt he'd had on the day before, and it looked like someone had used a wet comb on his hair. Before he reached their table, Alice called to him from the dartboard, and he ran to her without a hello to his uncle.

"He's too good for us, too," Gene joked.

"Nah, *he's* got his priorities straight," Harley said. He looked at his watch briefly and then back to the small stage by the front window. Then he propped his elbows on the table and smiled. His long gray hair just touched his shoulders. He said, "As long as we're on the subject of snobs, didjah see the Haytes bought a bunch of new signage over there at their shit ranch? Me and Annie were over to drop off some Girl Scout cookies for Bev, and they got those alleys between the tanks marked with street signs now—one of 'em is Niklaus Way."

"Shit," Ross said.

"I don't get it," Claire said. She leaned her back against Gene's chest at the booth where they were all sitting, and he wrapped his arms around her waist. His hands were rough, fingernails dirty. His forearms were deeply tanned now, the band tattoo turning ever bluish and indistinct. He had never been stronger since they had been together, or happier. When he rested his chin on her shoulder, she could smell Dove soap.

"Oh, they're naming parts of their property after golfers, is all, but I wonder how much the signs cost." Harley looked up just as Alice ran by, following Theo toward the door, and he caught her around the waist. "Hey, little Al, before you and your boyfriend start running off." He pulled a rectangular envelope out of his pocket. "I got you them bee-balm seeds from Annie."

"Thanks!" She kissed him on the cheek. She opened the envelope and peeked inside. "Thank you very much."

"Now, these oughta attract the right kind of insects to your garden," he said. "You let us know if you want some different variety, 'cause she's just got 'em all saved up and waiting. And don't forget, you gotta date with Annie to teach you how to make a slug trap with beer."

Alice hugged him around the neck.

"All right." Harley patted her on the back. "*Now* you can go."

"Where are you off to?" Gene asked Alice.

"The river."

"Pay attention," Ross and Claire said in unison.

"Don't go farther than the base of the bridge," Gene said.

"That's like two feet away!" Alice complained.

"That's right," Gene said, then turned back to the conversation at the table while the children ran out. "That dairy's had a pretty big effect on the surrounding land. I'd be surprised if anything within a few miles of where they're dumping their shit will be able to certify organic."

As always, this was a conversation killer. The table waited

for Gene to explain some technical thing about soil that would depress them, or describe some new dire situation with giant agribusinesses like Gen-Ag-Tech, then finish with the demand that they all go to more town meetings. Heavy as that topic was, Claire knew it pleased him to talk about it. He loved the fight. In the city, after he had left his job and started the greenhouse, he was out at meetings a few times a week, or up in Union Square with his urban farm buddies, getting the word out. In Haeden, town meetings were fine once a month, but nobody would come every time like he wanted. And they stopped giving him the "I'll try to show up" line because it meant he'd call their houses, offer to give them rides. Show up with Alice and a loaf of zucchini bread and a gallon of cider.

Claire hated to see this happen. She knew people should get more information in a town this size, but she also knew how far away everyone was from one another, how much time they spent driving or working during the day. Gene didn't get tired like other men. He never had. "You should be making this speech over at the Alibi," she said. "You're preaching to the converted here."

"I'm trying to *motivate* the converted," he said. They all laughed.

"Yeah, besides," said Ross a little drunkenly, "we don't need no Alibi, pardon the pun. They don't care about the dairy. They're all a bunch of rich folks over there—thinking *we're* the rich folks 'cause we went to college." He paused and nodded at them, then seemed to realize he hadn't quite made a point. "That GI Bill helped me make some cash, boy. Can't tell you how valuable my degree in American studies turned out to be."

"I'm sure," Claire said. "You get ten dollars more an hour on roofing jobs if you can quote from *The Pentagon Papers*." They laughed and clinked their pint glasses, but these things did disturb Claire. How little money they had and how much they'd all studied something else and had no training or history in the things they were doing. The fact that if they didn't have the garden, they really would be scraping by. They made just enough for rent and bills and thirty dollars a week for groceries; the fact that the garden depended on the weather and on their health—things largely outside of their control—was mentally exhausting. She was still baffled by how anyone lived on upstate wages. And despite all the cries of poverty at the Rooster, she suspected most of the people she was talking to had family wealth, had safety nets. She knew they did in Constant, though it was a sore subject.

"You know I'll show up, man," Harley said to Gene. "But this shit's been going on for years, and I mean like fifty years. The Haytes got more than a couple connections helping them out." He finished the rest of his pint. "Best thing is for everyone to just have their own garden. Don't eat from farmers that contract with them, so you don't get all the chemicals and shit." He patted Gene on the shoulder and went back to the circle of chairs by the bar's front window, where his wife was already tuning her stand-up bass. Annie was tall and strong. She had the knotty hands of a string musician, her salt-and-pepper bangs hung above dark blue eyes, and her face was lined from smiling. She winked at Harley as he walked toward her. Claire watched her mouth the words "Hi, lovey" to him. Claire adored them. Somehow they'd made it work here. And somehow Harley did manage to stay on top of all the politics without losing faith when things didn't go their way. She wondered if he'd been like Gene when he was younger. Annie and Harley reminded her of their friends in the city. They shared a similar fatalism. Playing out every week, planting their own food, bitching about the suburban mentality, trying to do what was right, not even entertaining an idea that regular people, people concerned about their status or standing, were anything but jackasses. Annie had told Claire one time that she and Harley were having financial troubles and they made themselves feel better by saying "Oh well—if it doesn't work out, we can always kill ourselves." Annie laughed so hard telling her that, she had to wipe tears from her eyes, and Claire was struck by how hard and how weird they were and she loved them.

The rest of the band finished their drinks at the bar or headed for the bathroom before the next set. The group was made up of older folks, men and women in their fifties and sixties who had moved to Haeden as hippies when they were young. And taken the "back to the country" idea seriously enough to start a band in which one of the principle instruments was a washboard. They were a beautiful spectacle, exuberant and especially buoyed by four or five pints as the day cooled down after work. They were like godparents to Gene and Claire, kind and grateful that a young, like-minded family had moved to town. Claire rested her back against Gene's chest and listened to Harley sing. *Shady Grove, my true love, Shady Grove, I say, Shady Grove, my true love, bound to go away.*

And just like it had in the city, the music suppressed her worry—or gave it the right sound track, at least. This was life now, and it was Claire who was grateful to be there with them. She thought of Alice and the things she would learn growing up in Haeden. How much time and quiet she'd have. Claire was glad they weren't bringing her up in Manhattan.

In that warm, buzzed, almost drowsy moment, sitting beneath the yellow lights of the cozy bar, Claire dreamed of her daughter's life of play and study at their little farm, her adventures with Theo on the riverbank. And she knew this was the world that would let Alice see things clearly, that would make her the right kind of woman.

Gene

GENE WORE BLACK knee-length shorts covered with paint and plaster, and a thin white T-shirt, the sleeves of his wool sweater pushed up to reveal one forearm tattooed with a band of binary code surrounded by insects. He was tall, quiet, sinewy, strong. His white-blond hair was shaved on the sides, a cowlick at the back of his head. He knelt in front of an eight-by-twelve-foot raised bed of black earth, pulling weeds from around pale green sprouts as thin as thread.

Behind him, Constant stood at the entrance to the roof, wearing pajama pants, his black hair an unruly mass, two days of growth on his face, heavy eyebrows, full lips. His dark skin was marred by a scar on his left shoulder that looked like a large white bruise; there was another one on his stomach that looked the same, a bruise or a burn.

"Can you just think about it?" Constant asked. "I want you to think about it."

"Well, that's good, man, it's good to know what you want." Gene was trying to ignore him. What he wanted was some help with the seedlings, or some good conversation to pass the time. He knew the news had taken Con and Michelle by surprise, but he wasn't ready for some brotherly sit-down.

"Be serious for a fucking second. You're not going to be able to support a kid with your stilt-walking skills, and the likelihood of you getting another fellowship doesn't seem too realistic."

"There's always washing dishes. Whatever, man. I'm DIY. We'll run away and join the circus before I do anything like the shit you're talking about."

Gene thought of Claire's smile, her elegant, delicate face. Her small straight teeth and big gray eyes. Sweet, smart eyes. He thought about how her shoulders looked as she sat in front of him on their bike, riding fast down the abandoned windswept corridor of Avenue A on the way home from the free clinic, metal grates pulled over doorways. He knew a baby would change things. But not that much. Not like Con was saying.

"If you take the position, it can afford you guys the time for Claire to finish this next year at the clinic and get things straight, take time off before the baby comes."

"Honestly? I can't believe you're still talking to me about this. Claire would fucking leave me, not be grateful, if I did it. I'm having enough trouble with *you* doing this kind of bullshit, so leave me the fuck out of it. Okay? Please?"

"Gene."

"No. No. You want to be a walking cliché? Go for it. Three years of idealism and the Hippocratic oath and then off to conduct clinical trials because all of a sudden you don't like the lifestyle? Seriously?"

"It's not forever, man. I didn't get a free ride everywhere I went to school. If you had the loan payments I have, you would find that salary reasonable for a couple of fucking years, too."

That was it. Gene felt his heart rate increase. His neck felt hot, and his hands began to sweat. The term "free ride" always did it to him. There was nothing free about institutionalizing his intellect for eight years.

"I'm sorry," he told Con sarcastically, meticulously. "Did you not start this conversation with the phrase 'repurpose the botulism toxin'? Am I wrong? It sounded like you were asking me to work for a cosmetic company to repurpose botulism. You came up here, where I am working on growing our food, and . . . and . . . and you said that I should take a job working on human clinical trials repurposing a deadly substance for nonmedical use in humans. Wait! No, wait. And the reason you gave is because

I am about to have a child." Gene roughly shook the dirt off his hands as he spoke. "Does that make any fucking sense to you? Does it?"

Con nodded. "Yeah. It does. You are broke, you have a medical degree that you are not using right now, you won't be going on assignment with the baby coming, and this isn't that big a deal. There is a price at which you could make this decision."

"That 'price'?—that 'everybody has a price' price, Con?— that's fucking bullshit, man. That price doesn't represent the value you assign to yourself. It's what you assign to everyone else involved. Three hundred K isn't how much you're worth. It's how much humanity is worth to you. Introducing some completely unnecessary, possibly dangerous procedure into the world, you'd give up a bunch of people you never met for three hundred K?"

"Dude. Spare me your grandstanding, all right? And your Dr. Moreau fantasies. Stop talking to me like I'm fucking stupid, okay? I'm trying to help you and Claire. I don't know how we're going to live with a baby in this neighborhood."

Gene was furious and knew it wasn't just because of Con's suggestion. It was because Con was talking down to him, echoing his professors and colleagues. Hinting that his current behavior really signified a "mental-health issue," not ideology. He would not let their vision of him replace what he knew to be true. He was not going to screw people for money. Fuck them. He was twenty-nine years old and had graduated before all of them. He knew what it was like doing that kind of research, and it was for the morally retarded. The fact that Constant now thought it was okay to do "just for a while" disturbed Gene beyond words. What the fuck was he talking about? Con was the one who had turned him on to gardening in the first place, describing the logic of it, telling him how his mother's vegetables had saved them growing up in Beirut when there were blackouts and food shortages. Gene resented being treated as though he were somehow a romantic for doing one of the most practical and essential things humans do.

Constant stared at him. "Why did you go to fucking Harvard, dude? Why did you even fucking bother? Put your ideology in check and do the right thing. This is asinine."

Gene turned away and raised his eyebrows, shook his head. Wiped his hands on his sweater, leaned against the raised bed of dirt, and lit a cigarette.

Why had he gone to Harvard? Because he got in. Because you don't know anything when you're a teenager and labeled "gifted." Nothing, not even why you're good at things or whether you like doing the things you're good at. Being good at things did not obligate you to do them. It was a mistake to think so. And he had made many mistakes, been told too many times that he was just the person for some special job or project or social movement. He'd picked medicine because it was fun at the time and gave him the most information. But it easily could have been engineering or literature or political science or what-the-fuck-ever. All he wanted now was to be who he was before he went to school. He could see flashes of it but had never been able to reconnect. Maybe now, with the baby, he could get there.

Back before Harvard and Columbia and research, Gene was a brainy, hyper kid who listened to reggae and Captain Beefheart. He learned languages because they were fun. He read small-press classics, historical books on pirates, and manifestos from the Situationist International. He ordered self-produced albums with Magic Marker covers through the mail. He was not athletic, though he had always been strong and flexible. Never played team sports and had instead taught himself tightrope walking and unicycle riding. And yes, he had to admit that most of those pursuits were romantic in some way. But they were also practical.

In grad school he spent summers at a trapeze camp teaching terrified kids to hold on, to let go, to hang by their knees, to fall. He would ride his bike back home after flying and hanging, listening to Joe Strummer or the Talking Heads on the Walk-man and going over his lab work in his head. Constant knew all this—was there for it. Part of it, anyway.

Gene was done with everything by twenty-six. And done all over again with his brief mistake in the corporate world by twenty-eight. He was very happy doing what he was doing now, could feel that it was right. His hands in dirt instead of washed and sealed inside of gloves. He could not believe Con would even bring this up. These things that had driven him up here on the roof, starving for something he'd planted himself.

He looked at Constant's face, looked into his eyes, and watched his friend drop the subject, watched him recognize that thing they both used to feel, a separateness, a lack of faith that had once drawn them all together, a knowledge that certain Ameri-cans could be made to live longer—but making Americans as a group healthy was laughable in the current economy, with the current labor and environmental laws. They'd had this unspoken pact not to be hypocrites, not to busy themselves, in their fancy suits with their prohibitively expensive educations, rearranging the deck chairs on the *Titanic*. It hurt his gut to think Con was taking a pharma job and was still a member of Physicians for So-cial Responsibility; that he wouldn't be doing Doctors Without Borders with Michelle, even though he easily could, that he had been so unnerved by the news of a baby. He saw disappointment in Con's eyes and wondered if his friend was simply mirroring his own expression.

"I just can't do it, Connie," he said tightly.

Con nodded, looked somewhere beyond Gene's shoulder. Finally, he said, "Can I borrow the sweater?" Gene took it off and he put it on, buttoning it up over his bare chest. He walked forward and pulled Gene up from where he sat. Then he hugged him close for several minutes. "You're going to be a dad, my brother." Gene smiled at the thought of it, relaxed, and embraced his friend, pounded his back before letting go.

"Hey, I gotta go buy coffee and milk. Since we don't have a cow yet." Con laughed, reached in the pocket of the big sweater, and pulled out Gene's rolling papers and some Drum, began rolling a cigarette.

"Soon, maybe," Gene said. "That'd be fucking great! Come up to the roof and milk it every morning." They laughed. Con smiled at him, spat out some loose tobacco, then lit his cigarette. They walked to the stairs and headed down through the building to Seventh Street.

"Did I tell you I got an uncle that used to farm?" Constant asked him.

"The one with the metal forehead?"

"Yeah." Con laughed. "Obviously I have told you."

"You'd think the magnets would be bad for him."

"He only really does it when he's drunk."

"Which is like . . . daily?"

"P-T-S motherfucking D," Con said. "Dude was in Vietnam. There's worse things than drinking."

"Wait. He's Lebanese?"

"Fuck no. It's my aunt's husband. She moved to the States for her postdoc research. They've been there a long time. He's not my blood relative, man. But I was just thinking, if you want, we could go up and stay with him a while."

"And do what? Where do they live?"

"You know just see what this organic-farming shit really takes. He has a good-sized garden now, but he used to have a few acres of crops. He lives in Haeden. It's this tiny place upstate, got a state park nearby or something."

EVIDENCE *P47908*

5/20/09 3:30 P.M.

Sgt. Anthony Giles

December 20, 1996
Dear Gene,

Without having to move, we now live in a pretty nice neighborhood. The bad news is there's no more "we." Micky got a new placement, this time in Zelingei. I am the last of us here. I know how I got here and now I know I can't do this for very much longer. I have to talk to someone whose been through this who will understand what all these fucking details mean, and how fucking sick they are. I feel like I've been poisoned or brainwashed and I don't understand why I can't feel what I am doing. It was a bad decision — not just morally — in every way. I mean intellectually I know that what I am doing is technically insane and wrong. But I can't feel it. There is some weird psychological pull that seems to keep me here at Pharmethik. One more month or one more year I tell myself and then I can take all this money and leave. Or I rationalize like: I couldn't have paid my dad's mortgage or helped you and Claire with the land if I wasn't doing this. You were right. This is sick. I have to do something else. I've already lost whatever it was I was going to be by spending an intellectually active part of my life here. And I can't remember anymore what it was like to think and feel clearly — really clearly about the broader ramifications of my part in all this — of which I can't give you details. This whole month I was actually angry at you for not fighting harder with me about this work — not telling me why you got out so fast and never went back. Well, we don't

tell people much in this line of work do we? Just tell ourselves
bullshit.

Lately I've been thinking that I could be a whistle-blower—
but I realize—and this is fucking sick too—I realize there's not
enough money in being a whistle-blower, and that I don't like
the personalities of whistle-blowers. Not that I like the person-
alities of my coworkers—it's just that they have accepted certain
disgusting realities and do not base their decisions on aesthetics or
ideology or even emotions beyond their own. They have a focus
that is outside the law and an attitude that is bizarrely similar to
many of us (Michelle especially). Like us, these people do what
they want. They know the system is fucked and use that to their
advantage.

You would not believe how I look or talk if you saw me. You
would think this is something out of Invasion of the Body Snatch-
ers. *I know you will say I have* CHOICES *even in what I am*
doing but honestly what I am doing is so ridiculously amoral that
to make any of those little lifestyle choices inside of this life feels
like hypocrisy and tithing.

I haven't worn scrubs, haven't seen gloves, in years. The pur-
poselessness of my own attire offends me.

My job has become one much more involved with speaking
than anything else. My hands are useless and require no washing.
Most of what I do is review the things other people do, and refine
them, developing simple 30-second messages. I stand in front of
a roomful of people and show a PowerPoint I have shown 300
times before as if I am delightedly looking at it for the first time.
I have five diagrams that will fit the bill regardless of the topic.
Flow charts with block arrows called "chevrons" can be used to
describe any process. I spend my entire day manipulating people
into doing something I think is wrong. I convince *them of the*
profitability of doing something wrong.

And I am sick of the way everyone talks. Lower-end business-
people use images like "I'm trying to shepherd along this process"

or they make reference to herding cats, circling wagons, taking conversations "off-line" or putting ideas in the "parking lot" to be addressed later. Or possibly making sure everyone shares the "sandbox" or contrawise, "stay in their own swim lane" (can you believe these? There are more).

Buzzwords are another story. "Leverage" as a verb is universally accepted in business. It is only used incorrectly: "Let's leverage this capability in another functional area." These are the little things that are driving me crazy. Very rarely do I engage in small talk about my life or feelings. People can tell if you are making things up. I do not discuss politics unless I can judge the person's ideology with a 99 percent degree of accuracy. I've made mistakes before and they have been very costly.

I can tell you things are far far worse than news stories and investigative pieces in the alternative press (which sucks as a source frankly and you should get yourself a subscription to the Wall Street Journal). I'm not just talking about ethical issues involving testing and pricing, or pushing psychiatric medication on whole populations, or the suicidal side effects of the products in which I am strategically involved and for which I am morally culpable. In fact I can't even tell you what I'm talking about until I get the fuck out of here.

*The difference, Gene, between now and then is that then I thought I could make something happen. That I could do this for just a little while in order to do other more important things. And I did think we could change things or at least **escape**—build within the wreckage. (Beneath the Paving Stones, the Beach!) Now I know I can't make anything happen. And I don't care if it all comes down tomorrow. Let it come down, honestly.*

I am coming to visit soon and will try to stay as long as I can which may only be a couple of days. If you have any ideas as to what I could possibly do instead of this please let me know. I'm serious, man, I need some suggestions. And not that I should just "drop out" and move in with you which is preposterous (though lately I think about it at least twice a day). I mean real ideas. You know what I mean. I'll see you soon. Say hi to LoudClaire and the terrible three and a half—I can't believe she's starting to read.

I love you, I love you. Constant.

Gene

"WHY IS DADDY crying? Claire! Why is Daddy crying?"

"C'mere, pumpkin sauce. Dad got a sad letter from Connie."

"But is Connie sad?"

Claire swept Alice's tangled blond-white hair away from her head, and the girl slumped down into the soft paisley couch to lean against her. "A little bit," Claire said. "But he's going to be okay." She reached a long arm out to Gene.

He shook his head and came to sit with them, tears on his face. He let his head fall back and looked up at the ceiling. "We should really be living in community," he said. "You're fucking right. You're right, you're right. God, Claire. We all should be together. This was crazy. Crazy stupid. They should be living here with us. I should have tried harder to talk him out of it. I should have told him all about this shit."

Claire just held his hand.

Alice climbed over her mother to sit on his lap and brushed the tears from his cheeks with her little hands. He put his arms around her. She was tiny. Three and a half, long-limbed and round-cheeked. So pale the skin on her face sometimes looked translucent. She gazed intently at him. Her light blue eyes were shiny, pupils round and slightly dilated. Her brow was furrowed and she looked worried, but something else about her was studying the whole situation, and he could see it: her worry and her thought, her intensity in trying to put everything together. Her smallness made this both funny and oddly powerful. She was figuring it out, taking it on to help them.

"Wait," Alice said gravely. "Where *is* community?"

Gene and Claire looked at each other and laughed. Gene was still crying a little.

"It's when people live *together* and help each other out, you little question bug," Claire said, smiling at her.

"Do we have to help Connie out because he's sad?" Alice asked, looking relieved that they could do something.

"Yes, of *course* we help Connie and anyone else who is feeling bad. We stick *together. All* people stick together," Claire told her. "It's brave to help out, and it feels really good."

Alice was getting restless. She stood up on Gene's knees, and he held her hands. "Daddy's feeling bad, so I have to climb him." She put one foot on his chest and leaned back, rappelling off him while he held her hands. She was intent and grave about the task, watching Gene's face for signs that it was making him feel better. He shook his head in disbelief. And then he and Claire started to laugh hard. Alice put her other foot on his chest and began to walk up so she could stand on his shoulders.

"You're going to climb all the way up Gene while he's crying *and* laughing?" Claire asked. Gene thought maybe she had inadvertently suggested Alice climb by saying "brave" and "feels good." The girl loved to climb, and they always called her "brave" or "fearless" or said "good job" when she was doing it.

"Gene likes to climb," Alice explained, shrugging. She put her feet on his shoulders, her skinny legs on either side of his head. He held her hands out to the side but then let go. He could feel that she was very well balanced, the arches of her little feet curved and strong, the heels resting just above his shoulder blades. And it did feel nice—like a massage. Her weight was just right.

Claire was looking at him, and though she was laughing at Alice, he saw that she was upset about Con. Disappointed. Pissed. "He's unhinged," she said quietly. "It's him. You couldn't have changed it." She looked deeply into his eyes, the way she did, keeping him company that way, better than a kiss, and pulled her knees up to her chest. She was no longer the skinny girl he'd known from the East Village; she was rounder now, a big-breasted, softer-featured woman, someone who had nursed a baby and had been high on the joy of caring for that baby. But her face and her eyes still expressed a knowledge that set her apart. Gene knew she had no sympathy for Con. The letter clearly disgusted her. He could see her weighing Constant's life against her own back at the clinic. Fourteen-hour days, crowded waiting rooms, funding cuts, staffing problems because people like Con found the work too boring or taxing, were unwilling to deal with the attendant features of poverty, illness, abuse. Gene knew that as far as she was concerned, Con might as well have sent them a letter saying he was sad he had only one Mercedes.

"Honestly," Gene said to her with Alice still standing on him, "he's just caught. He's been caught."

Claire

MICHELLE WAVED AT Claire and Gene from the front window of Downtown Beirut as Gene locked up their bike. She smiled and headed in, and Gene followed with his messenger bag.

"It's the breeders!" Michelle said as they pushed their way through.

"Sorry sorry sorry," Claire said. "I hope you haven't been waiting." She carried a bag from the thrift store connected to the shelter at St. Mark's. She was wearing pointy black knee-high boots and had just had her hair bleached the same color as Gene's and cut into an asymmetrical bob. She was wearing a black shirt with the Ramones smiling across her breasts.

Con leaned out from a crush three people deep to hand Michelle her drink. "I hate that you guys always want to come here," he said before ducking back to the bar. "I fucking hate the name of this place. I mean, Christ."

Someone had put Iggy Pop on the jukebox. Claire watched Con lip-synch the words, "I am the passenger. I ride and I ride," while he waited for the next drink. He was still wearing his blue oxford shirt from work but had left the tie and jacket somewhere.

Finally, he came to stand with them and kissed Claire on the cheek, passed a beer over to Gene. Claire knew their "surprise" had shaken him and Micky. They were more than nervous about the home-birth idea and conflicted about living with a baby. But when Gene and Claire moved, it would still be a bargain for Con and Michelle to live there, still keep them where they wanted to be—away from their asshole colleagues on the Upper East Side. Even so, they joked about how crack hadn't driven them out of the neighborhood, but the "miracle of human life" just might.

"Drink those now," Gene said, "and we'll buy a couple of forties to take over to ABC No Rio."

Con nodded in agreement, then said, "Lovely outfit, Doctor," to Claire.

"Thank you, darling," she said, and laughed. "You look very sharp yourself." Claire had felt elated since the third month she was pregnant. Everyone looked more beautiful to her, she loved riding her bike more than ever, and she found herself singing out loud when she didn't realize it, like in the checkout line at the grocery store. She turned to Michelle, opened her bag, and pulled out a red and black dress, holding it up against herself to show the diagonal hem that cut across her legs. "Two bucks!" she exclaimed.

"Nice," said Michelle, but her eyes weren't smiling.

"How was work?" Claire asked her.

Michelle yawned and nodded slowly, covering her mouth. "Cytomegalovirus," she said, and looked blankly over the crowd. She put her arm around Claire's waist and rested her head on her friend's shoulder. "Kaposi's sarcoma."

"It's bad," Con agreed. "I feel like at least seventy-five percent of my day used to revolve around opportunistic infections. I do not miss that."

His last words made Gene visibly tense.

"I feel so sad for this man I saw today," Michelle said. "He had his sister with him. Twenty-seven years old. He's going blind, CD4 below 140, boyfriend died this past winter. He should be out here drinking with us. His sister's sitting with him all day, reading him kids' stories." She drank the rest of her beer quickly, her arm still around Claire's waist.

Claire could see that Michelle was somewhere beyond angry, frustrated, exhausted. She had seen this on Con's face in the months before he gave notice at Beth Israel. It seemed that for

Michelle, too, everything had fallen away but the facts at hand. No tradition, no protocol, no gender, no oppression, no class, no status, no hierarchy guiding desire. No acquiescence. No will to power. Nothing but the stripped-down sense of possibility and fellow feeling in an animal looking after another animal. The psyche offered up. *This is what a healer should be,* she thought, proud of her friends. Michelle was going off to do the right thing. Con, she was sure, would come back to his senses.

"Did you guys eat?" Gene asked. He pulled two thin and knobby carrots from the messenger bag. Constant and Michelle shook their heads. "We ate at home, and then Claire had to stop at Katz's, and then she made us stop again for some seaweed salad."

"Jesus, girlie," said Michelle, "are you *trying* to make yourself puke?"

Claire smiled. Claire did not puke. Or cry. And her eating habits had nothing to do with pregnancy. She was always hungry.

Con set his empty glass on the bar, and they headed out into the warm night toward ABC No Rio to watch the Motivators play. The place was on a part of Rivington where they normally wouldn't go, but they went because Gene's friends from the community garden would be there, and because he was in love with the idea of a DIY community center. ABC No Rio proved his point about something. Proved that even when the artists moved out and the crackheads and junkies moved in, regular people still got together and got things done.

His theory made sense as they walked along, but it fell apart once they arrived and it became obvious to anyone who looked at them that they were the only "regular people" from the neighborhood there.

The opening band started with no introduction, causing the crowd closest to the stage to start jumping straight up and down, slamming, smashing into one another. Kids with their shirts off and overdressed kids in leather, a beautiful variety of bleach jobs

and shaved skulls, teased and dyed and flowing locks, safety pins
and pierced skin, studded wrists and necks and waists, torn shirts
emblazoned with missiles and mushroom clouds and swastikas
and American flags all slashed through with a red X. Or blotted
out with a circle A. Bodies, beautiful in exposed disarray, danced
and fell together, screamed along, wrestled and rolled one another,
then helped each other up, held hands and shouted and jumped
as one animal. The crowd and the band were in love. Pumped up,
elated, singing along unintelligibly through the industrial din.
Claire smiled at the sight of it. There was coercion and there was
play and it was not a fine line that divided them. She knew why
they were there. There was a power in the place and in the music
that they were in danger of losing, were losing every second. The
joy at the heart of anarchy. The feeling that you were born to
win. She looked at her tired friends, then pressed closer to Gene
to tell him that she loved him. Close enough to get the faint smell
of earth and sweat from his skin.

No longer able to crowd-surf or stage-dive, she stood happily watching, glad these traditions still existed. Hurtling toward
thirty, pregnant, sober, "professional," standing in a gutted pre-
war tenement on the Lower East Side, half dreaming of fields
and forests.

Gene

BEYOND THE PATH lined with lanterns and illuminated by pumpkins with grinning faces, dry cornstalks rustled gently in the field. Claire had hung white-handkerchief ghosts from the lower branches of the trees near the house, and Alice ran back and forth in the yard, waiting for Theo, the edges of her white gauzy costume floating behind her.

Claire, dressed as a fairy with wings made of crinoline, pants covered in faded daisies, and a blue pointy hat with a reproduction of Edward Munch's *Scream* painted on the front, was inside roasting pumpkin seeds and making vegetable stew. When Gene came in from outside, he said, "I need you to help me with this, Fairy." He handed Claire a large jack-o'-lantern with a hole in the bottom and then sat down in front of her at the table.

She stood between his legs for a moment and kissed him. "You've outdone yourself." She put a tea towel over his head and then eased the pumpkin down over it until it rested on his shoulders. The face had triangular eyes and nose and a big grinning mouth; a long twisted stem grew out of its crown.

"Perfect." She turned the pumpkin a little on his shoulders. "Can you see?"

He nodded and she kissed the pumpkin's forehead. He rubbed his hands over her daisy pants, touching her for some time before they noticed Theo staring at them through the screen door, his hair tangled, his face painted green, bright yellow circles rimming his eyes.

They started and then laughed at the boy's expression.

"Are your parents here?" Gene asked him.

"They dropped me off," Theo said. He turned his head to the side, about to say something else, but then caught sight of Alice and jumped off the step, ran all the way to the path that she was haunting. They heard her squeal as she spied him.

"Can you imagine anyone just dropping off a six-year-old in the city?" Gene asked Claire, his voice echoing inside the pumpkin.

"I can," she said. "But not the way you mean, no."

"I'm just going to take them into town for half an hour," Gene said. "They'll be ruined for dinner by the time we get back."

"That's fine. Maybe they'll have had so much sweet stuff by then they'll be craving real food."

Out in the yard, Gene watched Theo and Alice. They were holding hands and leaning back, spinning in a circle as fast as they could—periodically, they would let go and fall to the ground, laughing and yelling, then stand again and stagger like drunks. Alice tripped over the sheet and fell, and Theo lay on top of her while she struggled to get up.

The streets of the town were crowded with trick-or-treaters. Gene stood at the edge of the sidewalk as the ghost and the frog ran up to each door. They were squealing and talking nonsense, words and sentences that were half articulated, half hummed. They ran to catch up with groups of older ghouls, stalking along in packs with pillowcases filled with candy. Jason and Freddy Krueger, NASCAR drivers carrying their helmets, Ariel and Snow White, a hobo, a witch, Batman, G.I. Joe, and Cruella de Vil. A taller kid walked by in a Bill Clinton mask with five little Dallas Cowboys by his side. A black cat, the grim reaper, and a ballerina stood on the corner peering into their orange plastic buckets, and a pair of dice in matching black tights waved to them as they passed.

Just before they reached Town Line Road, Alice and Theo

fell silent in awe at the mist surrounding a house lit with green lights. It was the last house in the village, and terrifying screams came from somewhere deep inside. In the front yard, stripe-stockinged legs ending in pointy black shoes stuck out of the ground, alongside half a broomstick, as if a witch had crashed in the yard. A big plastic glow-in-the-dark skeleton sat crumpled in a chair on the porch. And an enormous nylon ghost, lit from inside and inflated by some kind of faintly ticking fan, billowed up from the front lawn.

"It's haunted!" Alice yelled. She ran in a little circle around Theo, who grabbed the edge of her protoplasmic aura and wouldn't let go until she was wound around him.

It's haunted by the ghosts of Indonesian child laborers, Gene thought.

"Come with us!" Alice shouted. "Come with us on the porch, Daddy, it's haunted."

Theo was still holding part of her costume as they walked nervously up onto the porch in front of Gene. They rang the doorbell and hunched their shoulders, waiting for someone to answer. When the door opened, they did not say "trick or treat." They did not even move. Gene watched as they raised their heads in unison to look up at Frankenstein.

Frankenstein looked at Gene and winked. His makeup job was fantastic. The scars appeared real, and he had a flattop that made his head seem square, with bolts coming out of his neck. Plus, the guy was enormous. Gene thought this must be Danny White, the White Walls Drywall guy. It took a minute before any of them saw the princess, a girl who looked to be about nine years old, standing beneath the monster with a bowlful of SweeTarts. She was smiling at Alice and Theo and trying not to laugh.

"Mom!" the princess called back into the house. "C'mere, you've got to see this."

A short round woman with feathered blond hair and freckled

forearms came from around the corner and looked out through the storm door. She grinned broadly at them. "Well, what do we have here?" she asked.

Theo and Alice were still transfixed. Wendy's mother looked up at Gene. "They're darling. How old?"

"Five and six," Gene said.

"Oh my god," the princess said. "Is that a real pumpkin on your head? Daddy, look!"

Frankenstein smiled. "Well, holy smokes, Wen—someone's trying to outdo my costume this year!"

"Aha! That's not a real monster!" Alice said. Theo let go of her ghost suit and held out his bag. The Whites laughed, and Gene smiled inside his pumpkin head, thought what a sweet family, what good people, standing together beneath their porch light.

"You don't often see a ghost and a frog traveling together," Wendy's mother said.

"Actually," said Alice, "it might not be that uncommon. In Hades, there are rivers! And if there are rivers, there are probably frogs, so if you are a ghost, then there are probably frogs who could be your friends. There are definitely frogs down there."

"Ribbit," Theo said, and held out his bag again.

The Whites looked at one another and laughed harder. "You got your hands full, don't you?" Danny White said to Gene.

Wendy came out onto the porch and gave Alice a hug. "You are so cute!" she said. "Mom, she is *so* cute!"

Alice looked up at the big princess and smiled unseen beneath her ghost suit. "There can be princesses in the afterlife with us!" she said, eager to include Wendy in their game. "We know there can. We've actually seen them there!"

Flynn

THE FIRST YEAR I lived in Haeden, I spent many evenings eating dinner at the bar in the Alibi, listening to people talk, and many nights at home on my computer, researching rural environmental problems. My intentions in moving to Haeden had not been rational. They were certainly not ideal for me personally. I left a place where I was happy; I had friends and boyfriends and colleagues and sources, I had broken stories, and people knew my byline and what I liked to drink.

In Haeden things were different. There were few friends to have. The eight or so people to whom I might have grown close were significantly older and had children or other preoccupations. Many of them were some kind of dropouts from rich families or good schools, sold on an idea of pioneering that was reinforced by an extreme lack of hardship in their formative years. I enjoyed talking politics with them at the Rooster, and I felt they were decent people. The Pipers were among this set, and Alice's father, who had a part-time job with Soil and Water, and who saw himself as part of some David and Goliath story involving factory farms, provided me with a lot of information about the land itself. They were witty, intelligent people, good cooks and well read, but there was something slightly off about them—they'd experienced one too many bedtime readings of *Peter Pan*, maybe, had the earnest gaze of one who believes Tinker Bell can be brought back from the dead if we all clap our hands. They were looking for a place to love and believed it would be somewhere that didn't yet exist. Somewhere they would create, a place that would materialize beneath their feet, no matter the real landscape of the region, a landscape that included nearly two thousand other people whose median income was less than $14,000 a year.

Haeden was also not the place to find a mate. Even a tempo-rary one. I was asked out by a variety of different men—builders, a plumbing and heating technician, a pharmacy student intern-ing at the Kinny drugs, a sixty-year-old professor, one of Dale Haytes's rangy walleyed uncles, the Sysco salesman who stopped at the bar every week on his route through the region, a neu-rotic middle-school teacher, two Vietnam vets, a Gulf War I vet, several high school seniors, and an acupuncturist who lived in Elmville. All of them but the high schoolers went to work and then went home, and all of them were looking for someone else with whom to do that. Three trips back to Cleveland took care of the only thing for which they might have been useful. And long phone conversations took care of the things they couldn't provide.

I lived those early years as best I could and felt many times that I was an embedded reporter, a correspondent from some postmodern ghost place, not even a town. I had never thought that anywhere in New York State, let alone the Northeast, could look like *Deliverance* country. And in some ways that made it all the more exotic, more surreal.

I have said over and over that I left Cleveland so I could work on a big investigative piece. That I left because the next critical wave of environmental reporting would be, as I told my friends at *City Paper*, rural, about food and water. And in many ways, this is true—close to the whole story.

If there hadn't been a major change in environmental legisla-tion, and if I had never learned about Seneca Falls, New York, I probably would have stayed in Cleveland. Seneca Falls is the site of Elizabeth Cady Stanton's speeches, the place where the wom-en's suffrage movement began. It also was home to the largest waste site in the state—a fenced-in dome as big as a ski mountain over which bulldozers maneuvered tons of waste between the off-gassing pipes that went deep into the massive pile. My big-picture story would be about how all the garbage and detritus not fit for cities ends up in rural areas, buried or piled up over expanses of unfarmable fields. Places where the brain drain has been so bad that only a handful of locals take offense to this shit, and the rest ignore it.

I knew that nothing like this could happen without people getting sick and other people benefiting from it. If I followed the money, I would find out. But somehow, in my anticipatory zeal about breaking open the story of this waste site, I got lost. I voluntarily left somewhere I loved because I had become an egomaniac. I honestly believed articles in the newspaper could change the way the world worked. And that meant *I* could change the way the world worked. And that's not the healthiest thought for a human being to have.

The tipping point in my narcissism came when I won a George Polk for local investigative reporting, a few months before I quit Cleveland. It was a proud day for me and my editors, a recognition that seemed to independently confirm that it was worthwhile for me to be busting my ass the way I'd been. That my instincts for news were sound. The award was for a series on a neighborhood that had lost dozens to cancer, MS, and respiratory illnesses. These were the legacies of the steel and chemical industries. After the mills and manufacturers closed down, Cleveland lost a huge swath of the middle class, but we still had all the illness from things that were buried, burned, dumped into the Cuyahoga, or washed into the earth. This may not sound important to you, but the old adage "If it bleeds, it leads" finds more purchase in this kind of story than in a local murder. Leaves whole neighborhoods— sometimes a few generations in that neighborhood—fucked, bereaved. Racist redlining is not just a problem in housing. In Cleveland, Buffalo, Pittsburgh, Detroit, Chicago, the redline of affordable real estate between one neighborhood and another marks mortality. Buy or rent a house past this point, this street, in the shadow of this building, and see if your baby gets leukemia, see if your husband gets to keep his nuts.

The Polk was meant to reveal good writing and get important stories more press. And it did. It was part of getting Superfund designation for the neighborhood and getting things cleaned up. What the Polk didn't as handily reveal was the character of the recipient. In my case: obsessive, addicted to every story I was assigned, unable to cut details or column inches, unable to go home at the end of the day. Unable to talk about anything but my beat. In Cleveland I never left the newsroom; I just brought it to bed with me. I slept with other reporters or with people like reporters (lawyers, cops) because we loved to talk about the same things and were smart in the same ways, had the same sense of humor, but also because they didn't notice how little space in my psyche they would occupy. And because they were too busy to saddle me with their attention. We were alone together, looking at the same things. And this was a very full life. It was as I had imagined it to be when I was a girl and first fell in love with newspapers and H. L. Mencken and I. F. Stone. And though I was now an adult and surrounded by a culture in which papers and magazines were disappearing daily, I felt my future as a 1940s-style muckraker was secure. All I needed was the sleeve garters and a drinking problem. The Rust Belt's environmental problems were bad, but they were waning, "outsourced"; rural America's problems were beginning to snowball. And I wanted to be there.

When the job came up in Haeden, close to Appalachia and less than a day's drive from New York City, I was thrilled. I was sure I would meet a lot of simple salt-of-the-earth people and that they just needed someone to put all the facts together before they said no to being buried in garbage.

I didn't know until I had been there six months that they were also being buried in shit, and drinking it and eating it. And that the only investigation into the health effects of the industrial dairy was being carried out by Scoop, who had a mysterious method for fact-checking called "he gave me his word." After explaining, he would fix me with an indignant look. "Places like this, a man's word is still worth something," he told me.

My methods of reporting were different. You do not find things out by "believing." Digging is the main method. I began filing Freedom of Information requests immediately, interviewing chemists and toxics geographers from across the state. I amassed files and photographs and research, wrote article proposals and pitches for every major publication in the country, then waited. I wrote only a few pieces for the *Free Press*. Covered a handful of town meetings about the smell and the waste dumping and what might happen to the drinking water. Sometimes people would talk about how the animals were treated, but for the most part, people accepted the Haytes and talked about how they provided for the community. For a while it appeared Gene Piper might become a galvanizing force among townspeople, the voice of reason and good health for all, but his outsider status, his quick, articulate way at meetings, sank any real influence he could have had before it even began. The stories did not spark the kind of response I'd seen in Cleveland. So I saved the majority of my research for other publications. And as you know, that big-picture story never saw the light of day.

For the *Free Press*, I wrote about Alice Piper's accomplishments, about town meetings and school board meetings and local women's groups, about pancake breakfasts, local elections, church trips to Mexico, and watercolor exhibits at the one-room library in the center of town. I did feel sometimes that in little places like Haeden, it meant something when someone gave you their word. And I did feel that there were salt-of-the-earth people waiting for someone to put the facts together so they could do the right thing, but maybe they were too tired to follow through. And that the builders who asked me out, and who I rejected, and the ladies my age pushing strollers or talking to one another at the Savers Club, were okay, were doing what

I couldn't really abide by, which was just to live, not dig, not achieve, but live.

This is a heartbreak I do not like to admit to. That there were times I wanted something they had. And I was caught off guard by the shock of learning what it takes for regular people to be at peace in their homes, in their communities. I was thrown, entirely thrown, by the price of their quiet lives, their contentment.

Alex Dino. April 16, 2009.

Like I was saying, if anyone knew it was going to happen, it was Theo Bailey. We interviewed that smart-ass little fuck and I nearly lost it. Parents too busy up at the college and letting that psycho Ross Miller half raise the boy. I nearly fucking lost it.

This did not happen without planning. She's a planner. And she's a studier, she's a leader. This shit isn't like workplace violence—it usually involves more than one person. And I swear to you, that other person was Theo. This is entirely on background. What I've said and what I'm going to say. And don't even think of fucking around with it. You're in no position.

We don't yet know what we're looking at. Typically, when you see things like this, there are a limited number of causes. We've got about twenty or thirty recent examples involving boys or groups of boys, but this is different.

We don't know much. We know she wasn't using drugs, not even prescription drugs, wasn't diagnosed with depression or anything, no recent concussion or anything like that. She didn't have a computer at home, no cell phone, which of course is weird enough, but . . . So no electronic information or correspondence or websites she went to, no blog. No Facebook. If there was more than one letter back and forth between her and that stupid little fuck, we haven't found all the rest yet. But I am sure they exist.

There's this idea that these kids are kids who are bullied, have bad social relationships and stuff like that, but honestly? Nothing actually connects these kids. Some have good social skills, good grades, family's got money. They're white. Some are bullied or picked on or come from tough home situations. Usually, this stuff doesn't happen in the city at all. It happens in rural or suburban areas, for the most part, which is why I don't understand why we can't get funding to do something about this problem. We used to have a school resource officer stationed here from the state police, but the funding got cut. Christ, we can't get funds for shit. It's like we don't even exist.

To tell you the truth, I don't know where half the ideas about teen crime come from, and I've been doing this for thirty years. Dumb petty-theft stuff, fighting and drinking, you might find in the less advantaged adolescents. But the *real* crime. The hard drugs, the drug dealing, the *real* theft, that's not coming from the wrong side of the tracks. That's a surprise, right?

Well, it's like this information they just handed out to us. We got these stats on incarceration last week says that white kids are seven times more likely to use cocaine than black kids, and you think, Oh, *it's 'cause the blacks use crack*, right? Wrong. Our kids are *eight* times more likely to use crack. Our twelve-to-seventeen-year-olds sell *more* drugs. So you know, a lot of folks around here, they think that crime and drugs is a black thing, but guess again. Then there's violent crime. White kids are *twice* as likely to own a gun than black kids. This is why *we* need more funding. This is why we need someone right in there, instead of giving all the money to the black schools and the schools in the inner city so the fucking niggers, pardon my French, can waste it. Yeah, they do, they just waste it. You think those black schools don't get money? They get more than we do for all the special ed and the whatchafuckingcallit cultural programs and shit. They just pour money into those schools, and they don't need it. And we sure as hell don't get anything in return out of those people, know what I'm saying?

Listen, we're looking at something here that's more like Timothy McVeigh. This situation sure seems like terrorism to me. Tell me how it isn't terrorism. It's just like President Bush said—this was like an attack on *our way of life*. We really need to figure out if there is some, some ideological base to these things—maybe there is to all of them—and I'm telling you, in the case of Piper, there sure as hell was.

We start out looking at motivations, maybe she was involved with one of those boys, got her heart broke. Well, that is just not the case. I can tell you this. We may be uncovering something a hell of a lot deeper.

The things those parents believe in are beyond the pale. It's not just some hippie stuff, the town's half run by those types anyway, but the Pipers, I don't know *what* you call them. They were like a cult. The three of them. Some kind of mind cult. Them and their friends. Environmentalists. I can show you documents we took from that house you wouldn't believe. Those smiling parents and that pretty little girl with all her awards, they associated with people, believed in things, that would curl your hair. You think environmentalists are harmless, but they're not. They're not tracked by the FBI for being harmless.

We know what they read in that home. We have boxes full of that shit. We know where they came from, what they'd been doing. But we don't know what she was thinking. We have one love letter and school papers. No journals, no home movies, no statement. Nothing. She's like a goddamn ghost. Going to have to try to trace it all backwards through the parents. And I know that punk-ass Bailey kid in his little blue blazer knows exactly what happened.

Claire

THE HAEDEN VOLUNTEER Fire Department was a vast metal pole barn on Route 34. It housed one fire engine; a gray tiled hall for dances, first-aid training, and speaking events; and a paneled lounge with low brown carpeting, a sectional couch, and a coffee table.

The VFD was a nice hangout, furnished and maintained by gifts and county money. The firemen didn't live there, but they did play poker there a few times a month with a couple of emergency medical technicians, and there were emergency pony bottles of Pabst Blue Ribbon in the refrigerator. They also barbecued chickens in the parking lot and held pancake breakfasts for Mother's Day, Father's Day, and Easter.

The VFD was making Gene's point about something. It was a living example of mutual aid and solidarity. Right there in the middle of nowhere. He convinced Connie to make a two-thousand-dollar donation to the place last year just by talking about it.

Gene loved the fire department in a way Claire thought was sweet and a little stupid. "I'm not all about pretending to be one of the boys in a place like this," she said.

Gene grinned at her. "Of course you are, baby."

She shrugged. "You know you're grasping at straws trying to make a neglected construction of corrugated sheet metal into some kind of community of unwitting first responders."

But the fire department was pretty nice, she had to admit. It was the one place in town that felt slightly familiar. She had taken Alice there to get first-aid training from a guy named Tom Cutting, who could easily be confused for an anarchist if he didn't love his ridiculous uniform so much. Cutting reminded her of Con when he was young, and she thought he might be good bait to get Micky to move back to the States and onto the land they now all owned together.

"You guys suck!" Claire told her on the phone the other day. "It's so pretty here, girl. And you! You just travel around and know your place is here, unoccupied by you."

"Connie and I are planning on having the field torn down to put up a metropolis," Michelle said. "That's why it's taking us so long, all the planning . . . Plus, if you didn't remember, Con and I have not lived together for the last seven years."

"Right—it's a very good time for you both to come visit. You can see your godchild."

"How's it going with the house and everything? Are you doing okay there?"

"I don't really get out much," Claire said. "I spend a lot of time with Ross. We'll be putting the garden in soon, which is always a lot of fun. We're planting soybeans this year. But mostly we're kinda broke. I doubt I'd get out much even if we weren't. Socially, nothing's changed. I don't really know how to describe the people here."

"Hicks?" said Michelle.

"C'mon, Micky."

"Aggressively hetero-normative? What did you used to say about those girls from upstate in our clinical?"

Claire laughed. "Oh, Jesus. No, it's somehow weirder than that. Like . . . that shit you said about paying attention to the obvious."

"George Orwell said that."

"Well, whatever. The obvious is all you get here. Try talking about anything else, and . . . I don't know. Whatever. Gene is pretty happy doing things at home, for the most part."

"What a surprise," Michelle said.

"It's hard. It's hard to go into Alice's school. You know, it's a little country school, and she's happy there. She has a sweet group of friends."

"So why is it hard?"

"Oh, it's nothing. It's really nothing. It's the moms, I guess. But the kids are sweet as hell, so they can't be all that bad. Most of our friends here are like Ross's age, they don't have kids in school. We see them like once a week at most." Claire could hear the crackling sound of the poor connection between them and pressed the phone harder against her ear. "I mean, this is what it is: The other day a woman wanted to talk to me about driving kids around, you know, what kind of car she had, something about shopping somewhere in a store in the mall. Like for twenty fucking minutes. Almost half an hour of saying a thing and then another thing. It's not like that's horrible on its own, it's just that there *is* nothing else. You could have five or six conversations like that back to back. Every day. There's no mass transit at all. You can't take the train somewhere else, or get some pad thai, or see anyone who looks different at all. A person comes up and just describes the things that are around in the lightest possible way, states various observable facts. The whole social context is missing. I hate to say this, 'cause it's my fault for not staying more mentally active on my own, but I haven't laughed out loud—you know, just felt myself laugh really hard—in a long time."

As Claire said it, she felt she was going to start crying. She was embarrassed she'd complained about it, about missing food and subways, especially to Micky, with the work she did, and when she finally said, "It's no big deal," her voice was hoarse.

In that moment Claire wished Michelle and Con were there or that she was in New York or Africa. Anywhere else. She could feel that woman's eyes on her, and the passive, trapped, haughty way she had spoken about routine things. A list of possessions. In that moment Claire doubted playing the MC5 was going to cut it anymore. It was just one more thing that made her different.

At least today was one of the most exciting days in Haeden — Mother's Day. Kind of like the town's version of the West Village Halloween parade, she had joked.

Gene and Tom Cutting and several other men were dressed in flowered aprons. This was supposed to be funny, and many residents commented on it while they watched the men flip pancakes and fry bacon. Some of the men acted like drag queens, which actually was funny but not for the reasons they thought it was.

Claire liked Cutting. He was thirty years old and still driving ambulances, which he had started doing in high school. Still helping people every day, not proofing textbooks, like she was. And it showed.

Cutting had crazy eyes and a huge gap-toothed smile, and he did not seem to assess the politics of every resident in the pancake line. He also did not pantomime "femininity" while wearing an apron. Something about him was completely engaged and completely detached all at once; he was a real studier of people, which might have been unnerving if he hadn't been so obviously dedicated to his job.

The other thing Claire admired about Cutting was that he was happy where he was, even though he'd been transferred there, the only paid employee affiliated with the Haeden VFD. He talked to everyone. If he didn't know someone's name, he asked. He asked about their grandparents or dogs or uncles.

When it was Alice's turn in line, he asked her how to restart a heart. "I need to know, I need to know!" he told her, flipping a pancake onto her plate. "Quick!"

"CPR will not restart a heart!" she said as fast as she could. "Its-goal-is to-circulate-oxygenated-blood-to-the brain-and-vital-organs, until-an-automated-external-defibrillator-is-ready-

96 · Cara Hoffman

to-use-or-advanced-medical-help-arrives-and-takes-over-the-victim's-care." She took a breath. "Nevertheless—once you begin CPR, you should continue uninterrupted until the scene becomes unsafe or a trained rescuer arrives or a miracle happens and a heart that technically couldn't have been restarted starts again!"

"Al's my best student," he said to the next person in line. "When she turns ten, I'm going to let her teach the class."

"Really?" Alice called back to him.

"No way!" He smiled. "You're just a kid! Didn't anybody explain that to you?"

Alice and Claire sat at the long folding conference table that was covered with flimsy red-and-white-checkered plastic table-cloths. After a minute Gene came to sit with them. It was stuffy and greasy, and the noise of forks and knives and several different conversations echoed in the hall.

The television was on in one corner, beaming CNN into the room—the familiar voices of newscasters and commercial jingles blending into the separate conversations like a song everybody knew. Everybody but Alice.

The Pipers had no television, and she sat transfixed. Staring at the screen, her mouth slightly open. Gene waved a hand in front of her face. Snapped his fingers right near her ear, and she didn't respond. "Better than dope," he said quietly.

Claire and Gene surveyed the room together: familiar un-knowns and some faces with accompanying names. It was a very round, blond population, sporting a variety of baseball caps, work boots, floral prints, and sweats.

A tall, sandy-haired man in a polo shirt, docksiders, and jeans came over to their table and clapped Gene on the back. "So here's what our scientist does on his day off, huh?" Gene looked up and smiled, offered his hand to the man, who gave it a firm shake. "This must be the missus!"

Claire looked at Gene and almost laughed. She smiled up at the man.

"This is Claire," Gene said.

"Weeell, pleased to meet *you*, Claire. I'm Bob Dyer. Gene here is helping us out, taking some soil samples up there at our property." He winked at Gene. "Got the first fifty acres pretty well taken care of by now."

Claire nodded encouragingly at the man.

"Is that your pretty little gal?" he asked.

"That's Alice," Claire said. Alice was still staring at the television, absently eating her pancakes.

"Well." Dyer grabbed Gene's hand again and clapped him on the back. "I better be getting back over to *my* little ladies— wouldn't want to get in trouble, now. Get DeeDee jealous on Mother's Day." He winked at Gene and somehow moved his mouth over to the side of his face to grin. He pointed a finger at him before walking away.

"Wow," Claire said. "My God."

Gene raised his eyebrows and nodded. "It's fascinating, really, if you think about it. Remind me to tell you later about that male pointing behavior. Everybody does it here. I have a theory."

"Is it related to tiny little penises?"

He laughed. "The term," he said in a hushed sarcastic tone, "is micro-penis, and in this case, it's likely the result of environmental toxins. Mr. Dyer's land borders the dairy."

Claire laughed. She loved her husband.

Alice was staring at a commercial for My Little Pony. "I love My Little Pony and new Pinkie Pie Plush Pony!" a little girl was shouting ecstatically at another little girl.

"I'm taking Newborn Pinkie Pie to visit Crystal Princess in her Curtsy Carriage!" The other girl replied. Alice's mouth hung open. Then she said the words "Pinkie Pie" out loud.

*   *   *

Later, in the car, Claire said, "Okay, you were right about the *Wild Kingdom* aspect of it all."

Gene laughed. "What'd you think of the VFD, though?"

"Nice. They've done a lot of work," Claire said.

"Those didn't really taste like pancakes," Alice said.

"It was an incredible turnout, baby," Claire said. "Where was Ross?"

"They were a different kind of pancake. Made from a mix," Gene told Alice, then "Why would Ross be at the Mother's Day breakfast? He's out shooting."

Claire shrugged.

"I'd like to go out shooting," Alice said.

"Ask Ross. I'm sure he'd show you how to shoot targets," Gene said, and Claire squinted at him and shook her head in disbelief.

"I'm going to make a papier-mâché centaur," Alice said, thankfully moving along to her next idea. "I need to get those kinds of dog-chew toys that look like hooves for the hooves. What are they made of?"

"Actual hooves," Claire told her.

"Really?" She was silent, thinking about it for a minute. Then said anxiously, "I have to check on my toad."

"We're almost home."

"Wait, though. Can we stop and get hooves?"

"I don't know where you saw them, honey," Claire said.

"Agway. They're in a plastic candy jar in the checkout line, and they cost a dollar thirty-five for two. Theo has a G.I. Joe, and we cut him in half for the upper body."

"What will you do with the G.I. Joe legs?" Gene asked her.

"Is it G.I. because it's gastrointestinal?" Alice asked. "Gastro-intestinal Joe?"

"No," he said, glancing at Claire and trying not to laugh. "Government-issue."

"What's the issue?"

"Issue also means like to release or send out," Claire told her.

"Oh, I get it. Well, I'm using the legs. I'm making a doll with a toad's body and human legs."

"How will you make the toad part?"

"Green leather change purse and a mitten! Those pancakes tasted like papier-mâché. I tasted that stuff once and they really did, seriously."

Alice stopped talking, and they were quiet for a while, driving into Elmville to the Agway. Claire was happy for the quiet as it was rare these days. Alice had so much she wanted to do and talk about, seemed to have left behind the contemplative, private world of her babyhood, the seriousness of watching and assessing. Now everything had to be discussed and explained.

Claire was content just driving with her husband and daughter together in their separate thoughts, but the silence was short-lived, because Alice began to sing Woody Guthrie songs. Lying flat in the backseat, she sang. *Let's go riding in the car, car.* Then she sang it again in a different key. *I'm gonna send you home again, I'm gonna send you home again, boom boom boom, rolling hooooooommmmmeeee! Take you riding in the car.* When she was done singing, she said, "Hey! Can you really spin straw into something you can sew with?"

"I doubt it. Not too easily," Gene said.

"Can you make a unicycle out of a bicycle?"

"Yes," he said. "That's doable."

"*You're* doable," Claire said to Gene softly. He touched her hand on the stick shift, and she glanced over to see him looking at her thigh as she pressed in the clutch. She could smell his hair, a faint waft of tea-tree oil. Claire knew Gene would want to take a nap when they got home, make love and fall asleep while Alice was out in the barn building centaurs and frogs and checking on toads. He would make the day's bread dough first and let it rise while they lay. And she would feel his weight and warmth, her cheek on his shoulder, their arms and legs entwined even in sleep. And when she woke, she would smell his skin, and seeing his face would be a gift. It was because of Gene that Claire knew she could want the life they had. She could have faith that it would all work out.

Alice and Theo

ALICE'S LEGS WERE long and nearly the same width from ankle to thigh. She looked down at them and thought about how walking worked, wearing her swim cap, chewing a huge wad of bubble gum, headed to meet Theo after school at the bridge on Rabbit Run Road. It was early June. In three weeks she would be free of third grade. Tomorrow Constant was coming for dinner and to stay for a while, like he had done every summer since she could remember.

Constant is Alice's uncle and Theo's cousin, but somehow none of them are related, really, in the genetic way. Constant was Ross's ex-wife's nephew. And Ross is Theo's mom's stepbrother. And Constant is kind of Gene's brother. In this way, it is like she and Theo are cousins. They look alike, too. They can pretend to be cousins.

"Blood relationships are weak relationships," she remembered her mother saying. Brain relationships are the ones that really matter. Sometimes you're related to people you have good brain relationships with, sometimes not. Being related by blood isn't the same as being a family. Alice thought about this as she walked to the bridge.

Genetics only make a difference because if you have sex with your relatives, you will produce babies with screwed-up bodies or brains—having sex with your relatives is what kings and queens and rich people do, which is one reason rulers tend to be crazy. Gene and Claire told her all about DNA and how humans are all made of the same stuff, and animals are made of mostly the same stuff, too. So the craziest thing in the world is believing you can tell other people what to do—or thinking that some people deserve better care or more things than other people—because all humans have the same biological needs and deserve the same essential things. Kings and queens and rich people try to make those with less than they have give them things. They also think they can tell people what to do and how to act, which proves they are crazy, maybe even from inbreeding or something like that.

She and Theo are not related. But sometimes they would tell each other what to do. And she knew that wasn't good. Sometimes she wanted to tell him what to do so badly she felt like she might scream. She asked Gene about it while he was splitting wood one day, and he said, "Go ahead, tell him what to do, he'll do it or he won't. That's up to him. Then there's nothing more that can happen. What do you want him to do, anyway?"

She had thrown her head back and groaned in frustration. "To catch the *second* trapeze on the *second* swing! NOT the third— the third gets everything off to the WRONG count if you're playing Peter and the Wolf!" She shouted because it was obviously so easy to catch on the second swing that she was still mad he wouldn't do it.

Gene had raised his eyebrows at her and laughed. "Yeah," he had said. "It would be a different count if you're playing circus to that CD, and you want the upward swings to be on the downbeat." He set the axe aside and handed her some split wood and lit his cigarette. "I wonder what sounds right with the third swing?" He seemed to ask himself, though he said it loud enough for Alice to hear. "Not Prokofiev, that's for sure. You called that one." Then he hummed. He picked up his own pile of wood, and she walked beside him toward the house carrying hers. He shrugged. "Theo could practice it and get it right or not. Or you guys could find something that has a different tempo; there's only a million circus songs in the world, punkin. Everything can be a circus song. It's not that big a deal."

When he said it, she was amazed that she hadn't thought of other songs herself. It was like she had completely forgotten other songs existed. She could tell Theo what to do, but then she would only be right about this one trick and this one song. Which didn't seem worth the bad feeling of wanting to tell a person what to do. It was like the scope in Uncle Ross's gun. It blotted out the entire world and placed a cross over the thing you wanted to see most clearly. The thing you want to look at up close. It was the opposite of Gene's old microscope.

She snapped her gum, still thinking about it as she walked toward the riverbank and saw Theo waiting on the bridge in the afternoon sun. He had a way of having all the right things. Magnets, matches, marbles, rubber erasers shaped like animals, a harmonica, beeswax, rolls of caps. Today she hoped he had brought a jar, because she didn't have one. They had planned to wade out into the river and catch crayfish, but they always forgot to bring a jar. He waved at her and stood on the rail of the bridge.

"Connie is coming tomorrow night!" she called to him.

He nodded. "Why are you wearing your swim cap?"

"Can I sleep over?" she asked.

"Yeah."

"In the yurt?"

"No. Ross said he quit his job. He's going to stay in the yurt for a while."

"*Really?* Why does he have to stay in the yurt if he quit his job?"

Theo shrugged. His hair was always tangled, and it stuck up in the back and was a little too long in the front. He brushed it out of his eyes.

"I wanted to make mobiles for Con," she said.

"We can make crayfish mobiles. Do you have any more gum?"

Crayfish mobiles are a genius idea, she thought, even better if there was a way to keep the crayfish alive. She reached into the pocket of her shorts and handed him the whole pack of gum as they made their way along the trail that led beneath the bridge and out along the muddy pebbled bank of the river. They crouched, looking into the shallow water for tiny gray-and-green-mottled lobster bodies camouflaged as stones. They wandered in up to their ankles, looking straight down. Seeing the armored insect-like bodies darting away got their hearts pounding. They were hunting, grabbing the crayfish fast, just behind their front claws so they wouldn't get pinched.

Theo hadn't brought a jar, so they took off their shirts, making them into pouches to hold the crayfish, and they left the shirts on the bank churning and crawling slowly in different directions as they swam.

This was where they used to pretend to be animals when they were little and their parents brought them there, and they felt it again now—the desire to change into animals. They avoided looking at each other for a while. But it was too much for Alice. She looked right at Theo and raised her eyebrows, hunched her shoulders. Then she waited. She could see when he had become Mole. He didn't need to tell her. When he first did it, she felt a little sick to her stomach, so embarrassed that they still did this—played Wind in the Willows and Circus and came to their special place when the rest of their class was trading Pokémon cards and going to Little League practice or watching TV. Something about what they were doing was wrong. No one played this way except babies. That was made clear to them when they were overheard on the monkey bars at recess. She felt queasy because it was actually dangerous for Theo to play like that. They pulled his sneakers off and hit him in the face with them. They slammed him on the floor in the hallway coming in from the playground, slammed their shoulders into his back. The kid whose hair was cut with dog clippers, who wore a Buffalo Bills sweatshirt, whose cheeks were rosy like in pictures of Snow White, he was Theo's age but a big boy. His wide-set eyes were too wet. He had big chapped lips and really straight teeth. He was the one who knocked Theo down for saying "Quite, quite, Ratty." That kid knocked into

Theo and called him a girl and a fag and told him he had a girl-friend. And that his dad was a fag. He called Alice a slut and said her parents were on welfare. She didn't know what welfare was, but it sounded pretty bad. He also said she was wearing queer Kmart pants. Claire had made the pants and Alice didn't know if they were queer. When she asked if they were queer or not, her mother laughed. She didn't laugh about what the kid said, though. She put out her arms for Alice to come lie on the couch and read with her. It wasn't just the kid with the straight teeth. Alice didn't want to think about the number of boys who had understood everything that kid said. And her not understanding what he said was the worst part about all of it.

Claire said, "When people do stuff like that, pumpkin sauce, they are in a lot of pain, and they want someone to keep them company, so they try to give them the pain, too. Bring them that bad feeling they have. You have to ignore what they say."

Claire obviously didn't know how much company the kid had, because Alice hadn't told her the whole story. There had to be another reason. The kid with the chapped lips wanted them to stop playing a game they always played—and even to stop wearing the clothes they wore. Somehow Alice really hated her pants now, which didn't make sense, because they had been her favorite pants. Bright orange with side pockets.

She thought about it. People hurt other people when they were in pain or if they were crazy—if a person is in bad pain or for too long, they go crazy on reflex, like a dog that bites you if you step on its tail. People tell other people what to do if they are crazy. Like the way inbreeding makes people crazy or retarded, kings and queens and that kind of thing. Claire had it mixed up. She thought the kid was in pain, but he was royalty. He was not in pain. You could see he wasn't unhappy. He was happy. He was so happy when he knocked Theo down that you could see it in the way he breathed.

"I'll never keep him company," Alice said, amazed and confused that Claire had even suggested it. You're not supposed to encourage the bossiness or crazy ideas of rich people. Or ignore the bad things they do. You're not supposed to be scared of them.

Standing in the river with the queasy feeling, she glanced at Theo to see if he had changed. She watched his eyelids droop, then he squinted. And somehow he actually made his nose pointy and his chin shrink back. He was nervous but dignified.

"It's ever so good of you to come here, Moley," Alice said to him, pulling a strand of her long hair out of her swim cap to make a wispy blond tail that would hang down her back. This was why she'd worn the cap in the first place, but didn't want to say so out loud.

"My pleasure, Ratty," he said. "But we've got to act fast today, I'm afraid. We've got to *do* something about Mr. Toad." Theo's English accent was perfect, and he was proud of it. He was the best actor in the whole world. She no longer felt sick or worried.

"Pretend we have to break him out of jail," Alice whispered.

"We need to take the train out to Elmville," Mole said, as if he hadn't even heard her—but he had. "I've an idea. A dangerous idea."

"Quite," Rat said as she put her hands on the silty, stony bottom and let her legs float on the gentle current. She blew a pink bubble. "Quite so, old chap," Ratty went on. "We should go to Badger's at once and bring him these lovely crayfish, and maybe he can help us. They're holding Toad in the dungeon, I hear." She gestured toward the only large building visible from the riverbank, the flat white architecture of Haeden Medical Center.

Mole was standing up to his waist in the river, holding a stick in the water and watching the current ripple around it. "Badger will know what to do once we've freed him," he said. "He has tunnels that go all the way to Elmville and even farther. But we need a plan."

"Yes, quite. A plan," said Rat. "Toad can't quite leave as himself, can he? I say we sneak him out, disguise him as an old washerwoman. So long as he keeps quiet, no one will know. Then it's down to the riverbank and past the wild wood to safety."

They stared into each other's eyes, standing shirtless in the green-gray water. She knew the gravity and danger of what they were about to do was immense. Outrageous! But she had no idea what it was or when they would do it, and suddenly, she started to feel like this had all happened before and she was remembering it, felt goose bumps break out all over her skin. She was filled with a sense of awe at their bravery. There was no one in the world they could trust more than each other with the task of saving Toad.

Mole looked at her and squinted. "Come now, we've a good deal of work ahead of us."

They got their crayfish shirts from the bank and began walking in the shallows, following the river in the direction of Alice's house.

Connie can be Mr. Toad, Alice thought. *He can hide out in the barn. We have to show him the new trapeze anyway.* Beneath the bridge, she and Theo began to howl, and the concave metal canopy drew their voices up into the sky and out into the town, echoing, their last ghostly tones still resonating as they left the riverbank behind.

Wendy

HAEDEN, NY, 2008

IT WAS HARD to tell at first why Dale Haytes looked good. He was tall and stocky, and his cheeks were often red. He wore expensive clothes. His teeth were perfect. He had a flattop, and his neck was shaved and sometimes pimply. He was always on his way to play golf, or coming back from playing golf, and he drove a shiny dark blue truck with an extended cab. He liked to play cards and was friends with all kinds of different men. Men who worked in business, men who traveled, and men who hung around the Alibi. People you wouldn't necessarily think he'd talk to, real different types of folks. Like Wendy, he had watched his friends leave for school and go on to college. Like Wendy, he worked for his father's business and was proud to sit in the office. The farmwork was rarely done by family members because the farm was a big corporation now. She'd heard them talking about it at the bar, how people didn't get that. It was a business. They had more than eight thousand head now that they were working as a subsidiary of Groot Dairy Development. Groot had offices in Holland and Argentina. Dale had told her how he traveled to Europe a couple times a year.

She liked the way he had explained it. Like it was simple, just another place. Dale was a hometown boy connected to the wealth of the wider world. But he wasn't phony, like the college boys who went traveling. He said what he felt, no matter what it was. And he didn't seem too worried about it. He didn't seem too worried about anything. Though Wendy thought sometimes he pretended to be worried so it would make people feel better about themselves, and that made her like him—the way he changed his confident attitude to help out the little guy. "Throw him a bone," as she'd heard him say.

At twenty-two, Dale possessed a demeanor that Wendy thought seemed suited to an older man. He acted much older than the guys she worked with, though he was ten years younger. That was probably because he liked to talk about tradition and said things like "Gotta play hard to work hard," "You snooze, you lose," and his favorite, "It's all about attitude." Sometimes he'd abbreviate this to "Attitude!" or say, "Attitude is more important than facts." Wendy had heard him explain this last phrase to some of the workers from the milking parlor, who came in one evening and stood around shooting the shit with him. It was part of a long inspirational piece his mother had framed and hung in their kitchen, where most people hung a "Bless This House." He told them the piece went on to say that attitude could color a situation "gloomy and gray or cheerful and gay." And that working in the office and talking to salespeople had improved his attitude and his vocabulary. Wendy didn't know how she felt about that. She'd had to talk to wholesalers and bill collectors on the phone, and she thought they were just people who spoke like they were on teams while really, they were sitting in cubicles and talking on phones. Still, it was no secret that attitude and communication and team spirit were the things that had made Dale's family so successful. Not college education. And Wendy could relate to that.

And she liked his voice. Dale had the flat upstate drawl and terse truncated way of speaking that was ingratiating to old-timers and funny to his friends. Parents and teachers loved him. And he had a kind of lost quality: charm. She could tell Dale read people and then adjusted his language accordingly.

The phrases he chose seemed at once ironic and full of authority and respect, a genius way of speaking that couldn't quite be pinned down—that he could turn serious or into a joke depending on the responses he got. Sometimes all it took was a quick wink. "A man's got work to do," he'd say about himself, or "You don't disturb a man when he's trying to eat." He might believe it or it might be sarcasm, or he might be mocking someone else by contrast. And it was brilliant when the things he said achieved all three. Dale was a joker.

This was part of his appeal to Wendy. He even said things out loud that she'd been thinking. He was a joker but also conscious that he was a man, tied to his family and property, his appetites, tied to his body. Maybe part of being a man was being a joker. He was definitely not like a boy—or even like a friend of her brother's, who worked in the trades. He was a part of the town's history, a name that could be found on a map, a fixture. And his square jaw and slight double chin could be traced back through family photos and old people's memories for generations.

Dale lived in an apartment in his parents' house, a big colonial on the corner of Haytes and Town Line roads. His brother, Bruce, and their parents lived in the main part of the house, and his uncles lived in the house next door that had once been quarters for farmhands. Not one of them had left that land yet.

The things that made Dale attractive to Wendy ran deep, and she knew it by the way she felt when he was around, the way she tried not to look at him when he came in and sat at the bar. She knew most girls didn't look at him this way. Even though he was a Haytes and had been a football player in school, her friends and other women in the bar acted like they were too good for him. Maybe it was the smell of the farm. Wendy thought it was pretty superficial for people to judge him because of a by-product of the family business. She figured the poor guy had to deal with it all the time. She'd heard him talk about girls from his class being stuck up. How they were off at college pretending they loved city life or faggy guys or some shit they'd never even heard of until they were nearly grown. Moving away to chase some career pipe dream. Some of them going to college after college and living like they were poor. It was one of the only times he sounded angry to her—but maybe that was partly in sympathy for the guys he was sitting with. None of them had girlfriends, though some of them had wives.

One evening when she set his drink down, he grabbed her wrist gently and looked up at her for a long time. It was a dramatic gesture, and she wondered if he would have done it if he was alone, if he were just doing it as a joke for the guys he was sitting with. She smiled at him and felt her face flush. Then, still looking in her eyes, he said, "You sure got pretty, Wendy. You're almost breaking my heart every time you run down to the other end of the bar and leave me all alone here." He'd looked down at her hand as if he just realized he was holding on to her, then he gave her a shy look and let go.

She glanced toward the kitchen, pulled her tickets out of her apron pocket, and set them nervously on the bar so she wouldn't look like she was doing nothing but flirting with a boy her boss already knew she had a crush on.

"A man can only take so much pretty walking back and forth in front of him." He said pretty like he meant something else.

"Well, I'm sorry, Dale. That's my job. I mean, the walking to the kitchen. I didn't mean being . . . I mean, that's . . . Are you kidding around?"

She watched his mask of confidence falter for a second as if he hadn't made up his mind yet, hadn't decided whether he was using her as a joke for the boys, or using her to show he had a serious and romantic side, or maybe right then, she hoped, right in that moment he had fallen in love with her.

Then he said, "You just bloomed like a rose right in front of us all."

She felt the corner of her lip twitch. She picked up her tickets again and shuffled through them for a minute.

"I'd be proud to take you out to the movies sometime when you're not working." He tilted his head down and looked up at her, raised his eyebrows. It was the kind of look your parents give you when you're in trouble.

Her stomach fluttered. She could smell his aftershave; she looked down at the smooth clean cuff of his shirt. It was like he was some kind of Haeden nobility, asking her out for all the guys sitting there in their boots and flannels, guys she might have said no to.

"Uh, yeah. Awesome," she said, and nodded, tried to sound like he was someone she only thought about as a friend. "That would be fun. I would love that. Yeah. That'd be fun."

My name is Megan Osterhaus. It's April 18, 2009.

Actually, you know what? I'm not going to talk about any of it. Okay? I just feel like even thinking about that kind of thing can't possibly be good for the world. My concern right now is to make sure I don't invite that kind of energy or fear into my life. And to pretty much make sure I can affect things in the moment. And keep breathing.

So I'm going to talk to you for maybe ten minutes. Okay? And then I really have to go. And this is off the record, like you said. Right? This is all off the record.

I graduated between Alice and Wendy and was not really a part of their everyday social lives. I knew both of them, of course, because of swim team, and yes, I know there are a lot of pictures of me and Alice together because of swimming.

All I can say is that I would never have lived the way they did or have done the things they did and that ultimately it's up to the universe the way these things shake out. It's karma. It's karma, and in a lot of ways, it's what people settle for. Because there's no doubt you get what you settle for, and harsh as it sounds, some people settle for things that end in death.

I mean, with Alice, it's a little hard to look at that way, because I spent a lot of time with her before I left for school and she seemed to have built so many good things in the world. But with everyone else. No, sir. No way. There was a lot of . . . a lot of, I guess . . . attracting negative energy. You know? And I think you need to look at it like kind of a flood or a tornado or something. It just builds and builds and it's inevitable. That's about the only perspective I can give you. The things we say and think about have bigger impact on the universe than we know.

There was nothing I could do about it then, and there definitely isn't now. There is nothing anyone can do about it but live their lives right now. In the present.

As far as Haeden and all this stuff about the economy or the culture or whatever, I don't think the place is different from anywhere else. Just smaller.

Not that I would set foot back there or set my thoughts back there, because it just doesn't do anyone any good. And I'm seeing an energy practitioner right now to help me get clear, because I did have kind of a close proximity to the event. Not physically, but whatever.

Anyway. I had in many ways a real emotional proximity to Alice, and she made some choices that were a part of a spiritual path I don't really want to intersect with.

As far as Wendy goes, I really really hope she has better luck and a lot of happiness now that she is not on the material plane. She was generally pretty happy in the material world, so I could see how this next phase of her existence, or nonexistence, would be a good one.

I am not going to say a thing about how she died. Because I don't want to tie her to another second of that kind of pain, even in my thoughts and certainly not in my speech, not in anything that would be carried in my body or mind and come out of my mouth.

And if there is one thing I would say as a general statement that *should* be quoted, it's that no one should bring that kind of . . . just . . . that kind of unhealthy thinking into their lives.

I did feel sad. I cried when they found her. I sent flowers to her mother and father, but I didn't go back for the funeral. I didn't feel that there was anything I could do. I built a really beautiful lantern for her out of brass and copper and glass, and I hung it off the front porch of my apartment. And I burned some incense and played some Gwen Stefani and . . . I'm sorry, just a minute. I . . . I think that's a lot better than what happened in Haeden. Which, if I am not going to talk about Wendy, I am certainly not going to talk about that.

I'm not going to talk about Alice. She didn't really know Wendy, you know? She was younger than us. But she was upset. I talked to her briefly, and I talked to a couple of other girls from the team who were away at school, too.

We were all just glad we weren't there. I think it scared a lot of girls who were living there. Which is a bad thing because there's nothing you can do with fear. Absolutely nothing at all. There are studies about how fear and negative thinking affect the brain. And how we are all really connected at a kind of micro level, that our thinking actually creates the world. So again, I am not going to talk about it. Any of it.

And as far as Haeden and Haeden High are concerned, to be honest, I barely remember anything from living there other than swimming and watching TV and playing Bigger Better. That whole period of growth, I think I just had to keep my head down and keep moving. Just keep swimming and pretty much stay in the art room as much as I could. Otherwise. Just. Forget it.

I would never tie myself to events there or to the things people said or did. Never. I couldn't use it for anything, and I didn't want to bring one bit of that with me to college or have it show up in my artwork. You just knew Haeden was a place that wouldn't exist as soon as you left. It barely existed while we were there.

Constant

CON SAT WITH Gene and Claire and Michelle, watching the children approaching, not knowing yet that they were being watched. He smiled when the two of them, lost in their own conversation, started at the sight of the surveilling adults, reclining on the grass near the barn, drinking out of big green bottles. The air was cool, and the maples shone bright yellow against the sky. Con was wearing a neon T-shirt, jeans, and dress shoes because he'd been late for the train to the airport and just slipped them back on after changing from work instead of looking for his boots. His hair was cropped close, and he was conscious of the luxury of not having shaved that day. Very happy to drink beer out on the lawn.

A light breeze blew, moving the brown heads of wildflowers and goldenrod gone to seed. From inside the house, the sound of the MC5 playing *Kick Out the Jams* drifted toward them, a muffled drum beating fast and regular like the crickets throbbing in the grass.

This was, Constant thought, a family reunion. Something very rare. Alice and Theo, so tall now and happy to see them. It fortified him, the idea that someone was so genuinely happy he was there. He stood as they approached, hunched over, and clapped his hands together in front of his knees, and they ran toward him. He caught them both and picked them up, squeezing them tight. They were starting to get gangly, nine and ten years old and all legs. They smelled good, like leaves and mud.

"Here!" he said. "Good thing you guys got here. We were waiting for the circus!" He kissed Alice on the head and then put her down, but he hoisted Theo up on his hip to carry him around a little. He looked into the boy's face. His matted hair had pieces of lint in it and looked like it hadn't been brushed in weeks. Con let the pity and disappointment at the boy's parents—and at himself for not being more of a presence—pass through him, then he smiled big at Theo to make him feel tough and special. "Things going okay?" They nodded at each other. "Yeah? Well, okay, then."

Depositing Theo onto the lawn, he watched and grinned as the kids took in the spectacle of Michelle, beautiful Michelle, who until that afternoon not even he had seen in a year. Micky who smelled like sweat and roses and honeysuckle. Who had lost ten pounds, who was so tan she looked almost orange brown. And the tattoos on her forearms and biceps—insects and numbers and an encircled capital A—had, like Gene's tattoos, faded. The symbols they'd lived by blurred to blue. Michelle's eyes were large and placid, her hair long and unruly, and she was wearing thick wool socks beneath her sandals. He knew she must look wild to Alice and Theo, who would have no memory of her.

The children stared, and Con admired her calm way, the respect she had for them.

"Oh my goodness," she said, and reached out for Alice. "Would you come here, please?" Alice went to sit in her lap. "You look to me like someone very special." She wrapped her arms around Alice, resting her chin on the girl's head.

"You know Micky is the doctor who delivered you, right?" Claire said.

Alice nodded, looking embarrassed.

"It was a joint effort," Michelle said. "There were two very good doctors and a women's health advocate with an MD there."

"Yeah, but she just swore the whole time," said Constant. Claire laughed and shut her eyes, leaning back against Gene. Their faces glowed with the same light of memory.

Michelle gave Alice a kiss on the head. "Apart from all the cursing, it was not what you'd call a primitive environment."

"Are you delivering babies now?" Gene asked.

"No, no, no," she said. "We were in a health center right in Seleia, where we were dealing with a lot of trauma and wounds, but we got evacuated. Now I'm back in Zelingei, and mostly what we see is malnutrition and some mental-health issues because of the displacement. And the war."

Alice and Theo listened intently. "Were there lions there?" Alice asked.

"Not really."

"Oh!" said Theo. "Then it wasn't that dangerous." He looked up at Con and nodded as if that would make him feel better.

"Not in that way, no," Michelle said to him.

"I can't imagine it," said Gene.

"You can't. Really. I have yet to see or read anything here that could give you an idea of the magnitude."

"There's psychiatric staff there?" Con asked.

"Yeah," she said. "Of course. The place is a mess every which way. But that's not for talking about now." She had begun braiding Alice's hair.

"Remember that 'street psychiatrist' when we were living over on St. Mark's?" Gene asked.

"Oh my God!" Michelle yelled abruptly, startling Alice. "And his orgone accumulator!"

"Oh Jesus," Claire said. "That thing was made out of particle board."

Con began to smile.

"What?" Alice and Theo shouted in unison. "What did it do?"

Claire spat her drink out on the lawn from laughing, and then Gene rolled her up in the picnic blanket. "Should have put *you* in the orgone box!" he said to her, putting his face close to hers. Michelle watched them and smiled, but when Con tried to catch her eye, she looked away.

"That part of our long-term plan is going remarkably well, at least," Con said, nodding toward Alice and Theo as they lost interest in the adults and took off for the barn. Michelle stared at his shoes, his three-hundred-dollar shoes, then meaningfully into his face. Gene nudged her to stop.

Then with a squeal, the barn door slid open, and Theo stood in front of them wearing his shorts and no shirt and a dog mask made from cardboard, masking tape, and round black buttons. The first bars of Prokofiev's "Peter and the Wolf" sounded too loudly and then were quickly turned down by an unseen hand. The dog's voice was muffled, but he said dramatically, "Today we will be showing *Dog in the Manger.*"

Con laughed, and Michelle smiled genuinely at him, looked warmly into his eyes for maybe the first time since they had arrived, and it made him feel how small his world had become.

"What will you pay us to enter our Russian-trapeze antigravity theater?"

"How about if we pay you nothing?" Gene asked.

The dog shrugged. "Okay," he said. Then he looked over his shoulder and nodded before gesturing expansively toward them. "Come in. Come in. Come in, won't you?"

The adults entered the barn and sat next to one another on a straw bale. The space was cool and smelled of mold and apples and motor oil. Earlier that week, Gene had raised the trapeze high above the barn floor, so Alice could learn to swing onto the loft and practice hanging tricks. She was standing on it now, balanced on the bar, confidently holding tightly to the ropes at her sides. She was wearing a white swim cap and a short white dress that she'd made from a sheet.

Michelle and Con exchanged an incredulous look. She seemed far too many feet off the ground for them to concentrate on the play.

Theo looked up at Alice, and as the clarinet solo began, he climbed up into the loft. "All right!" he announced again dramatically. "This is called 'Dog in the Manger'!"

Con smiled. He knew the phrase from Ross; it was one of

his favorites for describing businessmen and politicians. It was obvious how much time these kids spent with him, and Con was glad they were there to hear the old man's stories, and that Theo had Ross to watch out for him.

"I thought it was 'Peter and the Wolf,'" Micky said. "Don't you need a net?"

"No!" Theo shouted. "This is *Dog*. In. The. MANGER!"

Alice pumped her knees and swung on the trapeze, leaning back to get higher as Theo flopped down on a straw bale.

Gene began to laugh quietly again, and his eyes filled with tears. Con had seen this before. One time when he'd accompanied Gene and Claire to a play at Alice's school, Gene had to walk out twice because he couldn't stop laughing whenever she spoke, tears just rolling down his face. "Sorry sorry sorry," he had told them, still laughing as they waited for Alice in the parking lot afterward and then heaving a shaky sigh to try and break the absurdity. "God! I love her so much."

Theo lay fitfully on the straw, pretending to be a dreaming dog. He scratched his ear, feigned running in his sleep, and then moaned and howled, chewed at his shoulder. The full orchestra was playing as Alice swung back and forth, nearly touching the ceiling. Michelle cringed every time she leaned out over them, but Claire and Gene looked on, happily indulgent. *They must watch these things every day*, Con thought.

The play was growing monotonous, and Con guessed Alice was trying to figure out when to jump to the loft when she hopped like a bird and then slid straight down, still holding the ropes until she smacked her chin audibly on the bar of the trapeze, where she now clung with one hand. Gene and Claire gasped and stood up involuntarily, and Con raced into the center of the barn, ready to catch her. The trapeze was swinging out over the loft and back as she hung tightly, her face blank with concentration. Without a word or the slightest fearful sound, she pulled herself up. But instead of folding her waist over the bar to regain her balance and stand, she simply pulled the bar against her neck and rested her chin on it, continuing to swing her body so that the trapeze would reach out over the loft and she could drop. As if this had all happened before, Theo continued his fake slumber.

"Alice," Gene said firmly as they watched her right hand release its grip, "no."

"Goddammit," Claire whispered.

"Alice!" Gene called to her again as she took her hand away, stretched her right arm out at her side. "What the hell are you doing?" He took a deep breath. "Not when it's swinging!" he shouted, but she was ignoring everyone, concentrating on the trick. She tucked her chin forward and then took her other hand off the bar, extending it, her arms spread out like wings. They were dumbstruck. She pointed her toes, and Con could see the muscles in her arms and legs and back. It was amazing. She looked exactly like Gene, had a finer, compact version of his morphology, but clearly the same poise and strength. And the same idiotic sense that she could not get hurt.

When the trapeze swung far enough over the loft, she raised her head, spreading her arms wider and arching her back as she slipped delicately from the bar, landing nearly on top of Theo, ducking to miss the backswing of the trapeze as it grazed their heads.

Once her feet were safely planted on the loft, Con relaxed and sat back down, but Gene continued to stand in the center of the barn.

Theo began barking.

"For God's sake!" Alice shouted, grabbing the dog mask and flipping it up on top of his head. "Wake up! Wake up! You were dreaming!"

Those were the only words in the play. Then they stood together on the loft, held hands, and bowed.

No one clapped but Michelle. And there was an unpleasant

silence during which Alice folded her arms over her chest and shrugged down at her parents.

"What does 'dog in the manger' mean?" Michelle asked brightly. "Death-defying feat?"

Alice smiled. "No, it's like somebody's taking food away from somebody else who needs it. Like a dog gets into the animal's trough."

"How significant," Michelle said, raising an eyebrow. "But in this case, the dog is the main guy, the animals are gone, and the dog is having a nightmare."

"That was definitely a nightmare for everyone, as far as I'm concerned," Gene said, looking pointedly at his daughter.

"The dog ate everyone's food and fell asleep in the manger," Alice said, exasperated, "but when the moth flies around the ceiling and abolishes gravity and wakes him up, then he's never going to go in there and eat all their food again! She has to save him from what he does to save everyone else because he's always taking stuff. She wakes him up and makes him float up into the air. Didn't you figure that out? *God!*"

"Hm," Michelle said. "I don't know how I missed that."

"Well, the floating doesn't come across that great," Theo explained.

"I strongly suggest you never do that trick again," Claire said, simply nodding at Alice. "Does your chin hurt?"

"Yes," Alice said, looking down at them, laughing a little.

Con was stunned at the way they dealt with their daughter. He could still feel the adrenaline in his system and a hollowness in his stomach from having watched her slip from the bar.

"Certainly don't do it again until you have more practice," Gene said, "because you could die."

"How can I practice if you've suggested I don't do it again?"

"You practice with me," he said. "And we'll lower the trapeze. You don't want to land on your neck and break your windpipe. Claire has made a very reasonable request." Then he clapped his hands and said, "Hup," and she jumped off the loft into his arms with the same careless joy as a person jumping into a pool of water. Con was impressed and horrified. She was obviously much lighter and more coordinated than other kids her age, but her lack of fear was disturbing.

"Well," Michelle said. "I guess the show's over. Thank you very much, trapezists."

"We have another one tomorrow," Alice said. "Every day at four or seven."

Con was beginning to feel that the whole afternoon was surreal. This homesteading thing of Gene's, Claire so silent now, the shock of seeing Michelle. All this pretend and risk taking from everyone. And he was astonished that the children had made up this story, felt oddly sick and exposed by it, as if he'd seen some native interpretation of his life via imaginary animals. A living nativity of his troubled sleep.

Gene lowered the trapeze to a few feet above the ground and the children were now hanging by their knees side by side. "You better set up the tent if you want to sleep outside," Claire told them.

The adults left them hanging and walked toward the house. Once out of sight of the barn, Gene stopped walking, Claire put her arms around him, and he bent his head to touch hers. Constant watched her kiss the side of his face and wrap her arms around him, whisper something in his ear. Constant and Michelle walked ahead toward the house.

"I think that play was a sign you should quit your job," Michelle said.

"I think it's a sign they need a net in that barn. And it was definitely a sign I need to be more of an influence on Alice. Girl's a little shaky on the concept of risk."

"You mean Gene Junior," Michelle said.

"Yeah. Well, both of those kids, actually." He put his arm around her waist, and they walked in step along the mowed path.

"Come to Zelingei with me," she said quietly.

He shook his head.

"Haven't you seen enough of Manhattan after last year?" she asked.

"No. I love the city now more than I ever did. Now is not the time to leave."

And it wasn't just for himself that he stayed, it was for all of them. Didn't she know one of the reasons he kept his fucking job was because of her? Because they were all so unaware of how little they had? Their poverty and grandstanding were actually based in privilege. He literally hated his job. And if the opportunity arose to have a real impact on something, he would probably take it, but you don't just do that until you have it all figured out. How could they not know that throughout history, the difference between getting across a border at the right time or getting shot came down to money or a decision people couldn't influence without it. He was astounded by their ignorance sometimes. He was not the CEO of fucking Pharmethik. He was not Eichmann. Not a dog in the manger.

The fact that they didn't understand the value of a risk-benefit analysis was one reason they were constantly fighting the same monsters in the same ways. Why Gene believed he could "live the alternative" in order to convert people to organic farming. But that lived alternative was subsidized by wages coming from a pharmaceutical company Gene wasn't willing to work for himself. How was that sustainable?

"I'd like to live with you again," he said to Michelle. "But the problems you are trying to fix won't go away if I personally stop working. I don't know how to get out of it yet, baby."

He didn't say the rest, which was that things were so overwhelmingly bad, so redefined, in the world, and he was so entrenched in what he was doing, that he couldn't imagine a defining political moment that could possibly have enough impact to make him leave. If last fall didn't do it, what would? You keep waking up to a next day. Shredded documents on clinical trials, the lack of polar ice, the lack of any coherent community manifest in the incessant conversations people had *about* television that sounded like conversations people had *on* television. He did not know how to get to the core of it to fix things. And for all their staying on the right path and applying pressure to the wound, he knew that they didn't, either.

"It's morally wrong," she said. "Your work is morally wrong."

He nodded again. "I know that. I can do something that is wrong in order to achieve something good, something of a greater magnitude, down the line. I'm not afraid of doing something bad in an isolated circumstance if it can yield a greater result. I know who I am, Michelle. I can do this one thing and move on."

"When?"

They had reached the porch and sat looking out at the fields. Inside the house, the needle had reached the end of the record and made a static hiss and click over and over. He looked down at their feet. Her socks had dry leaves stuck in them. He knew she hated his shoes, knew the point she'd been trying to make by staring at them. He'd heard her talk about uniforms before, uniforms and language, heard her describe the world as Orwell had. And he had no disagreements with her. She was disgusted by the violence inherent in the businessman's uniform and by the power it conveyed. He could take the shoes off and throw them out into the woods for what it would mean to her. But he knew if he did, he would be buying a new pair on Monday. That was the kind of waste that was born from believing in symbolic gestures and poorly conceived individual acts.

"When it makes sense," he said.

She took his hand and kissed it. "I'll pray for you, then."

"Really?" Con asked, smiling. "To whom?"

ROSS

HAEDEN, NY, 2003

RABBITS ARE NOT something you wait for like a deer or ducks, unwitting sorts of creatures that walk or fly by while you hide. Not big visible things you track. It takes more patience. Rabbits you gotta get deep into the brush. Thick impenetrable thatches and fallen trees and briars. It's suited to a small person. A small person can carry the animal home and feel accomplished, which is why I started her out on it.

You don't wait for rabbits, you go after them. Some people like to go after them with dogs, which is just a hassle. I hate beagles. Fucking hate 'em. Get the rabbit running in circles and then they start baying, messing up the woods with all that noise. Plus, I don't want anyone to know my business. Know when I'm hunting or where I'm at. I got my own business, and I had enough of people talking about it after I got back from the war and grew my hair out. Then after I married Hediyah and again later after she left. I'll go toe to toe with anyone at the VFW who wants to talk about this war now. But I won't have them nosing around in my business in the woods or anywhere else. Plus the thing with dogs is, it's easy to put one of them RFID chips into the dog so you can track them wherever they go. And track the owner, too. No, thank you. Those things got recording devices in them now. I want to be surveilled, I'll buy a telephone. I tried to tell Hediyah about this when she got her ID tags for the medical center out in Elmville. She knew it had a chip in it, but she didn't think it mattered. Plus, that woman was dedicated. Always put her patients first. Even if she was getting her name made fun of or people asking all the time was she happy to be able to learn the newest things here in America, be somewhere she didn't need to wear a scarf on her face. Or was she Muslim and did Arabs have TV. Christ. Fucking embarrassing is what it was, but she didn't care. She was here to practice rural medicine and work with the poor and finish her research on obesity. If she wanted to learn the "newest things," or even have an intelligent conversation, she'd be back in Lebanon. Which she is now. So, I guess there it is.

Best thing that came of all that business, though, was the Pipers. And I gotta say they all remind me a little of Hediyah. Especially Claire, though Claire's more of a family kind of woman.

I was more than happy to move out of that house and rent it to them. Don't think I'd have rented to anyone else honestly. But I'm happy they're there and happy to sell the land to Constant. And in a way, it means that land's in Hediyah's family still; that they have a spot here, which they damn well should have. God-damn prejudice and stupidity. Christ-al-fucking-mighty people are ignorant. The way people treated my wife, who was here to fucking help their fat asses in the first place.

Well anyway, point is, the little Piper is old enough to hunt with me now, and I enjoy her company. Especially hunting rabbits, which is what I guess I started talking about. That child can learn fast, and it's a shame her people don't put more value on the gift she has because I believe outside of the service, I have never seen anyone take so much pleasure in hitting a target or put so much time into figuring out how to do it. Girl's a marksman and quiet as can be. I believe by the end of the year, she'll be using a rifle for rabbits. She's gotten very good very fast. I guess that's a tribute to her parents, as most people wait until it's "legal" to let their kid learn to shoot. And that's a huge mistake. Everyone knows a ten-year-old can learn quicker than a fourteen-year-old. Which is of course why they put them all in school, so they can make sure they're not out there thinking away about everything they see, putting things together they're not supposed to. Which they would if they weren't federally mandated to go get brainwashed every goddamn day. Gotta make sure we keep 'em pumped full of bullshit like the fucking Gulf of Tonkin. And Pearl fucking Harbor and Christopher Columbus and our great hero the Nazi Henry Ford. Don't tell them Johnny Appleseed was some burlap sack–wearing pervert moonshiner. It's all just a big whitewash. Keep them away from real people with real memories 'cause they sure as hell don't want them to meet someone like me who can tell them what I really did in a uniform. Jesus Christ. Anyhow. If you start shooting at ten, you have a chance. The more practice you get, the better. And when that girl's grown up, she'll be able to feed her whole family. If they eat meat. That's about the biggest mistake the parents have made, if you ask me. What kinda child goes out hunting but don't eat meat?

I come pick her up and say, "C'mon, Al, it's wabbit season," and she's happy as hell.

Right now she doesn't like to eat 'em, but she likes to dress 'em and makes things out of their pelts. Made me a pair of earmuffs.

First few times we just went out to Tern Woods, which is not much of a woods compared to when I was a boy, but it's still pretty, what's left of it, and easy for a kid to learn how to track through. Later, we went out to some old growth by the river. And that was just gorgeous and hilly and dark in the middle of the day. The "wild wood," she called it. And she was light and silent walking on the pine bed with a gun almost as big as she was tall. I was proud of her. Proud she'd call me her uncle.

Claire

COMPREHENSIVE FREE CLINIC
FOR THE UNINSURED, 1994

SHERRI'S SON GOT sick at school, leaving a bare-bones staff that Wednesday, lines to the door, standing room only. Claire was glad she had a stay-at-home husband. She called to let him know she'd be late. Alice was taking a nap. He said they'd been in the greenhouse on the roof all morning; she'd been playing with worms and a spoon.

"Oh!" he said. "And Micky found out where she's getting placed for Doctors Without Borders."

"Where?"

"Let's just say it's unlikely she'll be seeing less HIV. We're going to make a special dinner."

After the call, Claire went to the front to pick up paperwork for Sherri's patients. "Thank you," the receptionist said quietly, her hand over the mouthpiece of her headset. She handed Claire three clipboards. "Go to five first, she's been sitting there for twenty minutes. You'll need a kit."

Claire hurried to pick one up on her way to the room. Didn't want the woman waiting any longer. She shuffled the clipboards awkwardly as she knocked on the door, managing to get the patient chart on top just as a woman's voice said, "Come in."

Claire opened the door and looked up from the chart, quickly adjusting her gaze to match the height of the patient sitting on the examination table.

She looked to be about five years old. She was pale and had straight dark hair, dark eyes. Her shoulders were narrow and her arms thin. Claire could see from where she stood that the girl's earlobes were dark red and encrusted with dried blood. The gown was big on her, and she was wearing grimy white ankle socks with pictures of Princess Jasmine on them. Beside the girl, sitting on a low stool, was Amadi from rape crisis. Behind the screen, Claire could see the cuffs of the girl's jeans laid out on top of a wide white sheet of sterile paper, for her to take later and seal inside the kit. A clean shirt, sweatpants, and underwear were folded, waiting on the table. The room smelled strongly of urine.

"Lauren," Amadi said. "This is my friend Claire. She's going to give you a quick checkup."

Claire set the paperwork and kit beside the clean clothes. "Hi, Lauren," Claire said, smiling gently. Lauren lifted her hand, not quite waving. Claire wondered where the girl's mother was. Knew the injuries should not be extensive, or they'd have taken her to the emergency room, but was concerned to see the box of Kotex on the chair beside Amadi.

They talked about the Aladdin movie while Claire positioned the lamp. It wasn't until she was gently scraping beneath Lauren's fingernails that she realized she would be performing the same examination, gathering the same information, whether or not the girl was alive. She sensed the warmth of Lauren's small hand through the thin plastic of her glove and felt a surge of adrenaline and relief, something bordering on gratitude, to be able to touch her.

She walked home with the headphones on and the volume up as loud as she could stand it. Joe Strummer's voice in her head blotted out traffic and sirens, rendered the streets a ballet of random events and motions. But the day at the clinic was still there, it wasn't going anywhere.

Claire was in it permanently. And because of this, her family was, too, her daughter. And there was no leaving. If Claire were to abandon the city and her patients, she would be wrong. She would be morally wrong. She would hate herself. But she hated herself now anyway. Hated herself, hated her ambivalence about the job, hated someone. Some invisible person, invisible man; the same invisible man described again and again, committing the same act, in the same ways. A guerrilla war against a civilian population. The more stories she heard from patients—stories that mirrored one another to the smallest tactical detail—the more it was impossible to think of it in any other way. Hard to imagine there wasn't some organizational structure to it. Certainly there was an ideology behind it—an invisible ideology hiding in plain sight. In the language, in jokes, on the television, on sides of buses, in clothes and gestures and wallets and bodies and faces and minds.

Who was she to simply go home after this day? Lauren wasn't the only child she had seen; she was just the youngest so far. Claire wondered where the girl would go tonight, who would be caring for her. If her labs would come back okay. What kind of woman she would grow up to be. She turned up the Walkman until there was white noise inside her head and stood still on the sidewalk on Seventh Street. It was not enough. What she was doing was not enough. The way it was being done would never be enough.

Claire said nothing about work when she got home at eight. Alice was still up, and she nursed her and gave her a bath while Gene and Micky made dinner. Washed her blond-white hair, her strong, pale, and tender body, her impossibly soft skin. Claire dressed her in green footie pajamas. Then sat on the side of the tub as the steam rose and dissipated in the bathroom, holding her for a long time.

Haeden, NY

"Is she awake?"

"Holy shit, dude, does it look it? Could I fucking do this if she was awake?"

"Dude, cut that shit out. Wait till my brother gets here."

"Maybe she's playing possum."

"Shh. Shh. Fucking quit laughing."

"Fuck. What if she's dead?"

"We got the coroner here in a minute. He can take her pulse."

"Look at her face. Oh shit. I can't believe she doesn't feel this shit."

"Wait. Would you just wait till my brother gets here?"

"All right, all right. Hands off. Jesus. Remember when she used to be a fucking cow?"

"Yeah, dude, if this had happened six months ago, how were you going to fit her down there?"

"In pieces."

Theo

THE IDEA OF the next day arriving was impossible for Theo, a day that Alice was not there. That day couldn't be. He wanted to leave town, wanted to go to a good school, but not without her. Knowing this would happen had ruined his fourteenth birthday. He'd asked Claire then if they would be sending Alice to Simon's Rock, too. No, they wouldn't, she said. Theo was lucky because it would be so exciting. He would get a better education, he would be close to the city and Constant, and he would have fun. But Theo did not feel like he would have any fun without Alice.

He'd just begun to get taller than her, and now, when they did the trapeze catch, they had to wait longer than before because his weight had changed things.

She was already crying even though he would not leave until after dinner. She was crying out in the barn, upside down on the low trapeze, tears rolling off her forehead onto the ground. It smelled like fall. The things they had painted on the walls since they were little surrounded them. Maps of fake countries, extra circus characters, two-headed animals, a guy with a goat head wearing a business suit and holding a briefcase. A fake porthole with a view of fish and mermaids and Poseidon.

Theo held her hands and backed away, pulling her with him until she was stretched almost parallel to the floor, then let go. She swung backward, then forward to him again. Tears rushed off her face. Her hair hung down, nearly touching the floor.

She pulled up and stood on the bar. Pumped her knees to go higher and higher. He watched from below. She let go of the ropes and stood balanced on the bar, leaned forward, and leaped off to land in a pile of straw next to him.

"I will be ever so sorry to be leaving you, old chap," he said. "Quite."

He got into the straw with her and lay his head on her chest, and she put her arms around him while he cried. Her skin was warm. He felt like his heart was being squeezed. She wiped her nose.

"This fucking sucks," he said into her shirt.

"I'll send you stuff," Alice told him. "We can test our psychic powers. We can write letters from all the characters. It will be cool because they'll actually come in the mail. We can make the code even harder to figure out." She was talking quickly, making things up to comfort him. "We can stop using the ones with numbers and do the ones with author and character names, make them context-specific. You know, the more boring the letter seems, the more exciting the *real* letter is." He could picture it perfectly. It stopped him crying. "We can make a map of an underground river for them to meet in secret. Can you draw it?" she asked.

"I probably already have one drawn somewhere," he said. "I should keep my maps and all that shit with your stuff while I'm gone, so you can use them."

"Okay." She kissed the side of his face and said, "I love you," which made her start crying again. They never said it, even if they thought it. Saying it now proved they could read each other's minds. "I'm going to really really really miss you," she said, putting her cheek right next to his.

He knew she would. And he knew she would write. But he also knew she would replace him somehow with projects or research or a new game. He knew her. She couldn't help it. He knew they should not be apart. He was afraid of who she would become without him.

Video Record 0002
Bailey, Theophile

I'm not smirking. I know you think that I'm the key to all of this, and you're wrong. I went to elementary school with them. I played sports with them. Whatever. You don't seem too upset about it, either, frankly. I don't think I should be talking to you without a lawyer.

She was never violent, no, absolutely not at all. That doesn't even make sense.

She never even got mad at people. She just didn't care that much. I mean, she watched . . . she paid attention to people. Which every kid does. When we were little, we used to pretend to be spies, so we'd watch people.

I would definitely say she was my best friend. I think that's pretty obvious. There was never a time when we didn't play together. But she never said a word to me about this stuff. And she would have. She really would have.

Yes. She was really smart. Back in elementary school, she was kind of dorky. Then she got some influx of brilliance with her period. Seriously. She got like PMS that made her build stuff and talk faster and have weird dreams. It was pretty cool, actually.

Why wouldn't I know when she had her period?

A lot, I guess. We did every summer when I came home. Why? You think the sex made her do it?

Do *nothing*! I was kidding. Whatever. You wouldn't even be *talking* about sex if it was a guy that did this.

I mean, did whatever you *think* she did, which nobody else thinks she did. Which I know she didn't do. But if a guy did it, you would never find some girl he had sex with and ask her about it. Why do you want to talk about whether or not she had sex? Isn't that what people do? People have sex, right? Don't you have sex? I do. Whatever. You don't need to get so pissed off. I'm not a fucking cop, I didn't know that you like to talk to everybody about sex when there's a murder.

No. Why would I care if Alice had sex with people? I highly doubt she was having sex with a bunch of football players. I wouldn't say I was her only boyfriend, no. I mean, I wouldn't really say she was my boyfriend at all. What? I mean, I was her boyfriend. You're confusing me. I left here before high school. I already told you how close we were.

What I *do* know is that I should have a lawyer here if you're asking me this kind of shit. I was willing to talk about things, but now I know this is wrong. I know what you're doing is wrong. You're trying to get me upset. You're confusing me. I don't think I should talk to you anymore. No, I wasn't trying to be funny. I know this isn't funny!

Oh my fucking God. Jesus, please. I am not going to look at those pictures. I'm not. I'm not going to look at them. It must be illegal for you to make me look at them. Please. I need a lawyer here. Because! You said you were going to ask me one thing, and now you're trying to show me those disgusting pictures.

Call it whatever you want. I'm not opening my eyes and I'm not saying anything else and I want a lawyer here. I'm not the key to anything. Oh my fucking God! Why are you asking me? You know what happened. I was in Annandale when all this shit happened, and you don't have any right to hold me here and abuse—please put those things away.

I will not open my eyes until you take those pictures away.

Thank you. Now can I please go?

What? No, of course not. Do I look like I know how to hunt?

I imagine my parents are on campus right now, and I assume you already know that. Please can I go now? I actually know I can go. I actually know you can't do this unless a lawyer is here. Please just let me go.

I don't know anything about Wendy White. And the last time I saw those guys was middle school. Wendy was older than us. I don't remember her at all. Alice never talked about her. She was a waitress or something. You're the ones who know. I don't know *anything*. Alice didn't tell me anything.

Beverly Haytes

BEVERLY HAYTES HAD wide-set champagne colored eyes and a flat freckled face. Her salt-and-pepper hair was cropped, and her back was enviably straight. She played golf every Tuesday with a group of ladies who had named themselves the Haeden Homegals, all of whom she'd grown up with except for Ruth Tyson, who had come up from Florida with her husband who worked at the salt mines.

She was rooted in that town. Hell, her roots *were* that town. She had grown up in a house around the corner from the house she lived in now, so similar the two places could have shared architectural DNA. Houses built by the same workers.

She and her husband, Jim, had been together since high school, and even then they were living the dream, as Jim liked to say; she was a cheerleader, he a football player. She was Beverly Tamarack then, of Tamarack Road. Jim was a kind of rowdy boy, she thought then, filled with school spirit and a spirit about life that just made him so charming. They were engaged before they graduated—she had to say yes that night while they still wore their crowns and corsages. They were married before they were twenty. And there was no doubt about how they fit together. There was just no one else.

People got married younger then. She didn't really know why that had changed; it seemed to her people didn't make so many mistakes back then. Didn't confuse themselves. Trusted more— or knew who not to trust. Or just didn't expect the world from one person, so there didn't have to be disappointments, divorces, people handing their kids back and forth from one broken home to the other. Not like her family.

It's like she was saying to the Homegals, Jim wasn't perfect. He had a temper. He came off kind of gruff sometimes. But he got things done and said what he thought, and she was proud of what they'd made together with all those years. And let's be honest, you're not going to have a strong family without those "pick yourself up and get it done" values. Everyone knew that was how the Haytes had always lived, which was why she couldn't bear the rumors she was hearing about her boys.

And neither could the Homegals.

"What I don't understand is why people turn on their own in a time like this," Charlene Puitt had said that afternoon at the golf course. "My mother used to say that newcomers bring nothing but everything you don't want when they move in. And if you ask me, it's the outsiders who are causing all the problems. You take this reporter who's been asking all these questions."

"Oh, her," Beverly said. "She was up to look at the dairy. I'd never seen anything like her. Some kind of shiny shirt with horses all over it like it was her pajamas, and those glasses, and that hair hadn't seen a brush in I don't know how long. I think I saw maybe two smiles the whole time she was there."

"Probably wishing Dale was after her," said Ruth with a sniff.

"Now, I wasn't going to say that," Beverly said, although she *had* thought it.

"What I'm saying is," said Charlene, "people like her, they're restless. They come here looking for trouble because they aren't settled themselves. They want to stir things up. And they're the ones people are listening to."

"People are stupid," said Ruth, not reminding them that she was a newcomer once.

"We're not talking about people like you," said Beverly, giving her a nod. She knew Ruth was sensitive about that.

It was like what Jim said, and Beverly had to agree, that when you have the Department of Social Services providing trailers over on Route 34 for people who are going to come and go like a revolving door, you're setting yourself up for trouble. She wasn't saying all those people were bad, and Lord knew no one understood better than she did how hard it was to be low on money. But some people just didn't want to work, and she didn't have any sympathy for that. None. And if there was one thing her boys knew how to do, it was work. They might not have liked it all the time, but they did it. And how could anyone even wonder who it was out there doing bad things when you compared boys like hers to those children who didn't even have a real home or a mother and father right there for them?

True, sometimes bad people came out of good families. Like that boy in Dryden who took those two girls right out of their house. That family was good people. But the boy had been taking steroids, which was something his mother should have put a stop to. Beverly would have. Her boys were raised on a dairy. They did not take drugs. Where would they even get them? It was like she was telling the Homegals, "I don't know how much more wholesome you can get than a glass of milk."

Everyone knew she and Jim had given their boys everything. When they'd had nothing, she'd given them good values and time. When they expanded the herd for the second time, and got all that money from Groot, their toy closet was packed to the ceiling. And it was a pleasure to do it for them, give them a reward for being good boys and see the joy on their faces. See them looking sharp at school. Which people don't think farmers can be. They wore Adidas, Levi's, whatever was in style, but tasteful, not too flashy. Beverly gave them traditions, too. Every Fourth of July, the family went golfing together. They'd take the flags off the green and replace them with small replicas of American flags.

Even now she could see them all out there, rosy-cheeked in the sunshine, competing in their matching striped shorts and white shoes. Bruce so little but wanting to look just like his big brother. It had been a comfortable life, good nutrition and the strength to compete and a tight family. She remembered sitting on the bleachers drinking hot cider and cheering while her boys played football, first Dale, then later Brucie, and making the boys dinner when they came home. Dale was cute even then, and later, so handsome. If he'd ever had any problem with girls, it was that he had too many choices and never wanted to pick. She guessed this waitress was the closest thing to a farm girl around the corner for Dale. She guessed he thought this Wendy was the girl for him, like she'd been for Jim. She guessed he loved her, like he'd been saying for almost half the year now.

It was obviously all lies and gossip, what people were saying. So why was she still bothered? Well, because you got bothered when people were saying things, no matter how hard you tried not to listen. If there was one thing you had to learn in a small town, it was not to care what other people thought. But they were asking Dale questions about Wendy White. Where he last saw her. How long had he known her? Implying that he, who could have had any girl he wanted and was traveling around half the globe because of the dairy, would have gone and done something to a girl from this town. A girl he wanted to marry. It was ridiculous. And if it was someone in this town that took the girl, Dale sure wouldn't know who that would be, because he just didn't associate with that kind.

She'd met Wendy White once or twice—her father had some kind of handyman business—but she could hardly say she knew her. Dale had his own apartment, attached to the house with a separate entrance. But truth be told, the girl hadn't impressed Beverly. She seemed bland. Not stupid but not real motivated, either. She seemed a little coddled, like she came from one of those soft families, not too many expectations, trying to make up in hugs what they couldn't provide for the kids. She'd seen it before. Bad for the child.

Beverly couldn't respect that. She loved her boys, and they knew it. But she always told them to be something. Have an attitude. Attitude is much more important than facts. She'd also noticed that the girl had no problem parking her daddy's car by the apartment all night long.

Like everyone else, she didn't like it when the girl disappeared, just took off and didn't tell Dale, didn't even tell someone to fill in her shifts at work. It gave you a bad feeling when something like that happened. But Beverly had heard of that kind of thing before. Her great-uncle had wanted to marry a girl from Elmville way back when, and she ran away and was never seen again. Left him so brokenhearted, it was no wonder he took to drinking now and again.

People liked to talk then and they liked to talk now. Beverly felt bad for the girl's family, of course. What they were going through was terrible. Unthinkable. And if she could help them, she would. But she had no idea where their daughter was. She wasn't a police officer. She'd heard Jim say to Dave Fawcett, "Between the trailer trash and the tree huggers buying up a few acres here and there, there's sure to be drifters. They'll pick up someone who's not rooted in the community as sure as you're alive and take her away."

Well, she didn't know if that girl was rooted or not. The family'd lived there a long time of course but she knew their troubles had started long before. The mother had to take a job at Wal-Mart, and the girl's brother got some very poor girl pregnant after high school, and now that girl did hair over at Cut Above.

"I want you to leave it, and I don't want to hear another word," Jim said. "I've been hearing all about that girl all over town, and she ain't any kind of saint. She had her eye on more boys than Dale. And she wasn't as dumb as she acted. This'll all blow over, so don't make yourself crazy."

"I just don't like people talking about our boys," she said.

"Beverly!" her husband said. "I told you to shut it. Who cares what a bunch of ignoramuses gossip about. Dale ain't got nothing to do with White Wall's daughter going off to New York to become some prostitute."

The way he said it startled her out of her worry, almost made her laugh. She knew he didn't mean it about the girl being a whore, but he did mean Beverly was being ridiculous. Farming was a hard and dangerous job, and over time, it had made them not care what anybody thought. She was going against him by worrying so much. They both knew how they felt about Pollyannas who wanted to drink their milk but were angry about how it got to their tables. People who thought farms were quaint but didn't want to smell shit or think of animals not getting treated more special than most people. How they felt about snobs who thought farmers were dumb. Men growing up in the country, like Jim and her boys, knew a lot more about life and death than those who didn't. That was the nature of it. She needed to remember who she was.

"Now, Beverly," Jim said, "you're going to be sleeping alone in this bed if I get woke up at three in the morning again because of your tossing and turning. Now rest your gray head on your old man's chest and quit thinking so hard."

He put his arms around her, and she folded in to him. Even getting older and stouter, they fit like puzzle pieces. She closed her eyes and thought only about how proud she was of Dale. Dale when he was three, when he was four, when he was five, helping her around the farm and looking after his brother. His stocky little body. Telling her jokes from the time he was just little. Dale being shy his first day of school, how he looked so handsome like her uncles. Dale all grown up, walking with his clubs across the green, his shoulders broad and strong in the shirt she bought him for his birthday. *Attitude,* she thought. *Attitude is more important than facts.*

As if Jim was reading her mind, feeling her fight against that doubt again, he said, "Dale didn't do nothing different from any other red-blooded boy growing up in the country, and a lot of things he did a hell of a lot better."

Flynn

ACCORDING TO MY research, the Haytes dairy stopped being what was traditionally called a dairy at some point in the sixties. The Haytes were the first farmers in the area to become an industrial farm. Later, in the 90s, they signed a contract with Groot, a firm out of Holland, and increased the size of their herd by a whole order of magnitude. Most of the people they employ are outside contractors, other companies that plant corn and spread the cow shit. There's a handful of people who deal with the cows in the milking parlor. Yet somehow there is still a sense that they are the biggest employer in town. They are not. That honor belongs to Home Depot.

The thing the Haytes dairy produces most of is shit, chemically treated, pharmaceutically contaminated shit, which is spread on fields throughout the entire county, leaches into the water table, causes blinding headaches, nausea, and skin rashes in those living close to where they "fertilize," and is suspected of causing nitrate contamination of the local drinking water and massive fish kills. There are several weeks in the summer when the countryside and parts of the village smell of methane and ammonia—not the organic smell of hay and cow shit and silage, more like the smell of concentrated sewage.

I managed to get on the property "officially" for a piece I was doing on local employers in 2005—I got a tour from Jim Haytes and his husky little son Bruce. It was the only angle I could think of to get in there. I pitched it like a series we were doing in conjunction with the Chamber of Commerce. And that was what I'd write about for the paper, but it was not what I was looking for. At this point I had filed Freedom of Information requests with the DEC and the EPA and had environmental-impact studies for all the industrial farms in New York. I'd also found that Groot had contracts with corporations downstate dealing in municipal waste and purchase of a new "liming agent" that was an unregulated by-product of human sludge. In other words, they'd found a way to repurpose the countryside as a toxic-waste site. I had just begun to dig, but until that day I hadn't seen where the big players buried things. I hadn't seen how it worked up close.

Despite the smell surrounding the place, the inside of the buildings was like an operating room. All stainless steel—big high Plexiglas windows—with an observatory overlooking the milking parlor. The cows were kept in a kind of cow parking lot. They stood partially on cement floors with their hind legs on metal grating though which their shit fell directly into a drainage pit below.

I sat in the milking parlor observatory with Jim Haytes and talked about Haeden and the dairy and about Bruce playing Small Fry football while we watched the cows. It was air-conditioned and quiet, and the concrete was painted pale yellow, like cream. The whole milking process was something from a science-fiction film. The cows walked in a straight line and were attached to the multipronged suction apparatus of an industrial milking machine. Workers swabbed their teats with a sanitizer and then attached the hollow prongs to the udder. The cows did nothing but stand there, and then when the suction was taken off, each one walked forward, following the cow in front of it. They didn't need to be shoved or hit or led. They just kept walking in this line, stopping, then walking back to their stalls on the cement. The whole process was hypnotic. They did this nearly around the clock.

The cows were almost impossible to differentiate, and from where I was standing, even with a higher vantage point, I couldn't see the end of the line. After an hour or so, you really don't think of them as being alive in the same way other animals are. This is because they aren't. They are made through artificial insemination for the purpose of providing milk. And they are themselves constantly inseminated so that they will keep lactating. Haytes said the calves are picked up by a separate company that has contracts with a variety of businesses dealing in food and apparel. It is hard to look at something that has been created specifically to be a commercial product and think of it as alive.

Jim Haytes said the last time the cows were milked by hand must have been over thirty years ago. But people still liked the logo of the man in the straw hat sitting on a three-legged stool next to a cow. He had a lot to say about what the dairy had done for the town. How they sponsored the dairy parade, bought uniforms for the high school football team, how, way back, when his father did the first expansion of the herd, they gave money for the pool to be built. There were no girls' sports then, and he joked that Daddy wanted to give the boys something to look at. But seriously, not too many farm towns got a swimming pool. He said that was one more way you could tell Haeden was a little different: the town had a lot of old money, the kind of history you might not know about just to look at it. Wouldn't know about the country nobility or the country intelligence—hell, might not even know how to spot it if you came in from outside.

Haytes was like a block of wood who could talk. He had a loud clipped way of articulating his words and an almost mocking singsong way of discussing the town. It was close to impossible to tell if he was being sarcastic. He was one in a class of men I'd become familiar with over the years in Haeden, men who sucked attention toward themselves while pretending they were "stoic." Men who alternated between loudmouth and sulking personas. There was something of the hysteric or the martyr in them. Too ignorant to read the culture they came from or the corporations that owned them, they presented themselves with no sense of irony as heroes of tradition who'd been smart enough to modernize, invest, sell, or simply look away, when the time was right.

While I was there, he bragged about little Bruce and then rolled his eyes at me while the kid watched, as if every nice thing he said about his son was actually a joke. I think me and the kid experienced a similar confusion about how to respond to any of Haytes' comments. Neither of us said much that day.

Bruce was good at sports, apparently—but saying "All right, good job" to the kid resulted in one of Jim Haytes's sighs and exasperated comments: "Yep. Might be even *better* if he lost a little *belly fat*—'course, it's easy to make the time for playing ball when you don't quite finish all your chores, isn't that right, Moose?" The kid didn't seem to hear a word. I regarded his round flushed face until he looked up at me and smirked. He was just too quiet. It was hard to tell what was going through Bruce Haytes's mind or if he even had one. I remember thinking the kid was either just shy of taking the short bus or we're going to find out in twenty years he's a serial killer. His father had essentially poisoned the town his own family lived in for over a century, in exchange for a Range Rover and some golfing vacations. Their very property, according to DEC maps, was the epicenter of the contamination. Nothing that came out of that family would have surprised me.

Megan Osterhaus

IT SNOWED IN early October, a thin blanket covering the fallen leaves. Alice and Megan swung on the trapeze in the cold barn while Theo dug through boxes in the loft. They were bored. They were killing time.

Megan lived up the road, and the girls had shared a fort in the lilac bushes that separated their two properties when they were little, but Megan had strict rules, even though she was older and wasn't often allowed over. This was irritating, as there were no other neighbors within biking or walking distance, and the girls had become close again because of swim team. Megan was a very sweet-looking girl and knew it. She also had a filthy vocabulary. She tried not to swear so much, but she liked to, and half the time it was by mistake anyway. Also, if you swear, people think you are making your own way. They don't know you're the kind of person who has an early curfew or a million chores. She was allowed to swear all she wanted at Alice's, but somehow she never did as much. Things were confusing at the Pipers'. They all seemed like roommates or something, friends who lived together.

"Found them," Theo called.

Alice jumped off the trapeze and stood with her hands on her hips, looking up at him. Then raised her hands.

"I'm not going to throw it at you, dummy—it's the whole set."

"Why are we gonna play in the cold and dark, anyhow?" Megan asked.

Megan was often afraid she would get in trouble for playing with them. She never knew what the rules were there. Or if there were any.

Theo and Alice's parents let them sleep over at each other's houses, and one day last summer, when it was really hot, Megan went to Alice's and no one was home but her and Theo, sitting in the bathtub naked, reading comic books. They had dumped a bag of ice in with them. It was like they didn't care. Like it didn't matter that they were naked or anything. It wasn't sexy or anything. It was, like, boring. They were really bored, and it was too hot. She put her feet over the side and sat there talking with them. They read out loud from the comic books in funny voices, but the whole time she was afraid somebody's parents would come home. For some reason it made her even more uneasy when she found out their parents didn't care. Also, since Theo had gone away to school, he smoked cigarettes right in front of everyone, and no one said a thing. And she thought it was kind of gross the way they still played Circus, and once she heard them talking in a made-up language. There was something dirty about the whole thing. Like Alice and Theo were brother and sister but also in love and they didn't even know or care that other people thought it was weird.

Theo walked down the steps with a big square metal suitcase, set it flat upon the floor, and then opened it. Inside was an old wooden croquet set.

"Do we have the lighter fluid?" Alice asked.

Megan watched them from the trapeze.

Theo smiled. "Indeed we do."

"Do we have the soccer socks?" she asked.

"Why, yes, we do." He picked up the paper bag at his feet and dramatically held it at arm's length.

Megan slipped off the back of the bar to hang by her knees, dropped to the floor, landing on her hands, then folded at the middle to stand up straight. "I have to go home," she said. "It fucking sucks, but I have—"

"Okay," Theo said to her quickly.

Megan had wanted them to ask her to stay and was slightly

hurt. Alice and Theo were already choosing their mallets and pulling the wickets out of the canvas bag.

They walked out of the barn; the yard shone in the moonlight, and squares of light from the windows of the Pipers' house patterned themselves across the ground, making the snow sparkle.

Alice poked the edges of the wickets through some ratty tube socks, then wound the socks tightly around the arc of wire, handing each one to Theo, who ran to various places in the yard, jamming them into the ground and pouring lighter fluid over them.

"I guess I could stay for a little while longer," Megan said.

"Good!" Alice said, grinning at her excitedly. "This will be fun."

Theo came back and stood with the girls and retrieved his mallet and a ball, which he also sprayed with lighter fluid. "Ready?"

"Do it!" yelled Alice. "No, wait!" She scrutinized how he held his mallet. Then said, "Okay, now."

Theo lit a match and dropped it on the ball, which shot flames higher than they had anticipated. He quickly knocked it with the mallet, sending the ball through the first wicket, which caught fire. In the darkness, it shone blue and yellow.

Alice ran and set the other wickets alight, the pale gray cloud of her breath visible, illuminated by the fire's yellow light. Then she went through the course, disregarding the rules, eventually setting her mallet on fire and balancing the handle on the palm of her hand while she walked around the yard. Megan watched silently. Had they never heard of barn fires? Didn't they realize how close they lived to the woods?

She tried to see what they saw. The fire was beautiful against the dark and the snow. So bright and mysterious and blue at the center. But she didn't feel good. It was like Alice and Theo understood something about what they were doing that wasn't even there. Something she didn't know. And they knew she didn't know it. That was how they made her feel at school, too.

Dumb. They never said anything mean. They always asked her to play, but that was how she felt. Slow.

She looked over at the house and saw Gene and Claire watching them from the window with mugs in their hands. Watching. Just watching the little fires in their own yard as they grew.

Wendy

NOVEMBER 2008

SHE WAS NOT in Dale's truck when she woke up, and she was not in her bedroom. She thought maybe they had been in an accident. Her body hurt, her arms and legs and back hurt, and her mouth was dry. It was too dark to see anything, and she was facedown on cold cement, no stones or grass, and it smelled like mold. Her head throbbed. She touched her body. She wasn't wearing her clothes. She was wearing something. A shirt. It felt like Dale's shirt—there was a collar and a couple buttons at the top. A shirt and underwear. Wet underwear. She had peed her pants. *What had happened to them?*

Oh God. Where was Dale? Something happened to Dale! She crawled forward and bumped her face on something, put her hand in something slippery and cold. *What was it? Oil, soap? It smelled like mold, like bleach.* Maybe she was dreaming. She sat up on her knees and tried to stand, but partway up, something hit her head and she fell forward. Her stomach lurched, and she felt like she was going to throw up. She lay still for a moment with her heart racing. "Hello?" she yelled, and her throat was raw and sore. It felt like she had swallowed something hard, felt like it was still there. Blood, maybe? There was a taste in her mouth like metal. "Hello? I need help. IneedhelpIneedhelp," she whispered to herself. *They had been in a car accident. That was the only thing that could explain it.* She hurt all over.

She closed her eyes again and lay still until her stomach settled. Then she tried feeling her way forward. Put her hand into something soft and scratchy, cloying. *Insulation.* She knew it from her father's work. It made her heart race to touch it. *What's going on? What's happened?*

There was an accident, and she was somewhere safe. She was in someone's shed—they had brought her there, but they didn't know she was conscious. Dale was fine, or he wouldn't have given her his shirt. That was it. That had to be it.

Alice

AT THE WHISTLE, she was off the block and out over the water. She was smaller than the other girls and thinner, but she could tell she had more air, breathed better, cut through the water faster. She was smaller because they were varsity swimmers and she was still in middle school. The other girls had broader shoulders. More weight. Breasts. They were like sea creatures. Seals and manatees and selkies and mermaids. She flew through the sink and rise of the butterfly as if the water had a different weight for her than for anyone else.

Their coach, Mr. Dunn, was an enormous fat man whom they had never seen get into the water. They could only assume, since he knew what to tell them, there must have been a time when he could swim.

"Coach is a fucking fat blob," Megan told Alice quietly on the bus to their meet in Elmville.

"Coach is an incredible example of buoyancy to which we can all aspire," Alice said, raising her eyebrows a few times.

"They should have called that thing you won the verbal *dis*advantage," Megan said. " 'Cause nobody can understand a fucking thing you say." She grinned to let Alice know she didn't mean to be mean. Megan loved to talk shit.

The girls on the bus started singing that Gwen Stefani song "Hollaback Girl" and clapping. They were getting ready to beat the Elmville girls to a fucking pulp. Eventually, they were just shouting the song at the top of their lungs and bouncing on the seats of the bus. If they got too carried away, Dunn would tell them to shut up, but they also knew he liked it when they got pumped up to win.

They sang the chorus over and over, almost in a trance: *A few times I've been around that track, so it's not just gonna happen like that, 'cause I ain't no hollaback GIRL. I ain't no hollaback GIRL.*

Alice had never seen the video for this song, but she'd heard it on the radio in the locker room and she loved it, whatever it meant. It was the song that made them win. And they always won.

Now at practice, she was swimming like a fish, happy in the blue pool surrounded by the echo and the rush of her blood in her veins and the feel of her heart in her wrists in the cool water.

At lap twenty, a cramp started in her belly and a weakness, almost an itch or a vibration, in one of her knees. *Fuck!* She had four more lengths before she could get out of the water, and she had not brought tampons to practice. She sped up but felt a little sick to her stomach. She crossed her fingers and willed herself not to bleed until she'd finished the next four. And somehow she managed it. She pulled herself out of the water quickly at the blocks. One of the seniors—a fleshy blue-eyed girl with a strong back and shoulders—had reached the blocks, too, and looked up at her, read the anxiety on her face. She pulled herself up and hopped out of the water and then waved and yelled to Dunn, "Have to use the bathroom. I'll be back." She bumped her arm against Alice's shoulder. "You need to go?" They didn't towel off but walked right into the locker room. Just inside the door, Alice felt the release of blood hot against her cold skin, and it saturated the crotch of her bathing suit.

"Oh, shit." She was embarrassed she had no tampons, and the other suit in her locker looked different than this one. Not a racing suit.

"It's okay," Wendy said, smiling at her. "I've got some in my locker. It's not a big deal. And no one will say anything if you come out with a different suit on. If you're worried about it, say your other one had too much drag."

Alice was worried about it. She grabbed her spare suit and a plastic bag for the bloody one and walked into one of the stalls. Wendy came back from her locker and gave her a tampon over the gray metal door.

"Dunn has these on hand in his office, too," Wendy told her. "Though I don't think he needs them, being nine months pregnant and all."

Alice wished Wendy wasn't a senior and that they were going to the same school. Something about Wendy reminded her of Gene. The way she didn't say a whole lot and was no-nonsense and funny. Too bad she'd graduate before Alice even got to high school. She was worried about having friends after Theo left.

"I'd rather be at practice during my period than sitting in class," Wendy said, and her low voice echoed against the tile walls around them. "You feel energized, not all tired and crampy."

Alice came out of the stall wearing the new suit. Wendy raised her eyebrows and looked like she was trying very hard not to laugh. "Wow!" she said. "Cute. It has a *frog* on it!"

"Well, this is my old suit," Alice explained. "I've had it since fifth grade." She felt like she was going to cry, standing in her bright green child's bathing suit with this older girl who was being so nice to her. She groaned.

Wendy looked into her eyes and smiled, and Alice could see that the girl had felt embarrassed before, too, but was strong from it, that it had made her nice—a little different than nice. Wendy could laugh at the suit and laugh at the way things like that made you feel, but she wasn't laughing at Alice. Maybe she was laughing at everyone who cared about embarrassing things.

"Oh, Jesus, don't even worry about it," Wendy said. "It's okay. If anybody says something, just tell them it's your lucky suit."

Alice smiled then, and Wendy White's laughter echoed against the tile, leaked out, and hovered over the blue pool and the bodies of their teammates cutting through the water.

Alice

BY NINTH GRADE, Alice had cut the frog off her little girl's swimsuit and sewn it onto the side of her black TYR racing suit. The girls she swam with when it still fit had gone off to college, except for Megan, who was a senior now. Mr. Dunn had dropped sixty pounds. The girls still called him fat, but most of them didn't know how he looked before which had been almost obscene. Alice was now tall for her age and had well-defined back and shoulder muscles. Long arms and legs. A graceful, light way of moving. And she had cut her hair very short.

Her face had become more delicate, classic, but her high cheekbones and strong straight Roman features were still dusted with freckles. She was never very conscious of the way she looked, but she did put black mascara on her blond eyelashes the day she went to meet Stacy Flynn in the field outside the elementary school where the hoop house stood—where the butterflies were eating their way out of their cocoons. The sky was cloudless, and as she got closer to the school, she could smell the flowers that the team had planted for the garden; lavender and rabbitbrush, sea pink, burning bush, aster, columbine, and bee balm.

Alice had looked inside the hoop house. It was lush and warm and fragrant, filled with a diffuse green light. A separate world from the sprawling concrete of the school and parking lot and the mud and scalped grass of the fields. Wendy White, who used to be on the team and never went to college, sat sleepily inside, her skin damp from the humidity. Several butterflies fluttered above the plants surrounding her, lighting on them and closing their wings and then moving on. Alice didn't know if Wendy had come for the opening or if she had walked up from the Alibi, decided to take her break among the flowers. She looked like she was beginning to fall asleep, and Alice didn't disturb her. She knew how it was to sit and think, and it would only be a matter of time before the kindergarteners burst into the garden, running on the stone paths between the flowers, startling her and stirring the butterflies in all directions until the sound of their bodies striking against the tight green plastic arc of the hoop house pattered like rain.

She walked outside, eager for Flynn to arrive. She wanted her to write about the flowers and the butterflies, not the swim team or the kindergarteners. Some cars pulled into the parking lot, and she watched parents and little kids get out. They started running toward the butterfly house to meet her and to be in the paper.

Alice did a cartwheel while she waited for them, then stood on her hands and started walking in their direction. Three little girls ran to her in their jeans and flip-flops, and when they got close, she tucked into a somersault and then stood on her feet in front of them.

"Are there more hatching?" one of the girls asked.

"They don't hatch," Alice said dryly. "You entomologists will have to do a little more research."

The other two girls were doing cartwheels on the grass, showing off for her. She smiled at them and looked up to see the group of swimmers approaching just as Wendy came out from beneath the green plastic canopy, brushing her sweaty hair from her forehead and smiling, making her way around the short bodies rushing forward to see the butterflies' new house.

"No *way*!" Megan shouted, seeing her. "I thought you were working until seven."

"I am. I came for a little break 'cause I thought Kenzie and Beth Ann would be here."

"Yeah, right, you came because the team is here! And you want to get your pretty face in the paper!"

Wendy laughed. Only a few of the girls knew her from swimming. Most knew her as a waitress. Alice came over and bumped her fist against Wendy's. And Wendy said, "Hey, Captain. Awesome butterflies."

Before Alice could say anything to her Megan said, "How's your cowboy, anyway, Wen? Nobody ever fucking sees you anymore. You're always playing golf or something."

Wendy laughed and put her arms around Megan.

"Are Crystal and Kenzie taking swimming?" Megan asked her.

"Hell, yes. Like you have to ask."

Flynn's car pulled into the lot near the elementary school, and the girls watched her stub out a cigarette with her low mud-covered boot, then grab her camera and notebook off the front seat. Alice had known Flynn from the other stories she'd written, and she thought the woman was really funny. She always seemed tired and unfriendly until she started interviewing you. Alice liked Flynn. Before they ever met, she had imagined Peg, the reporter from the *Short & Sweet*, acting that way. Alice and her parents actually called the *Haeden Free Press* the *Short & Sweet*. And for a minute when Alice saw her coming toward them, she missed Theo.

"Al," Flynn said, "sorry I'm late."

"No problem," Alice said. "This is a good day to take pictures of the butterflies."

A boy wearing green gardening clogs ran out of the hoop house, laughing, and his friend chased him through the field to a stand of trees. Flynn quickly and with no expression took pictures of them as they ran past, then looked back up at Alice. "This thing is great. What made you decide to built it?"

"You have to see the *inside*," Alice said, eager to get to the real story. "We did it because our team and the elementary school have to do all these bake sales all the time, to get money to do things, and I really hate baking and sales. So I thought why don't we do a swim-a-thon instead and then give half our money to the kindergarteners for science projects—they never have money for anything fun. So we ended up doing a butterfly-a-thon to build a butterfly house. Some money went to the fifth-graders for this project, and then our money goes to support the team so we can keep winning." The swimmers laughed and clapped. "Right?" Alice said to them. "Right? They'll have to fly us somewhere *really* far away to find anyone who can beat us."

"That's right, motherfucker," Megan said.

All the girls laughed, and Flynn raised her eyebrows and nodded with a big smile. "Nice language for the newspaper," she said. "So how many miles did you guys actually swim?"

"We swam a combined one hundred miles," Megan said. They could hear chatting and squealing from inside the hoop house.

"All butterfly? How much did you make?"

"Three thousand two hundred and eighty-seven dollars," said Alice a little impatiently, "and yes, all butterfly." This was Alice's event, but also, how could they have built a science project for freestyle?

"You could have gone door-to-door and asked everyone in town for two bucks," Flynn said.

"Not everyone has two bucks," Alice said.

Flynn smiled, wrote something in her notebook. "Good point."

"And training pays off. Look at Wendy." Alice put her hand on Wendy's shoulder. "Butterfly was her event when she was on the team."

Wendy looked shyly at the reporter and smiled, shrugged. Alice noticed that all the girls were bigger than Flynn. Strong and broad.

"Why aren't you swimming anymore?" Flynn asked Wendy.

"I'm working."

"Okay," said Alice to Flynn. "Now you have to come inside and see these things, because they are amazing. And that's the real story."

"Wait wait wait." Flynn put her pen behind her ear. "I need a picture of the team."

The swimmers stood in front of the hoop house, mugging for the camera, making muscles. Wendy stepped away from them, stood back and watched them.

"Quit it," Flynn told them. "You got to get closer together. You." She pointed at Wendy. "Crunch in there. I want everybody in the picture."

Megan squeezed Wendy to her side and then shouted, "Ten and *oh*!"

"As in: oh! I just got my ass handed to me," Wendy said quietly.

"C'mon, c'mon, c'mon," Flynn said.

"Make sure you put that we are ten and oh," Megan told her.

"I will." Flynn snapped a few pictures of the girls laughing, then a few of Alice by herself, her smile bright and eyes shining.

Alice loved the butterfly house. The smell, but especially how the butterflies moved. She watched as Flynn entered the garden and her smile grew wider. Alice could see that the place made her happy. She loved the way everyone looked excited when they first saw the garden. People thought butterflies were beautiful, but really, they were strange, so strange, and almost ugly, resting and working, hovering camouflaged as one thing—so they could one day be another.

Wendy

BUT WHY INSULATION? No. Think. Think. Think. She knew houses. She could feel her way along. If only there were a light, she could figure out where she was from the spacing of the joists. It was a small space. As soon as there was some light, she'd be fine. She knew how houses were built. *Oh God. Please don't let me be behind a wall. Jesus. Crazy. That's crazy. It was impossible, what that would mean—behind a wall? Not possible. In a basement. That's it. A basement or a shed. Holy Jesus fucking fuck.* "Hello? Hello?"

Then footsteps and whispering. *Oh, thank God. She must have fallen asleep. She was asleep. This was a dream. Was she really calling for help?* She called again, then there was laughing. *Okay. There was laughing, so no one could hear her.* Or she wasn't really calling. *Maybe she was sleeping. Maybe she was dead.* She thought she might be dead, in between worlds. Her back and her arms and legs hurt. Her hands hurt. *Do hands hurt in the afterlife? No. Can't be.* She couldn't look at them, it was too dark. *This could still be a dream,* she thought because she couldn't really see. Or she could be blind. *Oh, Christ, please, God, no. Don't let it be blindness.*

"Please," she yelled, "somebody please help me. I don't know where I am."

Footsteps coming forward, getting louder. *Someone was coming, thank God.* "Please!" she yelled, screamed, hoped she was yelling, hoped she was not dead. Her throat burned. Sounds got louder, sounds were right at her ear, right above her, and this couldn't be right, she was dizzy now. Right above her head. *Was she just waking up? Waking up right now after an accident, maybe she'd been in a coma since the accident, when did this*

happen? Right above her head, footsteps, and then they, them—
someone—one foot tapped like someone waiting for something.
Right above her. She could feel it. The creak of a floor, the creak
of a ceiling above her. Of boards on the other side of where she
was. She heard laughing. Four, five voices. Maybe all the same
voice. Voices from the Alibi! She got hurt, and someone must
have brought her to the Alibi to recover. Thank God, thank God,
thank God, that was it. Oh, please, that's it. And she was not
blind and they didn't know she was awake and it wasn't that bad
or they wouldn't be talking or maybe she was drunk but didn't
remember drinking.

The tapping was right there at her head. Then more voices.
Doc Green? Someone must have known she was hurt and couldn't
find a real doctor right away. Must have been near the dairy and
Doc Green was already there. That was it! No. God! Was it Doc
Green? Was she dead? She tried to stand again, hit something
hard, and fell forward. There was laughing. There was laughing
when she fell, like someone heard it but they must not know
what it was. Where she was. What had happened. They didn't
know she was there.

Epic Themes in Monique Wittig's
Les Guérillères (The Warriors)
Alice Piper
Freshman English
Ms. Lourde
7th period
4/6/2008

Monique Wittig's *Les Guérillères* is an epic poem and a memorial to the dead. The right-hand page at the end of each scene is simply a list of names capitalized in bold that the reader soon recognizes as names of dead soldiers.

Les Guérillères embodies the traditional epic plot of "conquering the monster." The magical and practical things that society and its heroes have done to "kill the monster and return to harmony" are revealed throughout the text.

Les Guérillères is an epic of violence, battle, and conquest and the entire book calls for war—even a war on the language of the enemy.

"The language you speak is made up of words that are killing you. The language you speak is made up of signs that rightly designate what men have appropriated." (4)

Later she expresses that the central mistake people make is acceptance or happiness in either being dominated or dominating. She refutes this false choice:

"Better to see your guts in the sun and utter a death rattle than to live a life that anyone can appropriate. What belongs to you on this earth? Only death. No power on earth can take that away from you. And—consider, explain, tell yourself—*if happiness consists in the possession of something then hold fast to this sovereign happiness— to die.*" (47) (italics are hers!)

Like true epic heroes, Wittig's characters are only satisfied with freedom and fighting for the cause. This also turns upside down the "essentialist" (or what people call natural) understanding of women as givers of life, symbols of life, and nurturers.

In *Les Guérillères*, they become bringers of death, celebrants of life and death, and individuals who are active, violent, malevolent or protecting, or nurturing or funny, all kinds of things. (Which makes more sense because really if you think about it a person can't be a symbol of a thing or a metaphor. Unfortunately Wittig makes people into symbols of something else. Which proves that the whole thing is bogus. I don't even get how this works given the fact that people are biological entities. When I was reading about the epic and the idea of a person being a symbol I almost called you because it seems to be an enormous flaw in logic. And really takes the pleasure out of reading about characters and what they want to do or who they are.) (I know you hate my parentheses—but this relates directly to *Les Guérillères.*)

The form of the narrative itself is a symbol—a circle beginning and ending with a postapocalyptic society in which the sexes are divided and a war has already been waged. So, men and women are divided, come together, and are divided again. Like they are one creature that keeps destroying itself. The book could be finished and started over perpetually because of this form. *Les Guérillères* is also an epic in that it can be cut apart and any piece can stand on its own.

The description of the monster is my favorite part:

"He has enslaved you by trickery, you who were great strong valiant. He has stolen your wisdom from you, he has closed your memory to what you were, he has made of you that which is not, which does not speak, which does not possess, which does not write. He has made you a vile and fallen creature. He has gagged abused and betrayed you by means of stratagems, he has stultified your understanding, he has woven around you a long list of defects that he declared essential to your well being, to your nature." (130)

This is a far better monster than the Cyclops or Minotaur or Golem.

Wittig's book is also about wrath. For example: Men are skinned, tortured, hacked to pieces, and buried in mass graves. Some men have joined the women in battle, must be reeducated, and then are heroes. An end of violence is declared and "Paradise," Wittig says, "exists in the shadow of the sword."

This kind of idea can only be taken seriously in an epic. (Skinning men or killing suitors all day long, like Odysseus, or fighting for years because someone is beautiful, or gods wanting battles to take place or even that "monsters" exist, etc. . . . it's absurd.) The epic overlooks the causes of war (gold, land) but it is meant to be a story *about* the causes and outcomes of war. It replaces real reasons with symbolic reasons and inserts human characters as symbols, too. Which I said earlier I think is completely illogical. Wittig's piece is a classic example of an epic poem (meets ALL the criteria discussed in class). The real question is what is the value of the epic—even if you change who does the killing? It might be the worst form of literature. (Ms. Lourde, can I stop in during lunch Thursday to work on this more? I want to get it right. Alice.)

Beth Ann

AFTER THE RAIN, Beth Ann and Wendy put the girls in the double stroller and walked through town so they could see how the river had risen and throw sticks into the muddy water.

The air smelled like wet pavement, and there was a light mist rising up from the sidewalks. Getting warmer already, that late-summer rainy season made Beth Ann feel drowsy, made her want to spend all day with the girls, stay up late and eat dinner on the porch and look at the stars. Summer made her love the simple things, and she wished Wendy were around more these days to do all the things with them like they used to. Crystal and Kenzie kicked their feet as they rolled along. They wore matching jelly shoes with Ariel and Sleeping Beauty on them, their hair in ponytails on the top of their heads.

Wendy had been talking about Dale since they left the house, and Beth Ann was beginning to get a little tired of it.

"It's like it's a whole different life," Wendy told her. "I feel like we can do everything together. And I feel like I can learn to do stuff I never thought of, how to play golf or drink shots or even how to draw better. You know I can really draw? I don't know why I never took any art classes. I don't remember even going in the art room at school except when I was really little. Like Kenzie."

"*What* wike Kenthie?" Kenzie shouted.

"Like me, too, right?" Crystal asked.

"Like both you girls," Beth Ann said matter-of-factly. Then she said, "Yeah, Wen. Love makes you feel pretty sure of yourself, but you know what? So does just getting older."

"My Widdo Mowmaid thoeth awe wike Cwythtal'th!" Kenzie shouted. Beth Ann mouthed the words "Oh my God" to Wendy, and they laughed. Some sentences came out all lisp, and it was hard not to laugh at her daughters no matter how hard she tried.

"That's right," Beth Ann said. "Now you girls talk amongst yourselves while Mommy and Aunt Wen talk. Big girls talk to each other now."

Wendy in love was something her family was happy to see, and they didn't care if it was Dale or somebody else. She was happy, she laughed even more than usual, and she seemed confident in a way she hadn't been at school. At school, Beth Ann thought Wendy looked a little worn out. Now she looked so pretty, had such a dark tan from being out playing golf and swimming.

She was growing up, Beth Ann thought, wouldn't be such a daddy's girl anymore. A little more self-sufficient. Wendy had always had so much more than Beth Ann—she didn't know hard work or worry. She got to work in an office. Take whole weekends to drive places with the swim team. It made Beth Ann mad sometimes, and she'd hate to see Wendy become one of those people who was out socializing all the time, not have time for family. Her family, anyway, not just Dale's.

"It's nice to have a first love," Beth Ann said finally. "But don't sell yourself short. You're a really pretty gal, Wen, and maybe you'll want to date other boys."

"You don't like Dale."

"I do, honey, I just don't like golf that much. And that shit smell coming from their whole place up there bothers a lot of people." Wendy looked offended for a quick moment and then touched her arm and they both laughed.

Beth Ann also thought Dale was stuck up, that Wendy was too smart for him, and sometimes she couldn't stand the way he talked. But she didn't say so. Plus she knew it wouldn't make a difference if she did. Wendy loved him, and Beth Ann figured a big boy like Dale was probably fun in bed, and that mattered. She wanted Wendy to be happy and have fun.

The little girls were singing a song from preschool, stopping to say "No no no, like this," to each other and then laughing and starting over with made-up words. Suddenly, Beth Ann remembered she wanted to tell Wendy about a story she'd read in *House Beautiful* at the salon. It was about a lady architect.

"Oh! You know what architects do, right?" Beth Ann asked her.

"Uh, yeah?"

Beth Ann said, "They draw houses out on paper. Like what you and DW used to do when you were a kid. You ever think of doing that? You looked at plenty of blueprints."

Right then Beth Ann thought she could see Wendy's whole future. See the girls going to stay with Aunt Wen in some nice house for the summer while she and Davy had their own fun time. Thought Wendy could be one of those women who didn't just get out of Haeden but got everything. Wendy could be one of those people you read about, who started doing math and drawing houses when she was five but didn't know what it all meant until her sister-in-law asked her one day, out walking, did she know what architects did. Then she'd go to school. Beth Ann could do interior decorating, and then the two of them could have their own business. Maybe buy the old Masonic temple, put up a sign that said WHITE AND WHITE ARCHITECTURE AND DESIGN, and call it a studio, like in *House Beautiful.*

"No," Wendy said. "I never thought of it." Beth Ann could see she was still distracted, thinking about Dale.

"Well, you might want to," Beth Ann said.

They stood on the bridge, looking down into the river, while the girls sang and swung their feet in the stroller.

"You might want to do a lot of things, Wen," Beth Ann said. "You got the whole world waiting for you."

Claire

THE LINE OF volunteer searchers stretched halfway across the field beside the intersection of Himrod Road and County Road 33. Gene and Claire and Alice walked holding hands over the blunt and broken stalks of harvested corn sticking up from the frozen ground.

Alice had asked to come with them, Claire kept telling herself. She had asked and they had said yes, but now she believed it had been a horrible mistake to bring her. It didn't matter that she was almost grown up, that several boys from her school had wanted to come, too. That it was the right thing for the community to do or that Alice shared Gene's constitution. Those things didn't matter. This was not the way a fifteen-year-old girl should be spending her day—looking for the body of another young woman. That's what they were doing, and there was no pretending they were looking for anything other than a body at this point. It was a show of community solidarity, standing together to do this for the Whites. It suited them better than joining a prayer group, but in the back of her head, Claire knew it would have about the same impact on the situation.

For all of Claire's worry, Alice seemed fine. Talking with them about raising money for the team and about school. Eventually, she got around to talking about why they were there.

"Here's an example of an ethical obligation, right?" Alice asked them as they walked. "What we're doing right now?"

"How do you mean?" Claire asked.

"We're ethically obligated to care for a resident of our town— it's part of the greater good."

"That's always true," Gene said.

"Well I guess we're not caring for a resident," Alice said. "Because we don't know where she is. Technically, we're showing care symbolically, right? We're more like caring for her family."

"I don't know if this falls into the category you're talking about," Claire said.

"Connie said stuff like this is better suited to a cost-benefit analysis."

Her words chilled them for a moment. Claire could feel Gene's tension as they walked on either side of Alice.

"Not really," Claire said.

"Does finding Wendy benefit her family and the town more than the difficulty or fear or whatever *takes* from the town? Isn't that like talking about a greater good, anyway? Con says what's practical is almost always ethical."

"Not quite," Gene said.

"Why not? If we find clues that prevent another person from disappearing, or that lead to catching someone, or if we find her alive! We might find her alive. It's not out of the question at all. We don't know."

Claire put her arm around Alice's waist and walked in step with her over the hard clumpy earth. She could feel her husband's sadness meeting her own when Alice said it. They walked quietly for a while.

"So the risk benefit is the right thing to base all this on," Alice said almost to herself.

Claire didn't speak for a moment. She was genuinely surprised that Alice had been sold on the kind of business-speak Con used. "Sometimes you have ethical obligations to do things that are hard or not practical for you as an individual, or difficult to understand within the social context you're in," she said, stopping to look into the cool blue of her daughter's eyes. "Like, none of the things people did during civil rights were really practical for themselves or their families, right? The individual risk benefit to sitting at a lunch counter where you know your head is going to get knocked in by racists or the police doesn't work out, right? Or the Panthers arming themselves when obviously the police and the army can take them out pretty quickly."

"In the short term, things like that don't work out," Alice said. "But in the long term, everyone knows it made sense."

"Right," her parents said in unison. "Exactly," Gene went on. "And that's why Con's idea is not always a good model for reasoning. That's the model that gets you companies like Gen-Ag-Tech doing what they're doing."

"Oh. My. GOD!" Alice groaned. "How did even *this* conversation get around to Gen-Ag-Tech that quickly?" They laughed, and Claire felt some tension lift from her shoulders.

"You know Daddy doesn't like to go too many hours in the day without saying Gen-Ag-Tech," she said.

"He's like a ten-year-old talking about Darth Vader."

Claire laughed harder.

"We were at the Rooster with Ross and Daddy and Annie and Harley," Alice told Claire. "Me and Megan were listening to them talk about some kind of music copyright thing because those old-time players were worried about it, and he goes, 'This is exactly like what happened in India with Gen-Ag-Tech.'"

"It is," Gene said, shrugging.

"Okay," Claire said. "You know what? That stuff is important, but it's not like the stuff we're talking about now, about Wendy. And we should probably give some thought to why we're here right now. Instead of trying to make it a puzzle. That's all Daddy means, I think—that you can't *just* use the cost benefit. You have to take a lot of other things into consideration. Really observe and study the topic you're concerned about."

Claire looked down the line of people walking in groups in their coats and flannels. It was nearly everyone they knew. Four regulars from the Rooster walked in a loose configuration next to the Haytes boys and a group of their friends. Mostly it was a line of men. Many wore only baseball caps and sweatshirts despite the chill and overcast sky. They shared a proprietary swagger, Claire realized, as they walked through nothing toward nothing like dogs set out by instinct to wander, or to rescue what they might have, under other circumstances, hunted.

When she and Gene and Alice stopped talking, it was completely silent, just boots crunching along and bodies moving under the pale gray sky. There were no houses visible in the distance, just more fields, and somewhere—how many miles ahead, she didn't know—a low hillside.

For a moment Claire felt overwhelmingly dizzy, like there was nothing to orient the three of them in space, like she was falling. Her stomach turned, and she thought she detected a slight arrhythmia in her heart. She was dehydrated, maybe. Easy to forget to drink enough water in winter. She held tighter to her daughter's strong and taller frame. Felt grateful to be able to hold her.

These weeks that Wendy White had been missing were disturbing for her and Gene. It had been an effort not to mentally replace Wendy's face with Alice's in the missing posters. She thought so much about the Whites—couldn't imagine the parents having to go to work every day, having to worry about making ends meet with their daughter gone, having to wake up in the morning knowing she was still missing. She and Gene had been changed by the girl's disappearance, but it seemed not to have impacted Alice and her friends as deeply.

Claire had felt this before on occasion, working at the clinic— thinking about "what if"—but the difference was those girls and women she saw were right there, were alive. The likelihood that Wendy White was alive, she knew, was very slim. And she felt again what she had always felt in the clinic when she saw patients with sexual-assault injuries. It was what you did to *prevent* these things that really mattered. Not the collection of evidence and the prosecution. Not the kind of thing they were doing right now.

*   *   *

Back at home, Gene put the bread that had been rising all day into the oven, and the three of them sat around the table drinking mint tea. Soon Theo would call, and Alice would be on the phone for the rest of the evening. Making origami butterflies or sewing or throwing darts against the black and yellow dartboard while she talked.

The walk had chilled Claire to the core. She sat with her feet in Gene's lap, and he rubbed them, his hands still warm from holding the mug. It was then she began to cry. She tried to stop because she knew it would disturb them, but she couldn't. She wasn't simply sad. She was exhausted. Exhausted from trying to run the little farm, from being isolated, from having no one to talk to but her family or Micky on expensive long distance. From having nowhere to go, from hearing nothing new for half a year at a time—not even a new joke or figure of speech—from constantly explaining what she'd said or what she meant, or putting the places she was talking about into context. Tired of being poor now for almost twenty years.

And she knew she was exhausted from way before all the things that had happened in Haeden. She was beat from the free clinic and from constantly thinking about how to do the right thing. From doing the right thing and ending up in the same fucked-up world. A million decibels of Iggy Pop would not help anymore, no matter the compassion for rage or the grace in his voice. She was too old to slip into a man's angry voice to get away.

Gene continued to rub her feet while she cried. Looking into her face. And she knew then, looking back at him, that he understood she'd been tired from long before. From birth, maybe, from all the things that made her become a doctor, from all the things that had happened to her friends and what they saw and heard and pretended every day not to see and hear. Tired of it.

"It doesn't matter," she said finally, an unformed rage building. "It doesn't matter what they do now. This woman is already gone. It's the next abduction or murder or rape. It's stopping it before it happens. If I could get away with it, I would kill every single suspicious fucking redneck sexist fuck in this entire town."

At this Gene winced and shook his head. "That's Ross talking."

"No," she said bitterly, tears running down her face. "That's me saying what I have always known to be the real fucking correct cost benefit! The real greater good. No women's clinic or search or prayer or self-defense class is going to prevent these things. When the kinds of men who do these things are eliminated completely or live in fear for their lives—not just their time or livelihood—if they act, when that happens, we'll have progress. And no sooner. No sooner. How else do we stop it? How?" Claire took a breath, then tried to relax, but it was no use. She put her hands over her face and wept hard, her body crumpled in defeat.

Alice sat stunned. "Mom." She leaned forward and took Claire's hand.

Claire said nothing for several minutes. Then: "I'm sorry, sweetheart, I'm sorry I said that. I'm feeling alone, is all it is." She wiped her face.

"Maybe she's alive," Alice said. "Or maybe she ran away. I'm sure she's okay, Mom. And if she's not, they'll take her somewhere like the free clinic where they'll take good care of her."

Claire nodded and looked into her daughter's eyes, saw the strength and earnestness with which the girl was trying to comfort her. "Maybe she did, babe. I'm sorry. I'm sorry I said that. I hope she's okay."

Alice stared past her into the other room, her eyes unfocused, thinking. Claire squeezed her hand, and Alice looked back down at her, and she felt awful at what she saw in her daughter's face: pity and shock and something that looked close to shame.

"If things are really this bad," Alice said quietly, "why wouldn't you tell me?"

Haeden, NY

He PULLED THE insulation away from behind the door and crouched in front of where she lay on the old crib mattress that had been stored there. He handed her a Gatorade.

"You've really lost your tan, honey."

Her arms were skinny now. Thumb-sized blue circles shone clear in the pale skin around her shoulders and wrists. He climbed down into the crawl space and sat next to her, held the plastic bottle for her to drink from. "You need these electrolytes—they're good after a workout." She had a rash on her face, maybe from the fiberglass insulation. But it was really ugly. Her breath was terrible. She had some white shit coating her gums. They should probably brush her teeth at some point.

Wendy's pretty days were really short-lived. He watched her swallow; her skinny throat covered with raised pinpricks of red, like her face.

"Man, I'm not going to get on that thing again until you give it a shower."

"Go on back to school, then. More for everybody else."

"Nah, I'll wait, if you can give me a ride."

He nodded. "Yeah, man, no problem."

"She don't even try to talk no more, does she?" He ran a thumb over his chapped lips. "She don't even want to tell us about her day."

He laughed through his teeth in agreement, tipped the bottle up for her to get the last of the Gatorade. He searched for something in it that could still turn him on. He was starting to wish she wasn't down there anymore.

"Are you hungry, sweetie? Man's got to take care of these things. Yeah. 'Cause we got company waiting." He pulled out a brown paper bag containing his leftover lunch and got out a white napkin, which he tucked into the front of her bra. "Yep, just a little more company." She started crying. After they were done, he'd give her her sweatshirt back.

"What's wrong, baby? What's wrong?" He took out a white Styrofoam container and a plastic fork. Inside was a cold baked potato and part of a salad. He held a forkful of potato out to her. "If you finish this, I have a surprise for you." He looked up at her, pointed his chin down in a little nod, fluttered his eyelashes for a moment for the comic effect. Shit. She was so fucked up. It was ridiculous. "Come on. That's better. That's the girl I know. The girl I know loves to eat. Right?"

She chewed and did not wipe the tears that were rolling down her face. He noticed one of her eyes was puffier than the other.

"You're going to be so happy when you see what else is in here." He took out another Styrofoam container. "They had peanut-butter brownies. I know you love them. C'mon, Hun, cheer up."

Flynn

I KNEW SHE WAS in that town. I knew she was in that town. She was in that town. She was not missing.

Point-blank, I said it right to him. Right to Dino. "Have you searched the Haytes property? Have any of your people searched the Haytes property?"

"My God, Flynn. Please take it easy. It looks to me like you're having trouble with this case. Who do you think's been paying for all the 'Pray for Wendy' ads?"

"I know who. It's my paper. I send them the bill every month. For five months now. Have you searched the Haytes property? The answer is no, right? It's no. It's no, isn't it? Just say you haven't done it. Out loud. Say it out loud."

"I haven't done it, Stacy, and I'm not going to do it unless we get some concrete evidence. I've pestered those good people enough."

"Yeah? Yeah? Like what would that be? What would be concrete evidence? She didn't come home from work, she'd been spending all her time with her boyfriend, Dale Haytes, and then she didn't come home from work. Didn't show up to work. Everything in her life is exactly the same as it's been since she was five fucking years old, except she has a new heavy relationship with someone older and outside her socioeconomic sphere. He's the only variable."

Dino raised his eyebrows and sighed in an elaborate show of patience. "Stacy," he said in a tone so relaxed it made me clench my fist inside the pocket of my hoodie, "we talked to Dale. He's the one who reported it. He's the one who called her parents. He's the one who went over there. I'm not going to direct this investigation by rumor. I saw him—I never saw anyone so upset, nearly as bad as her parents. Said she must have got cold feet about marrying him. He was in a panic that night. He thinks something awful happened to her because she prolly was trying to get away and clear her head a little, and he thinks it's all his fault. He's been blaming himself in here just about every day."

"When? On his way home from the golf course? Why would she get cold feet? Because she's only twenty? I highly doubt it. Her brother's wife was eighteen when they had their first kid. Where would she go if she got cold feet? Home. That kid was living on her own for less than six months—and it was down the road from her mom and dad."

He shook his head and gave me an expressly pitying look. "Dale's out playing golf because he's trying to keep himself sane. Man's feeling pretty bad. C'mon, now. He's playing golf to keep busy because he feels it too deep. He's a big doughboy lives at home, too, Stacy. That's not a guy going around doing bad things to the girl he's in love with. I've known that family since I was a boy. I'll tell you right now, you need to take a step back."

But there was no stepping back for me.

"You are bored," Brian from *City Paper* told me that night on the phone. "What else do you write about? I thought you were there to write about meth labs or some environmental shit. A cold case and some paranoia about yokels giving each other shifty looks is all you got."

"It's not a cold case, it's an obstructed case."

"I recognize that tone," he said. "You have maps on the apartment wall yet?"

"Fuck you, Walsh."

"Started writing articles that aren't for publication? How many you have? Got an extra sixty column inches lying around here and there?"

"I'll use them eventually."

"I seriously urge you to consider the last time you got laid. It's possible you will feel less obsessed and more clearheaded if you got a little action. When was it, Stace?"

"I don't know. You would remember, right?"

"Oh, Jesus. Word?"

"I don't need to relax. The last thing I need is to relax."

"C'mon, Tasty Flynn."

I stood in the doorway of the living room and drank my third bottle in a few long gulps while listening to Brian and thinking about how his ass looked in a torn pair of jeans at the paper's staff picnic. Thinking about how he took off his shirt.

There were maps of the whole county pinned to the walls. Stacks of transcribed interviews, marked in a patchwork of yellow highlighter, spilled across the floor. The place was a mess.

"I'm afraid she's alive," I told him, and knew I never would have said it if I hadn't been drinking. "I'm afraid every night that this is the night she gets killed because she hasn't been found. And I don't know where she is, man. But she's in this town. I know it."

He ignored what I said. "Listen to me. That place fucking sucks. And I am sure by now you got everybody convinced you're some badass ice queen that's never cried or smiled at a baby. But you are an animal. An *animal*, okay?" He laughed a little under his breath. "And it's not good for animals to be all cooped up alone and drunk and eating garbage and listening to interview tapes of weeping inarticulate hicks. You feel me? You're going to need some downtime, whether this girl is alive or dead. And you *know* that. See what I'm saying? You feel me, Flynn?"

"No."

"Well, you need to feel somebody. You need some weight pressing against you, and eight hours is a long drive for me, so I suggest you get it taken care of."

"I'll consider it."

"Good. You know we miss you, man. It's gonna be okay. Things are going to get better. Don't get caught up in this shit—write your big-picture story and come the fuck home to Cleveland."

"What if this *is* the big-picture story?"

"It's not," he said. "I'll call you later."

I hung up the phone and opened the refrigerator to find no more beer. I knew Brian was right. I'd written seven articles about this case and related cases that I would never file, in addition to my quota of fluff pieces and coverage of community events. I had a houseful of stories on abducted women. And I hadn't listened to anything but the interview tapes for weeks. I downloaded them to my iPod. I hadn't listened to anything else in the car for five months. I was living inside the story, and I had to get out of there, at least for a little while.

I put my hair up in a knot, grabbed my hoodie, and walked two blocks through the nowhere that led into town, past my office and into the Rooster.

It was later than I thought, nearly closing time. The bar was almost empty, just the bluegrass band that had been playing, a few regulars, and the crazy-eyed guy in the ambulance-driver uniform, so I sat next to him. I'd seen him set a broken leg at a high school football game and pull a drunk out of the mashed hunk of metal that had been a car. But I'd never really talked to him. I ordered a double Jameson's and then asked Mr. Uniform if he always drank on duty.

"I'm off. Just haven't taken *this* off. Yet."

"Shift just end?"

"Nah. It ended this afternoon, but I fell right asleep and didn't change."

"You just really like your uniform, don't you?"

He looked over at me and smiled, and it was startling. I could feel a whole world of exhaustion and pain and pride recoil and then rest heavily against me. I was not prepared for his look. Hadn't seen that kind of expression from a human being since moving to this godforsaken town.

"I do like it." He nodded. "Yeah. Do you like your job?"

And then I saw what it was in his eyes. They looked glassy. They looked like they were coated with something thin and shiny. Something that hurt him a little to see through. He was drunk and going mad, like I was, and it was all pouring forth. I had to talk myself down from putting too much meaning in his look. They were just eyes. Glassy, tired, beautiful.

"I do like my job," I said. "I love my job. I wouldn't do anything else."

"Me either, man." He grinned. "If you had a uniform, you'd probably wear it all day, too. Wait. Don't you? I think I seen you in that outfit before."

He was making me laugh, either for real or because of the Jameson's, and it didn't matter which because I could feel something other than a knot in my stomach.

Then he said, "I read that thing you wrote."

"Oh yeah?" I laughed again. "Kinda hard to read the paper otherwise. It's just me."

"No shit, man. I feel that shit. It's just me over at the VFD, too. I switch shifts with Elmville's guys—otherwise it's me, me, and me. I sleep with the scanner."

"Jesus. I sleep with the scanner, too," I told him. "It's actually kind of comforting."

He nodded like it was a given. Then he closed his eyes for a minute, and at that point I realized he was actually pretty drunk. "The problem with being the only one on the job," he said finally, "is I keep worrying someone ran over a kid in the middle of nowhere—and there's no cell phone, or there is a cell phone and I'm somewhere too far away taking care of a stubbed toe, or I get there and it wasn't fast enough. I get out there and it's too late. You know?" He looked at me, and his eyes were wet. "Yeah," he said. "You *do* know."

Clearly, I knew. And I didn't want to talk about it.

"Fuck, though!" He smiled his big goofy grin again. "You get used to it. But there's no way it's good for sleeping, you know it? It'd be nice to have some help, but whatever, I guess we just do it that way, huh? You know? We're just wired that way."

"Let's get out of here," I said.

He stood and grabbed his short blue jacket off the chair, put his arm around me, and we walked out of the bar, said nothing for two blocks, and said nothing as we followed a little trail down to the river's edge beneath the bridge on Rabbit Run Road. And I said nothing as I unbuttoned and unzipped his pants and he was already hard, pressing me up against the side of the bridge. I was holding him tight against me, holding his ass, feeling his sinewy muscles, his thigh muscles pressing me against the wall and his warm stomach pressing against my breasts. He smelled like pHisoderm and alcohol and dryer sheets and sweat. His mouth was all over mine and my hands were in his hair, on his neck, on his chest, up his shirt to feel his body, thin and strong.

I slipped down the wall, and we sat on the cold stones, his back against the bridge, kissing, and he was making a soft humming sound. That made me stand and step out of my pants, and then I pushed him back gently into the stones and mud and brush and straddled him with one hand pressed against the concrete arch.

He cupped my head and neck in his wide palm, and then we were moving slowly, uncomfortably, my knees pressed into the rocks, until he sat up and leaned against the bridge, held me in his lap, kissed my neck. Breathing steadily now in some incredulous joyful exhale. I kissed his mouth, and he was holding my hips and pulling me down on him, and then I felt it all at once in the base of my spine. And I was contracting and fucking him faster, so fast, until he grabbed my hips tighter and pushed me up and off of him, and he was gasping, spilled into the mud, onto my thighs. Then he was laughing, breathing, exhaling.

I squinted in the moonlight to find my pants, pulled them right side in, and put them on. By the time I got it straight, he was zipped up and standing, his hair wrecked, smiling, leaning against the concrete arch. "C'mere," he said lazily, and held out his arms to me.

I walked in to him, put my face on his chest, shaking my head, laughing but amazed, really. My whole body felt good, my back, everything. My shoulders. My thighs. My gut. My jaw. He held me to his chest, leaning there, kissed the top of my head. Breathed in and smelled my hair.

"My name is Tom Cutting," he said quietly. "And right now I'm pretty sure I was put on this planet to fuck you."

I leaned gratefully against him and felt the heat of his skin. "I better be getting home," I told him.

"Oh yeah?" he said. "Don't want the scanner to be waiting up worrying."

We walked up the embankment together and stood on the bridge for a minute, looking into the river. I said his name under my breath while I walked home. Partly to remember it. Partly to hear how it sounded.

EVIDENCE *P47911*

Sgt. Anthony Giles

December 12, 2008
Dear Theo,

You were right about that Carolyn Merchant book. Especially her thing on nature existing in three states: liberty, error, or bondage. How is soccer going? Swim is fan-fucking-tastic and we are faster than ever. This is going to be our season! (I hope.) I have meets the first part of your break so maybe you'll see what I mean by fast. We have awesome songs for practice too. The Yeah Yeah Yeahs for warm-up and to psych out the little fish from Elmville. And the Distillers (my picks with your help).

In other news . . . Thinking much about that last night in the tent? I am. I wish I could get a real boyfriend here—but the natural state for Haeden guys would seem to be error. When you and I fall asleep together, there's always this point where I wake up and I don't even feel you holding me or me holding you. It's weird. I feel like I am alone. There must be some ratio in our respective morphologies that causes this. Nature is filled with these complementary numbers. And ours add up. Or as Claire would say—maybe you're in love with him. HA!

I also can't stop thinking about the conversation we had about correcting errors. (Is this why you wanted me to read Death of Nature?) *Also thinking seriously about the idea of "the world having nothing to learn from evil" and all that stuff you read from the Gnostic Bible that night in the tent—or was that just to get me inside the sleeping bag?*

And you're right. It's hard to believe we tolerate the things we do. Like being good is going to make it all go away. The tent's packed up and under the bed and there are no Gnostics in town.

They still haven't found that girl. I shouldn't call her that girl, because she was a swimmer and I know her, but for some reason I have been. Last week Gene and Claire and Ross and I walked through 30 acres of fields with a bunch of other people—looking for her. It was really cold out. And I was glad we didn't find her, because I guess it means there's still a chance she ran away. Claire was really upset about it. I like to think she must have gone somewhere more interesting.

But in the newspaper her parents said she never wanted to leave Haeden. (I know, bizarre.) She worked at the Alibi. I don't know why these people don't know where she is. No one else is missing from town. I guess she could have had a secret life or hitchhiked away. Megan knows her pretty well and is friends with her friends. Also a couple of seniors on swim team. And you remember her cousin Donna White from elementary school? She was really nice. It's some weird shit, man. I only remember Wendy from a couple of times, swim things and when Ross took us to the Alibi (bluegrass night).

I wish you were here sooooooo much. I am learning to ride a unicycle. Gene made it out of the old no-speed. I'll show you when you get home. Pretty easy—though I still have to pedal fast. Your legs might be too long. Megan can't ride it. She freaks out after it starts moving and takes her feet off the pedals.

What's going on with what's-her-name? As your relationship consultant I advise you to immediately quit messing around and just fucking ask her!!!!! T, you know she's going to say yes. You are so beautiful. Last year maybe not—but since the summer? Come on. And you're funny!

Which, speaking of, I finished your hat with the rabbit-fur dog ears. They flop—but only on the tips. Amazing craftsmanship, I have never knit anything this thick. It could stop a bullet. The stitch is like the one we used to make the dinosaur cave that was *under the couch. I wanted to keep it for myself. But it would go better with your nose.*

I really miss you, Tea-ho. I can't wait for break. School is so boring and I have some good ideas for Circus but need you to be here because you're tall, and they involve me standing on you. And no, to answer your question, the parents will not be getting me a computer—which is fine.

Also! I've been target shooting with Ross (the little Glock). Sooooooo much better now it's not even funny, though I don't know how to work it into my Comprehensive Life Plan (the CLP keeps getting twistier) and Gene hates the whole gun thing. So this means hours of discussion on the nature of power. B-O-R-I-N-G. They are still blah blah blah about Hannah Arendt.

G&C say I should get a camera to "shoot with" and focus on "becoming the media" (I am so embarrassed that they said "become the media" I didn't even want to write that part to you). Wow, what a shock. Becoming the "new" farmers really worked out well for them, and it actually changed the world too!!! GAH!! Whatevuh. I know you love them. But they're not your parents. Where are your parents anyway? (I know, not funny.)

The other part of the CLP is volunteering at the Haeden Medical Center. THIS is truly fun. You should think about doing it this summer when you're home. We can ride our bikes there in like ten minutes—you can actually take the trail from our spot right to 24 and then you're there. Mostly it's crappy work—but you get to wear scrubs and watch what everybody does.

Claire keeps asking me if I am anxious about Wendy and if that's why I'm shooting and thinking about studying medicine. And then they said they think I'm angry about something. Claire's probably right in some way. But Jesus, what if I have to catch food to eat one day? What would she and Gene do if they had to? Ask the animal if it was okay to kill it? And besides, they're the ones who gave me the Ward Churchill and Derrick Jensen books! But now Gene says Pacifism as Pathology is "flawed." (Did you read Jensen's Endgame *yet? That's the one that's more flawed in my opinion. He fully thinks hackers are going to save the day and people are going to blow up dams in the name of salmon. Seriously? I mean seriously? In the name of salmon before in the name of humanity?) And what about all that Simone de Beauvoir and Monique Wittig and Naomi Wolf they gave me in like fucking middle school? I mean okay—you probably shouldn't go through puberty without it, but seriously? Try to apply these conceptual models in a sixth-grade health or history class. I'm fucking sick of it. I'm sick of reading about things. All I want to do now is swim and play magic and shoot. You are the only person with whom I want to discuss books. I will say it. I am alone. I am totally alone.*

So that's what's going on with me, Moley. Sorry for bitching. I can't wait to see you. Good luck with the Keira Knightly look-alike. She will fall in love with you if you tell her those string jokes. Hope you like the kissing pictures. Write soon. Dog-hat-on-its-way. Love. Love. Love. Love. Alice.

Haeden, NY

HE DIDN'T KNOW when he got the idea, but it was like it was always there. Not like he got it but like it had just been uncovered. Like it was sitting there in the corner with a sheet thrown over it. He laughed now at that thought. "Sounds a lot like somebody we know, doesn't it?" he said out loud, waiting for the light to change.

He also didn't know if he'd planned it, but when he started doing it, it all felt familiar, like he could just tell what was coming and what to do next. It felt good in a way nothing else had. If he had planned it, he would have had to put things in order—but things were already there. He had space, privacy, noises from the farm, animal tranquilizers, a few friends and relatives interested in the same thing. That's not a plan, that's an invitation.

He was fulfilling a dream. It was like taking a trip to Cancún or the Virgin Islands. He chuckled. The sun was beginning to rise. If he had planned it, it was planned in the same way you would plan a trip. You talk about it to your friends. You joke about it. You say you wish you were lucky enough. You make sure you don't tell people who will be jealous or rude. Maybe you bring some friends along. Guys you love because they love the same things. A golfing or hunting trip from heaven, he thought. You look at brochures of the exotic. Then, when you're brave enough, off you go.

"Off. You. Go," he sang to himself and Wendy. He was getting tired of driving around. If it wasn't for his respect for her family and his, he would have dumped her naked in one of the manure lagoons or somewhere out of town. He didn't want her father to think she was still alive somewhere or that she had just run away. He wanted them to know it was her. That she hadn't run out on him. She'd been taken from him. From them. She was dead. He looked over his shoulder at the sheet on the floor in the truck's little backseat and thought distractedly that he was glad he got an extended cab.

He planned it, but he didn't invent it. The idea to do it was there all along, and so was the knowledge that he'd never get caught, he'd been watching movies or the news about it his whole life. He was not a dirtbag or a pedophile or a black guy some cops would be looking out for, or a creep that stalked prostitutes, or a quiet old pervert. And he wasn't some super-rich guy everybody paid attention to. He was just a guy who lifted up the sheet to see what was underneath. Braver than most, like his mother always said.

He finally settled on the ditch near Tern Woods because he was getting tired and wanted to stop at the Savers Club to get a coffee before starting the day.

He felt kind of sad leaving her as he pulled away. Sad for her for one breathtaking second that traveled through his intestines and then made him slightly hard. He remembered what her eyes did to him, put something in him. He wished he could have that exact feeling of what her eyes did again from remembering it, but he just couldn't, and it was sad. Now he knew for sure things would be dulled. Nothing would ever be sexier and funnier and scarier than her eyes, than her squinting up from the crawl space with her mouth bleeding, saying please.

"Please." He would say it to himself in her voice. "*Please,*" he would whisper for the rest of the afternoon.

"Nine-one-one, how can I help you?"

"Yeah. Hi. I think I just passed an emergency situation. I am driving on Route Thirty-Four right now, just past the Savers Club in Haeden."

"Where is the accident? Is this a car accident, ma'am?"

"No. no. I think I saw a person hurt by the parking lot. It looked, I'm not sure actually, I wanted to call just in case because I can't stop, I'm late for a meeting, but it looked like a person was lying by the parking lot near that woods. I don't know. It could be someone dumped some garbage."

"You say it's a person?"

"I think so. It looks like an old lady, maybe someone walking fell. Maybe someone out walking early morning. Oh. Maybe got hit by a car! Usually I'm not driving this early. I think she may have fallen. I couldn't check. I think someone should check. I'm pretty sure I saw a hand reach up from the edge of the parking lot. I think someone maybe some lady got hurt. I would have stopped but I'm almost late. Someone should go check on that. I'm sure actually. I'm sure I saw an arm actually. Looked like someone fell down the embankment."

"We'll send someone over."

"Oh good. Good. Now that I think about it, I am sure it was an arm. Do you need my information? Do you need my phone number?"

"We have it, ma'am. We'll send someone over."

Flynn

THERE WERE VIOLETS at the edge of the woods, I remember. Violets and red trillium. I could see the ambulance approaching in the distance, flying toward the site with just the lights on, no siren. I stood beside her body, watching.

There were plenty of things I could tell were wrong right away. There was no medical examiner, for one. And Giles stood snapping pictures with a small square digital camera. One I had seen him use at his kids' ball game.

The ambulance arrived beside us with its loud engine sucking away the silence. Tom and a kid who looked about twenty stepped out and walked around to the back doors to unload and unfold the stretcher. The kid was visibly high on adrenaline and fear, barely contained in his own skin. Everything else from here on in was just waiting and formality. A series of actions that had to be undertaken. Tom looked up at me, and I nodded at him and kept watching, knew without knowing anything that we were both shut down, had gone somewhere else. He laid the length of the black bag on the ground beside what could not really be described as a grave.

Alice

April 5, 2009
Theo,

Here is the clip glued below. I sent you the whole paper too.
Burn this when you are done and then call me.

A body found yesterday morning in a drainage ditch at the eastern edge of Tern Woods in the village of Haeden has been identified as twenty-year-old resident Wendy White, who had been missing since November 2008.

Police and rescue workers found the remains after responding to a call from a commuter on Route 34 saying she believed she had seen an injured person on the side of the road that ran between the woods and the Savers Club parking lot.

White disappeared last fall after working late at a pub in the village.

Haeden Police Chief Alex Dino said a full investigation is under way.

At this time police have stated they have no leads pointing to the identity of the killer.

"We are pursuing all avenues," Dino said. "We are working with state police and investigators from Elmville and we'll be examining DNA evidence. At this point that is all the information we have."

I will probably call you before you get this. I need to talk to you.

This is what we've been talking about. I figured out today when they were having a "moment of silence" for her at school what was really going on. We need one more moment of silence? Oh my fucking GOD. Do you know what is going on? I know you do. You must.

I think I have fallen through the hole in all the logic of the entire world and I can see now that nothing holds up and I feel that I am going to keep falling. This is what Claire was so upset about. What everybody sees and then hides from, just bows down to.

Read the paper. The whole thing. Stacy talked about this stuff in every article, every single one.

All these girls at school are scared and weirded out, because the woods are so close to the school. Like the fucking woods did it. I want to tell them to shut up. SHUT UP. And don't be scared. Fear makes you run in circles. I need to call you. We need to figure all of this out somehow.

Then Ross tells me this whole thing is one reason why it's good I'm such a good shot in case someone is going to fuck with me. WTF? Like I walk around with my gun? It was the first time I had ever really seen him. I know you love him and I do too but it made me so mad. He looked like a sick old stupid war vet who had done bad things and was now "protecting me" by teaching me how to shoot 'cause he thinks I can redeem what he did.

It was like I could see ALL the differences I'd never known existed. But I'm the fucking fool for not looking close enough. For not putting it all together from the books Claire gave me.

Then there was this picture of the ditch in the paper, with police tape around it. The fact that they had this place, this grave, in the paper, where there was no way she could say "No, please don't take my picture," made me infuriated. It reminded me of that time I was telling you about—that asshole Jim took pictures of Trina with his cell phone when she was sleeping after they had sex—and he sent them to everyone. I could see Trina in that grave in the woods. Then the principal comes on and he says all this *pious fucking shit, that there's going to be a moment of silence. Seriously? More silence?*

And all these boys that want to walk us home now. Like we're supposed to think they don't just want to get laid or have the chance to get in a fight with each other and are using us as an excuse. Or to prove they're not bad. Be a prince or a hero. You would throw up if you saw it. It's everything you've ever hated. It made me feel so sad for you, to see these things. Love you so much and feel so sad that you are a boy, and that because of your body you could be mistaken for a thing that is all (T)error. It's an unfair camouflage they walk around in, Moley. Not fair to either of us. I don't want any part of it.

During that moment of silence I wanted to scream at the top of my lungs. I wanted to flip my fucking desk over and smash every window in that classroom. But of course I sat there and didn't say a word.

I can't write anymore. I'm going out to the barn to do pull-ups.

p.s. The Dairy Prince has maybe one more chance to reveal himself as actually human, someone who better have been joking.

p.p.s. Burn this.

Flynn

"NASTY MORNING, HUH?"

I looked up, and Cutting was there, holding some pale blue flowers. He said, "These were growing in the field across from the VFD. But I thought they'd look better surrounded by computers and stacks of paper." He set the little vase on my desk and I pictured the woods.

He was not the person I wanted to see that afternoon, given that our last two encounters involved partially clothed bodies in brutally contrasting states. I opened the bottom drawer of my desk and got out a bottle of Old Thompson and two shot glasses, and he smiled and said, "I thought that was a stereotype."

"Are you fucking kidding? It's one of the more accurate public perceptions about how newspapers work."

I poured him a shot, drank mine, and then was happy he was there so I could finish up my story. "It was White," I said.

He nodded. "Her parents identified the body."

"On the record now?"

"Yeah."

As long as we were talking about the concrete operations of our jobs, I felt completely fine, felt nothing. I thought it might have been that I felt fine, period. That I just wanted things to be resolved and didn't care how they were resolved. As long as all the details were out, were in print. Fine. I didn't find Wendy, and Wendy is dead. That's another story that can be filed. That's another body Tom Cutting packed up. *Fuck it.* I poured us each another shot.

"What else did you do today?" I asked Cutting.

"It was pretty busy, actually. A farmer had a heart attack just after lunch."

"Did he live?"

"He's going to be okay. One of his workers made the call as it was happening. Got there well within the golden hour. He needs to lose about fifty pounds. They'll tell him to lay off the bacon. What did you do?" he asked.

I didn't answer because it was fucking obvious.

"Did you just have to write about this stuff?" he asked. Something about the way he looked bothered me, like he was embarrassed, ashamed. At least he had changed out of his uniform.

"Where was the coroner, or whatever they call him around here?"

"He was out of town working."

"Working?"

"You know, coroner is a part-time job in this county."

"Do they have a cause of death?"

"I don't know what the autopsy is going to find." He looked away from me and pinched the bridge of his nose.

"What did it look like to you?" I asked.

"I didn't get a close look after I unpacked the body. There was definitely trauma. The cause of death, though, I don't know. It could have been a drug overdose."

"A drug overdose."

"Yeah."

"It doesn't jibe with her history."

"Not at all, no. It doesn't," Cutting agreed. "There were bruises, but I can't say what that means."

"Why can't you say what that means?" I was getting sick of the short answers. Why was he being cagey about it? I stopped thinking about the question and looked at him for a minute, looked for the reason he was being short with me. Something in my body supplied me with a reason I couldn't fully get behind. I experienced a second of vertigo, a flutter in my stomach, and then quickly took another sip of my drink.

"With certainty. I can't say if the bruises contributed in any way to her death. I saw no significant trauma to her head or torso."

"Do you think she was murdered?"

"Yeah. Of *course* I do. Or put in a position where her death was a likely outcome."

"Then why can't you say what it means?"

"Because you asked me the cause of death. Murder isn't a cause of death."

I nodded. "I'm asking you to speculate."

He reached out and touched the petals on one of the flowers he had brought, and I realized he was trying not to think about it at all. "I don't know what they're going to find," he said.

I tried, but there is no way to say "Do you think she was killed here in town?" more gently. So I just said it.

"Probably. I think she had been dead almost an hour before we got there. There was a good deal of lividity."

I listened and typed while he talked, then I poured another shot. The stuff was vile, and it didn't matter. "Is it common for the medical examiner to not show up?"

"Around here? It actually is," Cutting said. "He has another job."

"Yeah, you said that. Where?"

"He's a large-animal vet in Elmville."

"Can I have your notes?"

"They're at the hospital. I don't have copies or I'd give them to you," he said. And I thought he sounded pretty sincere, but maybe I was drunk. I nodded again. I needed a glass of water and to finish my stories. All the research, all the work, down to one fucking useless day. And if I wasn't out fucking Mr. Uniform last night, I would have had twelve more hours to find her, and if I had, she would be alive. She was dead for an hour before they came, just an hour. And now there was one thing left to write.

"Do you get off work at any point today?" Cutting asked. "I'd like to make you dinner."

"Do you have an appetite?"

"It helps to have somebody to cook for." His chin dipped as he looked at me shyly through his eyelashes. "You know, it's a good idea to eat if you're going to drink or work."

"I've heard that somewhere. I have to put the paper to bed. But I guess I can do that in the next couple of hours. Most of this week's stories have been written for months, anyway."

"It's not a big deal. You can come over whenever you get done. I just—It's not a big deal if you don't want to. I feel kind of weird about . . . I just know what days like this are like."

I looked at him and read his expression, the awkwardness of it all. But I didn't feel what he felt. I was an observer. I was okay as long as I was watching and writing. And I would not trade that for "feeling" with him today. Thinking that his "feelings" about this could be anything like mine.

Then before I could sell him short, he said it. "For me, Stacy, what days like this are like for me. Not for you."

Political Movements in 20th-Century Europe:
*Boredom Is Counter-revolutionary. What Started the
Paris Revolt of 1968?*
Sophomore Global History
Alice Piper
Period 2
10/17/08

The student worker uprisings of the late 1960s in Paris
were significantly different from the American student
movement of the same era because their philosophical foundation began in art, not politics. The group at the forefront
of this movement was called the Situationist International
(SI). Founded by artist and revolutionary Guy Debord.

The SI combined Marxist Theory (which criticized Capi-
talism) with Surrealist art in order to "construct situations" that would change an oppressive system and way
of thinking. (In other words, they believed in personal
freedom and autonomy over constructed cultures. And the
right of people to destroy not just the systems but the boring everyday aesthetics that oppressed them.)

Because of this, their attack was not directed toward a
specific political entity but "everyday life" in the 50s and
60s. They proposed "a radical front" that could create a
union of play, freedom, and critical thinking to take on
authoritarian forces that were controlling people through
boredom and oppression.

In 1967 Debord published *Society of the Spectacle*, where he argued that advanced capitalist life reduced life to an "immense accumulation of spectacles."

"All that once was directly lived," he states, "has become mere appearance."

Debord argued that society had become an "advertising, media, mass-marketing complex," a superficial giant that depleted people's everyday lives of meaning. (16)

In the "society of the spectacle," Debord argued, knowledge is not used to question or analyze but is used as a mask. While this might seem a purely political philosophy, Debord believed the SI needed to complete the work started by the Dadaist and Surrealist art movements, bringing action at last to art movements based in dreams and desires of all people.

While the SI became popular for their playfulness and pranks (such as dressing like monks on Easter Sunday and declaring the death of God at Notre Dame Cathedral), their real influence was seen during the student and worker uprisings of May 1968, the largest general strike in the history of the world. More than 11 million workers and students shut down the city of Paris and brought common people into the streets to fight the government for two straight weeks. (53) This strike was the beginning of people all over the world seeing technological and authoritarian rule as morally wrong (not just because it exploited people but because it went against people's most personal desires—it bored them and was ugly) and anti-authoritarian movements gained strength and popular support.

Members of the Situationist International graffitied streets and buildings with phrases that became defining slogans and battle cries for protesters, among them:

"I take my desires for reality because I believe in the reality of my desires,"

"Be realistic, demand the impossible,"
"Live without dead time,"
"Boredom is counter-revolutionary,"
"Beneath the paving stones, the beach,"
And my personal favorite: "Run, comrade, the old world is behind you."

Constant

"Hello?"

"Hey!"

"Loudclaire!"

"No," she said, "this is Alice."

Constant was shocked. In the space of a month, her voice had changed.

"Kropotkin? Oh. My. God. You sound exactly like Claire."

"I know, everyone says that."

"How's it going?"

"Good."

"Your dad around?"

"He's out with Claire, picking edamame for dinner." She sounded bored and pissed off, another unexpected change.

"Nice. I wish I was eating there tonight. You have enough soybeans to go around?"

"More than enough. They're totally delicious, but I am starting to get sick of them."

Constant laughed. "How's school?"

"I hate tenth grade. My parenthetical existence is dead in the water."

"English teacher cracking down on you?"

"I hate that class. It's my worst class. I wish there was a way to write everything like an equation. She says my essay style is too chatty. And no more parentheses because they look immature. Why do they think it's some kind of one-way street where I just present stuff to them? Why don't I tell them exactly what I want to learn and then they teach me? I don't know crap about literature, and I have to ask questions as I go, otherwise it's a waste of time. All the stuff I loved to read has been ruined. Plus, for half the questions I ask, they say this really isn't for English class, or this isn't a philosophy class, or some other excuse. I'm not even trying to write good papers anymore because I get A's for whatever I hand in. Everything is all divided up. How long does it take you to figure out that every single story is the same because there's something wrong with the assignments? Why would anyone want to hunt for the 'universal theme' in something? It's like working on a million different problems that all come out with the same answer."

"It's weird you don't like that class. You've always been into reading."

"Yeah, well, not anymore. Math and chemistry make sense, right? Because the symbols are actual symbols—they stand for real things—they're not made-up characters that are supposed to represent ideas or a moral or some shit."

Con laughed. "Oh my God, you sound exactly like your mother, not just your voice. This is actually weird. Is this Claire?"

Alice groaned and then laughed. He was happy to make her laugh, happy to make her feel better. It had been a rough week there, and he wanted to get her something special. "What do you want for your birthday?"

"A robot to attend school for me."

"Probably can't find one. What do you really want?"

"One hundred and eighty dollars."

He laughed again. "Really?"

"Really."

"Wow! Kropotkin. Times have changed! You must be growing up. I don't think you've ever asked for money."

"I haven't."

"What are you going to buy?"

"Meat," she said, and they laughed.

Flynn

TOM CUTTING'S APARTMENT did not have maps pinned to the walls or beer bottles piled in one bay of the sink. It was neat. It smelled good. It had a view of the firehouse across the street. No one lived upstairs, and the nearest neighbor was a mobile-home park three quarters of a mile down the road. He seemed too social to be living in such a remote place.

"Free rent," he told me, grinning as he read my expression. "I made pasta. You'll like it—it's tomatoes and olives and olive oil and garlic and other stuff. I bet you didn't eat at all today. This Mediterranean shit is good for you. This is what I eat when—well, whatever, this is what I pretty much always eat."

He opened the refrigerator and got out two Labatts, handed me one. "About last night, Stacy. I don't usually do things like that, and this morning makes me really never want to do things like that ever again. I'm just uh . . . ah, fuck, I don't know. That was just—"

"It's okay." I was exhausted and wired and a little drunk. After filing and going home and staring at the water running in the sink for half an hour, I had driven to Cutting's house, hoping it would be loud or there would be music playing or he would be very drunk and we would just fuck again. To erase it somehow. Otherwise, I knew I would talk about it, start reviewing the case.

"I really like you," he said.

I had finished my beer already and put the bottle in the sink.

"Oh, here—let me," he said. "The recycling's in the closet." He put the bottle away and then tested the pasta, strained it, poured it into a big bowl, and tossed it with the tomatoes. Set the bowl on the table and got out two forks. Pulled out another beer for me. "How did the paper come out?"

"Good," I told him. "You'll get it tomorrow."

"We're not going to talk about this while we eat, okay? It's a stupid thing to do. I'm sorry I brought that up, okay? Forget work."

I nodded and raised my bottle toward him. "Good call. Back in Cleveland, we always talked about what we were writing over dinner. It got boring."

"Stories like this one?"

I shrugged. "Sometimes. I had a friend whose favorite happy-hour topics were crime scenes and his Hearst Fellowship." I laughed, but Cutting didn't, so I started eating. The pasta was delicious, and I realized that it was the first time someone had cooked a meal for me in four years. It made me feel lonely and grateful. Happy I had met him.

"So when can we get the autopsy report?" I asked.

He put his fork down and raised his eyebrows pointedly.

"Oh, right." I laughed, wiped my mouth.

"I'm sorry. We can stop eating and talk about stuff, if you want, and I'll reheat this for us later. I just can't do both."

What he said annoyed me. I felt like things were unfinished, like I didn't have enough information yet, and I was not about to give in to the feeling that this dinner marked the end of something or was a cause to grieve together. He was the closest thing to a colleague I had, and I needed one right now. Needed someone to think with.

"You know, I spent most of today on the phone with the Bureau of Crime Statistics," I told him. "I looked up the names of all the women who were murdered this year—and the subcategory of all the women who were murdered by their boyfriends or husbands or guys they'd dated."

"Y'see, now, this is what I'm talking about. This is *not* good." He stood and picked up the bowl and carried it to the counter. "We're not going to eat while we talk about this."

My fork was still in midair over the table. "Anyway," I went on, "if you wanted to make a memorial for those women who died in that kind of violence throughout history—which no one does, of course—but if you did you would be carving names at roughly the same rate the crimes are being committed. If you wanted a historical monument—you know, one that had casualties, beatings, rapes, disfigurations—you'd need something like the Great Wall of China."

He stretched saran wrap over the pasta and put it in the refrigerator, which was immaculate. "There have been people I have not been able to save," he said simply. And then I felt that thing in my chest like I did when I first met him and we talked about our jobs.

"Let's sit on the porch until we're hungry again," he said.

I said, "I'm hungry now," but I wasn't. I was drunk and exhausted and fighting a feeling that even Tom, the man who'd relaxed me so skillfully last night, and brought me flowers, and fed me, could have killed Wendy, could be thinking of things to do that might hurt me. I saw him for a moment as simply his size and weight and speed. The kind of nearly conscious assessments that arise, that become, at times of evening and in certain places, autonomic. And then I followed him out and sat beside him on an old couch covered with a wool blanket in front of a low weather-beaten coffee table.

I said, "This is a bad day for a date, Tom Cutting."

"Yeah, I know. But it's a good day for me to be with somebody like you and for you to be with somebody like me." He looked steadily into my eyes, and I thought about how maintaining eye contact was part of his job—he was trained to do it. Thought of how many eyes he must have looked into with his own hazel eyes. How many expressions of pain or fear he had taken in, he had worked to allay. That same sense radiated from his body as well, a kind of steady, calm coordination, a readiness. This was what he had brought to me beside the river the day before. I wanted very badly right then for my feelings about him to be real. To have him as my friend. To be as angry as I was and not be alone.

We stretched out and put our feet up and looked at the parking lot and the fields in the distance beyond the fire department.

"What do you do, though?" I asked him. "It's such a small place, and you know that White was probably killed by someone just walking around here, going to the bar, sitting at the Laundromat. Somebody we might know, might pass by every day. Did you know Dino hasn't even searched the Haytes property?"

"I didn't know that, no."

"Yeah. This whole fucking thing has been bullshit from beginning to end. Did you know thirteen hundred women are killed every year in the U.S. by intimates? Boyfriends or husbands. What's that like, three, maybe more than three, women a day? That fact alone should have that motherfucker Dino all over that shit pile up there." He nodded in agreement. I went on, "The statistics are fucking staggering, man, the number of women every year murdered or disappeared. And raped, my God, you know what those stats are? You want to talk about rape?"

"No!" He shook his head and covered his eyes with his hand, leaning his head back. "I really don't. I know the numbers are high. People sure do get hurt and killed, and it's overwhelming. I know that, I do. I used to be obsessed with the traffic fatalities. Thirty-eight thousand people die in car crashes every year. Four hundred and fifty thousand die from heart attacks. Seventy percent of murder victims are men killed by men. People *die*, Stacy. All day long, every day, for a variety of reasons."

"You know that this is not the same. You know it's not. What do you think the autopsy is going to show?"

"You asked me that this afternoon. I don't know. Malnutrition, drugs; it will show trauma. Sexual assault, I'm sure, based on the pattern of bruises. Hopefully, we'll get some DNA evidence. That would help." He looked at me. "It was a really bad idea to have dinner tonight."

I studied his face for a time.

"Honestly," he told me, "I didn't want to be alone. I've never seen anything like that in my life. You may have, but I haven't. And I didn't want it to be the only thing I could see all night. I didn't want the image of you at the scene stuck in my head, either. You know especially. You know . . . I'm sorry."

I reached over and took his hand. I was tired and drunk and would have liked to cry, but I didn't. The quiet was still there. I couldn't make it go away with tears or fighting or quoting statistics. We slumped lower on the couch, and I rested against him. He put his arm around me, held my hand, leaned down, and kissed the top of my head. And I remembered, then, him talking about the golden hour and being afraid of kids getting hit by cars. And I felt like a fool for talking statistics. I didn't find her. And he didn't save her. Because these are things you don't do alone.

It was dark out when I looked over at him again, and the porch was dimly lit from the kitchen lights. His head was resting on the arm of the couch, his lips were parted, and he was breathing deeply, his long black eyelashes resting on his cheeks. I pulled the blanket down to cover us and closed my eyes.

Scoop

Scoop WAS ALREADY there when Flynn arrived at the paper, and he was trying not to lose it. She looked like hell. Her clothes were wrinkled, and her hair was matted in the back.

"What is this?" Scoop yelled before she had the door all the way open. He had meant to sound more controlled but found he was too enraged to manage. The bell tied to the handle of the door jingled as she shut it and walked to her desk. He waved the paper at her again. "What in the hell is this?"

She looked a little more awake but not alarmed, just disappointed. She must have been expecting it. "*This* is called a special edition. You might remember it from J-school," she said as she walked across the room and put a filter in the coffeepot.

"It's called terrorizing the town!"

That had the effect he'd desired. She looked startled, completely shocked. "This is called terrorizing the town? *This* is?" She fixed him with a look of such complete malice that he forgot what he had planned to say. The phone started ringing.

"See?" he said. "*You'll* see. I got calls all night."

She glared harder at him and picked up the phone. "*Haeden Free Press,*" she sang reflexively into the receiver. "Yes."

She paused, and he watched her blank tired face as she listened. "Yes."

She paused again and took the pen out of her hair and wrote something on the back of her hand.

"The National Bureau of Crime Statistics. And the New York State Division of Criminal Justice."

She winced. *Good*, Scoop thought—*someone's getting through to her.*

"Yes."

Flynn hung up the phone, and Scoop said, "I'd fire you if I had anyone else to do this job right now."

She continued to stare at him. He was so angry at her disrespect that he could feel himself begin to tremble.

Then she gave him a quick crazy-looking smile, something horrible, actually frightening. "You are not the publisher *or* the editor of this paper anymore," Flynn said. "I answer to *Weekly Circular*, and they're not going to fucking fire me! They're going to give me a motherfucking *raise* for the work I did on this Podunk white-trash bullshit! I won a George Polk when I was twenty-three. Do you even know what that *is*? Or did you just read it on my résumé and think I made it up? The paper I worked for employed real fucking writers. And what I fucking wrote yesterday was a real story. One I am going to keep investigating, so you might want to change your fucking tune. Stat."

Scoop felt his face flush. He raised the paper again and clutched it in his fist. "Do you have any idea what this has done to this community? To the families in this community? To people's professional careers?"

"*What* community? Is there a *community* here? Don't you fucking get it? Are you from fucking Mars? When the average income is fourteen K and the average educational level is eleventh grade and the so-called dairy is a factory fucking farm that employs next to nobody in town, and the Home Depot is where you all fucking work—*if* you even work. *That's* not a community, and it doesn't become one because people shoot clay pigeons or endearingly call women 'the missus' or have fucking parades where they crown a dairy queen! That's for actors in some anachronistic passion play about a town that never was, in a country that never, ever fucking was."

Scoop was overwhelmed by how fast she was talking and how

quickly she had become furious. He had come here to reprimand her, and she wasn't the slightest bit concerned. She didn't even look like herself. Her eyes were slits, and he could see how hard her jaw was; the skin on her neck and chest was flushed and blotchy, but her face had gone white. She wasn't about to stop.

"Community? Professional careers? Are you talking about your large-animal vet coroner who didn't show because he was yakking it up over at the Haytes dairy? Or your buddy who fucked up every aspect of this investigation, thinking that the killer was some drifter? You ever even heard the word 'drifter' outside of movies from the 1950s? You don't have a community, and you don't have professionals. Do you know where you are? *Do* you?"

The phone rang again, and Flynn picked it up. "*Haeden Free Press.*" Then she snapped, "This *is* Stacy Flynn. What can I do for you?

"Oh. Mm-hm. Uh. Sure. Yes. I would be happy to talk to you about it."

She slammed down the phone. "There! There! Do you *see*? Channel Seven!"

Scoop had no idea what he was supposed to see or say. He was irate, but he was scared Flynn would do something crazy. He didn't think he'd ever seen a woman look that awful. She was obviously not all right with the body being found, and she must be in shock. He wished that he had approached her in a different way or at least come to the scene with her yesterday. He had heard from Dino it was very upsetting. But what she was saying was nonsense. The coroner never showed up, so the body got taken by the EMTs. Big goddamn deal. He had been waiting for her to say something about that. Dino said she was hounding him all yesterday. Something about the Haytes dairy again—she just couldn't let anything go, thought everything was on purpose, even little mistakes. Just because someone knew someone or worked for someone—to her, it meant they were connected.

Think the county can afford a full-time coroner? Jesus. Of course the dairy uses a large-animal veterinarian. No shit. She thought people were looking away or covering things up when it was just the way things were around here. Around everywhere, as far as he knew. He was angry too, goddammit, and he couldn't just throw some histrionic tantrum like a lady reporter.

In fact you know what? He was furious. He'd just had breakfast with Dino and Jim Haytes. Jim said his son was so broken up about the murder that he'd been crying all night, and then about what he read in the paper. So upset he was moving to Argentina to take a job with the dairy's parent company. With Groot. Too many memories in Haeden, even if he got over Wendy, said he'd never be able to walk down the street without people staring at him. Now that farm was going to have to fall to Bruce, and everyone knew Bruce didn't have Dale's responsibility or social skills. That whole family's living stained with the shame of rumor. Even if she never said anything specific, why would she print all those ladies' names? Pages and pages of names. Or ask those questions. Like it had anything to do with Haeden. He wished she'd done something truly libelous so he could make *Circular* fire her, but she was right, he didn't work for them anymore, and they never much cared about who was running the paper in the first place. Jim was meeting with the family's lawyer to see if there was a case. Jim wanted to send her to jail for what she wrote, but Dino said he doubted it would happen. If she only knew how much Scoop had already been doing for her this morning, she would never have blown her top like that.

He remembered calling her references in Cleveland, and one of the editors had described her as a "pit bull." Scoop laughed out loud at that after he met her, thought it proved something about city people being a little queer. But now he could see it. She didn't let go of anything.

Flynn's face was no longer pale but had become completely red. A vein stuck out in her temple. No one had ever looked at him like that.

"You know where you live?" she shouted again. "It's called Appalachia, motherfucker! You are in motherfucking Appalachia! Even if you're one of the little lords of Appalachia and you play golf and drive a snowmobile! You're here because you are comfortable around stupid people. You know they're easy to exploit. And the cost of living is cheap. There's about one hundred of you who are even capable of abstract thought! And even those people are nearly unintelligible. Hyuk. Hyuk. Hyuk. Well, guess what? I don't need to learn how to speak your fucking language, because your language is being *eradicated,* thank fucking God! Do you know that word? 'Eradicated'? Your life, your way, your language. And for a good fucking reason. It's all bullshit! You sold all your precious land that was fucking stolen in the first place! You betrayed your fucking neighbors. And you! You personally sat by while a kid *from* this town was somewhere *in* this town *dying*! And she died yesterday. She died *yesterday fucking morning*!"

Flynn was trembling with rage. "*Fire me?* Fucking fire me, then! *You can't!* YOU CAN'T! And don't you *ever* threaten me for doing my job. Wendy White is *dead* because I couldn't do my fucking job!"

Scoop had sat down for the last of Flynn's attack. He had never in his life seen anyone behave like that. And he knew then that people were right about her being ethnic of some kind. He sat down because he wanted to hit her or grab her, and he felt that if he remained standing, he might do it, and then he would be charged with assault. He should have called Dino while she was still raving.

All he really wanted to tell her was that Wendy White was dead because somebody killed her and it had nothing to do with any of them or the town. And that she shouldn't have run all those stories about women getting killed, or printed those pages with just names on them because it wasn't good for people to think about. He sat there not saying a thing until he wasn't angry at her anymore. She ignored him, turned on her computer, made a pot of coffee.

He was suddenly painfully aware that she was about five feet tall and couldn't have weighed more than his granddaughter. He hoped to God she would start crying and that this was some kind of girl crisis so he could comfort her, but she kept ignoring him. He knew she would leave town and he wouldn't have to fight with her anymore. She was just bluffing that she would keep investigating. He should have come with her to the scene. He should have invited her over more. The phone rang. She picked it up and slammed it back down. Then she unplugged it from the wall and pulled a tape recorder out of her desk, put it in front of Scoop, and pressed play. It was the voice of Wendy White's mother:

"I'm Lori White, I live in Haeden, New York. It's January fourth, 2009. Uh, okay. I'll try to get through this for you. Don't know if I can."

Her voice was low and soft, and when she paused, he realized it was the sound of someone quietly crying as she spoke.

"Well. I guess it was Beth Ann first realized there was something wrong, because Wendy usually comes early to watch the girls so they can gossip a bit. And she was waiting and waiting, and she called Wendy's apartment. Then she called me to see if I could babysit because Wendy hadn't showed up, and we were a little pissed, you know. Thinking it's that boyfriend and she forgot. So I went over to stay with the girls while Beth Ann went to her ceramics class at the Y in Elmville.

"About, oh, maybe a half hour forty-five minutes later, Dale come over to Beth Ann's, and he was real serious. Not himself, you know how he is, joking always, well, his face was white and he looked like he had been crying, he was all sweaty, looked sick. And he said he couldn't find Wendy. Well. She'd been at work, so it was only a couple of hours.

"You know, I think now it's real strange he was that upset right then. You know now I think that. I told Alex Dino that.

"He'd called her friends, he'd talked to people at work. You know she didn't have her own car, so she probably hadn't gone into Elmville. And I told him I'm sure it's fine. Maybe one of her girlfriends drove into town and they were up to the mall. Well, we went through all the places we thought she could be. And I started to feel really uneasy because Wendy had been such a homebody before she started going with Dale, and I just figured when she wasn't around, she was with him. So it did frighten me right away, like I said. I called Danny, and he took the truck out looking for her. Dale sat with me there, and we played with the girls and waited in case she showed up. He was too worried up to go out.

"So finally, he just goes and tells me he had asked Wendy to marry him—which was a shock to me, honestly. A shock that she didn't come and tell me about it. And he was so worried because he thinks that she ran off. She said yes, of course, but he thinks she got to thinking and was overwhelmed.

"And then that did make me feel better because I figured she wanted to share that news with her friends and probably they had driven down from Geneseo, where she's got a few girlfriends at school. Probably wanted to tell them before us. And I was able to make Dale feel a little better, explaining that to him. I made him some hot chocolate, and after the girls went to bed, we watched some television and ate popcorn and talked about Wendy while we waited to hear from her. Waited to hear from Danny. Dale went home before Beth Ann came back. We told each other we'd call if she showed up.

"It turned out Wen didn't go out with her girlfriends. We called everyone the next day. By the end of that week, I just—"

Here her voice broke, and she sobbed.

"That was two months ago. I don't know what happened that night. Captain Dino keeps telling us they are investigating but . . . *what* are they investigating? There was nothing in her apartment gave anybody a clue. I mean, she was just *gone*, and nobody we talked to had any idea. She would not walk out on work and family, she never did a thing like that her whole life, that's just not our way. And for weeks I could feel that she was out there—like she was right here in town but I was just missing her somehow. I feel it now, I know she's here. I know she's got to be. I know somebody here has got to know what's going on.

"Please tell people if there is anything at all seems strange, please tell us. Tell us directly, because we don't care what's gone wrong at all. No, sir. We just want to get our baby back home safe. Anything. Anything at all that seems out of the normal—we don't care if it seems small, even if you just think you saw her, or you think you saw her in a car, or if you've seen a strange car or a stranger in town or even not a stranger. Please. Please. We will do anything and give you whatever we can, but we can't do this alone. And if she is here, we want her to know how much we love her."

The pitch of Lori White's voice raised but somehow became softer, almost a whisper. "We just love her. Her daddy and her nieces and her brother and Beth Ann. And me." There was a long pause on the tape, and Flynn looked at the ceiling trying to keep the tears from sliding out of her eyes while White's mother's voice whispered the word "me," one more time.

Alice

I SPENT MOST OF my time that spring with Ross. Megan was at the Rhode Island School of Design, working on losing her sense of humor. I spent most of the time swimming, hunting, volunteering at Haeden Medical, and waiting for Theo to come home from school. Gene and Claire wanted to talk about colleges because colleges and teachers wanted to talk about me. Whenever they brought it up, I would tell them I planned on living in a trailer with Theo. Me and Theo and a bunch of books. I was lonely.

I built a lot of things and went shooting with Ross. But people make you feel alone if you think a certain way. Eventually, you give in to what they say is real. What they insist is normal. And of course it's easy to excel at normal things—get praise for normal things—the grades, the sports, telling jokes, not being mean. The regular things you really do like: EMT class and pancake breakfasts and sledding on Tamarack Hill, practicing trapeze, going to dances at school. Reading at home.

Sometimes I could see why Gene and Claire lived the way they did. I could see how it had become important for them. I respected them, the life they led. I loved them. But I was not going to become a doctor or a circus performer or an organic farmer. And no matter what they thought, that was not what they were raising me to do. Those were things they did, not things they really thought were important.

When I look back on it now, I think I was slow to understand. Before Wendy White was found and the newspaper came out, I was very slow to put things together about the way things work.

But after they found her, everything changed. If anyone still had a question about what was going on, there was just something wrong with them. When the paper came that week, I had to revisit my responsibility as a person who lived in that town. And in the world. I was so awash in rage, I was weightless with it. Falling or rising or swimming deep underwater, holding my breath, hovering.

I would have to think about jokes I had heard and what they meant and what my responsibility was. Or had been. What responsibilities I'd already shirked. I would have to think about what was funny or not. What was real.

Bruce Haytes, whose brother had dated Wendy White, told a lot of jokes. And for some reason, I didn't pay close attention. Because Wendy jokes were common. Because Wendy being gone was a source of fear and gossip and, oddly, something funny. But why would *he* be joking?

I would have to revisit the things Kyle and Bruce and Rick and Taylor and a few of their other friends had said. I would have to revisit their mannerisms and the way they looked at me and other people from the time we were all young. Think about the things they said in class and did outside of class, things they yelled from their trucks. What they did after practice when people were walking home. The way they walked. The way their bodies moved and the sounds of their voices, how they smelled. The clothes they wore, how they changed their demeanor around certain people. Changed the phrases they used, shifted something inside themselves.

I would have to think hard about all of it. Because there were details I had missed or never bothered with, and now they had to be parsed out. Otherwise, they blended together, were a way, a manner, instead of a body of evidence. I would have to consider all the evidentiary details. After Wendy was found, I studied them for another week. To see if things changed. To see how they changed. To think about the level of anxiety they each telegraphed, the way they spoke in the months between November and April. How some of them seemed more relaxed and more confident. How there were days when I looked at them and knew exactly what was going on, but something stood between me and that thought, that understanding. I saw and sensed and knew, but some awful animal thing blocked that information from reaching my body, my voice. I saw but stood frozen like an animal. I saw the way I see when I know the answers, when I know what people will say just by looking at them, when I can remember nearly everything I have ever heard or read to take tests. And because I was slow this time, I would have to replay it for myself to double-check.

I would have to hear Bruce say over in my head what he had said out loud in February, that Wendy wasn't dead. Because he just fucked her last night.

"Probably dead by now . . ."

". . . not dead yet. I just fucked her last night."

"Oh, shit, dude. That's fucking cold."

"Too bad you were last in line."

"Your dad was last in line."

"Miracle of Viagra."

I would have to see all the details in my head. The picture of them looking up at me and the slight startled hunch of shoulders before Bruce threw his head back to laugh. Because it was funny I was there or funny that he was startled or funny that what he said was so sick.

I would have to revisit that moment to see if I had caught the slightest bit of fear or remorse in his look—if he had telegraphed some need for help. Because that would be a different kind of information. Would have changed the cost-benefit analysis.

I felt bad when Wendy was found. I knew that I would not feel the same again about my school or my friends or the place I lived. The whole world. And I felt sad about her body. Which was like my body. Being able to devote myself to the study of

Bruce and his friends made me feel better because I was doing something. Because it was a rational thing to do, to consider my ethical obligations.

It would hardly be rational to accept that I live inside a thing made of flesh that people capture, hide, and then wait in line to rape.

Gene

I HAVE HER BABY teeth saved in a box in my dresser.

Yesterday I was getting dressed for work and saw the little wooden box, and I had to pick it up and squeeze it as hard as I could. Just squeeze it. Careful not to shake it and hear them rattle. I started to think again about those parents. About how they probably have baby teeth saved somewhere. Or hair caught in a brush. Clothes on the floor. Muddy boot tracks inside.

I picture their houses, every possession, every space in their lives now filled with pain. Not just the photos of their children, which in some way must be a comfort, but things. Things ringing with the ghost of a baby's or child's touch.

The bike in the garage, the basketball hoop, clothes in the dryer. A dish in the sink. This day frozen forever. The worn path under a swing or worse; the swing that was asked for and never built. The tree standing bare without it. The smell of food. The sound of a door closing or feet on the stairs. All these things that must bring so much pain. Even now I am missing them. Missing Alice.

I have never in my life prayed or believed I knew what it meant to pray. But when I first heard the news and thought, *My God. My baby is in that school,* I was praying for her wit and her speed. The things she surely used to do what she did. Her wit and her speed. Those were things for which I prayed. And I cannot stand this thought.

Alice

NOT TOO MANY people know about Andrew Golden and Mitchell Johnson, who were eleven and thirteen when they dressed up in camouflage like soldiers and shot fifteen girls in their middle school in March 1998. Five of the girls died. Some were very little girls. These were things I didn't know about. My mother and father never told me about these things. They gave me books to read. Theory and philosophy. Ideas about why the culture is the way it is. But we didn't talk specifically about who was doing these things. We didn't talk about these kinds of current events.

Then there was a couple of years ago, when girls were molested and killed at school by men who came in from outside. First in Colorado, at Platte Canyon High School, where a man took six girls hostage in a classroom and molested all of them, killing one, a sixteen-year-old. He entered the school with a list of the girls' names. He'd looked them up in a yearbook. Later that same week, a thirty-two-year-old milkman took ten Amish girls hostage in a one-room schoolhouse, molesting them and killing five. He told the boys to leave the classroom, and they did. He said he was doing it as an "act of punishment" for something that had happened years ago. What could have happened, you think—was he molested by some Amish girls? Could be. He lived out in Amish country his whole life. Was he hurt by a teacher? But no, it turns out the thing that happened years ago was that *he* had molested some little girls. Hmmm. It's hard to see what he meant by "punishment." Punishing *these* girls for the crime he had committed against *those* girls. Because of course, they caused his actions by their mere existence.

The list of girls is long and not confined to one country.

It isn't just helpless schoolgirls, though. Jamie Leigh Jones. That's a name you don't remember. She was working in Iraq when she was drugged by a firefighter named Charles Boaretz and gang-raped by Boaretz and an undisclosed number of co-workers at a place called Camp Hope. Her body required extensive reconstructive surgery. Including reattachment of her pectoral muscles.

Stacy's article didn't talk about these killings in great detail. But she did a good job of talking about other rapes and killings in New York State, almost none of which I had any idea occurred, even though two hundred cases happened within thirty miles of here. It was a big gap in my education. The newspaper made me do a little more research. Research is essential in making any rational decision. Wendy White was raped, killed, and dumped. Men raped her, men killed her, men dumped her, men found her, men are examining her remains, men are looking for the men who did it. Then the men who did it will be represented in court by men, and a man will make the decision based on laws men made throughout the legal history of this country. There may be some women involved off and on throughout the process. Witnesses, maybe, family members, lawyers. But this is Haeden, so besides Stacy, who are we kidding? There's no one here.

And that's a little hard to take. It's a little hard to take these days.

I'm Cheryl Lourde. I live in Haeden, New York. It's April 18, 2009. I was Alice's teacher. She was a beautiful girl. She had pale, very pale blue eyes. And she had this look like she was imagining something funny most of the time. It was a pleasure to watch her think. She never ever took notes. She had an incredible memory. She wrote papers and completed her tests, but otherwise, she would sit and listen. I don't know if she had a photographic memory, but she could certainly remember everything she had heard or read, and she paid attention. She had a very intense focus. She asked lots of questions, and she had an extremely agile intellect—she often connected things that I wouldn't have thought about, even now, after twenty-five years of teaching. She brought life to subjects that I was going over by rote at that point, not thinking about. She said English was her worst subject. I think it was a subject she struggled to understand, but she had no trouble with her work that I could see. She was very well read and a very critical reader.

Despite all this, Alice was unpretentious, you could almost say unaware. A lot of adolescents like her thrive on their difference and stick together, but she wasn't like that. She had a sweetness and an openness that you normally see in much younger kids. She gave off the sense of being incredibly loved and cared for. Open to the world. And I know she was an only child. She liked to argue and explain things in class, and she had a loud, distinct musical laugh that was a pleasure to hear. Standing in the classroom, you could hear it out the window or down the hall, and it just made you feel happy.

I'm Theo Bailey. I live in Annandale-on-Hudson. It's April 21. Again, I don't think I have any insight here, unless what you're looking for is evidence that she was my friend.

My memory practically begins with Alice. We used to fall asleep on the couch. Her parents had this big long paisley couch, and we used to fall asleep lying there when we were like six years old. If Claire and Gene and Ross were having a party. If they were playing Scrabble or Boggle. If Connie was in town, they would stay up talking, and sometimes we'd listen to them, but mostly, we played. Sometimes we'd lie on the couch and braid our hair together on the side and pretend we were switching brains. We always ended up falling asleep there.

I don't know how we ended up together later. It was like being in love was a thing we already were, and it was a thing we needed to practice to be grown up. We were lucky to have each other to talk about how it felt or how it would work. I don't remember a time when I didn't love her. I'd rather you not write any of this. But I think it's important to understand, considering everything. She was an incredibly happy, gentle person.

Nothing seemed to connect who we were then and who we are now.

We were always talking about who would go out with whom. We had crushes on other people, we dated each other's friends, and then we were somehow together. Always.

I thought whoever I married would be like this. I thought I would marry my best friend. But I never thought I wanted to marry Alice. Most people who met her at school thought she was my sister. Like we had imprinted on each other before we could even talk right or understand things, and after a while there was no question how it would go.

We were free to love anyone else, but I don't think anyone else wanted to be with us. The other was always so present. And for us, other people seemed foreign. Their voices, their bodies, their ways of speaking.

I want you to know this stuff because I think it makes it pretty obvious that we were happy together and that she didn't have conflicts with any guys.

With Alice, the world was a secondary place. A place that was already false because it existed at all. The way objects are imitations, and ideas are originals. Our world was the real world. Everything else was a mass-produced tenth-generation copy.

She would never place herself in the center of that false world. She was too smart for that.

Alice

MY PARENTS USED to say "Beneath the paving stones, the beach," and they used to say "Demand the impossible," things they told me the situationists and the surrealists and the "modern primitives" said. I grew up on these expressions. Axioms of an underground and unrealized wish. Today is the day I stop wishing.

After Wendy White was found, I got that saying stuck in my head—"Beneath the paving stones. Beneath the paving stones." It upset me, and I didn't know why until I had this dream. Body after body. You lifted up the sidewalk on Main Street and there were bodies, lined up, pressed together, naked. Women's bodies. Their skin was blue and white and dirty. Their hair was sticking out like grass growing up through the cracks, but it was like it had been caught between the stones. Their fingers were broken from trying to push the cement away. Some of them had begun to dig down instead of up. It wasn't just one grave or one mass grave—it was the sidewalk of the whole town. In the dream, I knew this was what was beneath the sidewalk that led away and also beneath the roads. Underneath it all was this white-blue skin and skeleton and hair. And I knew that my parents, whom I love, were utterly wrong.

Beneath the paving stones and the fields and the parking lots and the woods lies something else.

And all the boys I had ignored or pitied or excused throughout school were also something else. They were something entirely different.

My parents' lives, the rooftop garden, our little "farm," were all just another way to ignore the fact that there is no beach down there, and there never was. That's not what you find when you go digging. There are bodies and bones. Women's bodies, which first became their coffins at puberty, a skin coffin. A place from which you will never be heard, except maybe by those who are buried nearby, or those with their ear to the ground.

After Wendy White's body was found, I saw the world as it was for the first time. When her body was found, I was also found. I woke up in her grave and gazed down at my legs, took in the power of my lungs, my biceps, my hands, and knew what they were for.

EVIDENCE *P47914*

4/15/09 8:00 A.M.

Cpt. Alex Dino

Video Record 0003
McClean, Gavin

My name is Gavin McClean. I'm a senior at HHS. I was there yesterday. April 14.

She was standing in the middle of the four corners where the downstairs hallways meet—she was, I don't know who it was. I guess I don't know if it was a girl, but I know it was a swimmer, dressed like a girl swimmer, because she was dressed like they did for Spirit Day in a green mermaid wig and the Titans shirt and glitter makeup. I remember they all wore glitter. She was in the middle of four corners when I saw her pull the gun out of her backpack. No. It wasn't. I didn't actually see a gun. She had a little bag or stuffed animal or something, I don't know what it was. I know I saw a swimmer there. There were a few swimmers there. And everyone was coming back from lunch, and the bell had just rung.

I guess all I know is a swimmer pulled a smaller bag out of her bag. She set the backpack down like she was going through it to look for something. And when she stood up, she had another bag. A makeup bag, maybe. I don't know, I guess it wasn't Alice's pack. 'Cause hers has a frog on it. And this was . . . I don't really remember. It was crowded because of lunchtime, and people were walking outside. Paul and Bruce and Chris and Kyle were walking from the cafeteria up the hall. I heard this pop, like it was definitely a gunshot and really loud. Then Paul fell, and then the other three, but they fell like it was fake. It looked fake. Just shocked faces or no expression at all, and they fell. Then I saw blood, and at first I thought, *This is not real, they're trying to make some point about school violence.* That's what I thought. I thought, *This is a play.* Then there was just a ton of blood. I didn't really know where the shots came from at all, but I guess it must have been her. People started screaming and running. People were screaming and crying, and I ran back up the hall and outside and kept running. I live two blocks from school. I didn't really know what had even happened. When I got home, I locked the doors. I called 911, but they already knew. I called my mom at work and told her I was okay and she said what was I talking about and I told her and she started crying. She said, "Stay right there. Stay right where you are. Don't go anywhere, don't leave the house." Then I couldn't believe what I had seen because it didn't make any sense at all and I was sure it was a big hoax. It really looked so fake. They must have been faking the whole thing.

But then I knew they weren't. I knew Paul and Bruce and Chris and Kyle were probably dead. And they were dead. They died right there in the hallway.

She killed them right there while they were walking.

EVIDENCE *P47914*

4/17/09 8:00 A.M.

Cpt. Alex Dino

Video Record 0004
Rumsey, Leslie

I'm Leslie Rumsey. I am fifteen. I was in global studies at the time.

We heard shots, and our teacher closed the door and locked it and told everyone to get under their desks. She called down to the office on her cell phone. The loudspeakers told everyone to get inside the classrooms and lock the doors. Some of us crammed into the closet because we were afraid to get under the desks. And everyone had their cell phones out and were texting their parents or other kids, telling them to get out. And someone said don't get under the desks, everybody expects you to get under the desks now, and they just shoot the lock off the door and then shoot you under the desk. Those kids at Columbine were hiding under the library desks, and it didn't help them.

We were all dressed up for Spirit Day, so everyone was easy to see. People had glitter in their hair, and the football team had fake horns they were wearing, and the cheerleaders were in their uniforms, but they all wore the same blond wigs and glitter face paint and glitter lip gloss. The track team had on black shirts with pictures of tridents on them. We were all dressed up and scared. Then we heard a whole lot of people screaming down the hall. There weren't any more shots, so you didn't know why people were screaming.

Someone said, "What if it's the guy who killed Wendy?" My heart was pounding because at the time I really believed that was probably what it was. What if the guy who killed Wendy White had come into the school?

We were there like that for an hour, listening and freaking out. We heard four or five shots, and a few minutes later, another I don't know how many, then sirens. The scary part is that after we heard screaming and people running and doors slamming all in a row—like boom boom boom—then it was really quiet. We were afraid there were bombs in the school because people always say they're going to blow up the school. Everybody says stuff like that, I couldn't even tell you who. But we were scared. I could feel my heart beating so fast. The kids at Columbine put bombs in their school, but they didn't go off. I saw the movie of it on the Internet. They left a bag of explosive stuff in the cafeteria, but it didn't go off, and they tried to shoot it to make it go off. "If there's a bomb in the school, we should probably get out," I said, "we should get out. Get out." But our teachers said, "Everybody is going to have to breathe deeply and try to be quiet. We're close to the police station, and we're going to be okay."

EVIDENCE *P47915*

4/17/09 8:50 A.M.

Cpt. Alex Dino

Video Record 0005
Salinski, Crystal

My name is Crissy Salinski. I'm a junior at Haeden. I had lunch and was going to bring my stuff to the music room.

We were coming out of the cafeteria right behind Paul and some other kids, and then there was this big crack and Paul fell to his knees and then over on his side. I looked up the hall and couldn't see anything. Anybody. I was so startled, I didn't look down again, I ran as fast as I could. There were more shots, but I kept running and I didn't see anything. Everyone was dressed up for Spirit Day and people were screaming. People were screaming and running. I have never heard such a loud noise as people screaming like that. It's like at my uncle's farm when the pigs get scared and know something bad is going to happen and they all start squealing at once. But there was nobody with a gun that I remember. And I thought, *Maybe he killed himself and we're all panicking.* Some of us ran and shut ourselves in the shop room.

Alice came running down the hall away from the shots, and she pounded on the door of the shop room—she wasn't screaming or anything, she just looked freaked out, so we let her in. She was wearing the swim team's Spirit Day stuff. She had blue glitter nail polish and was wearing the green mermaid wig all the swimmers were wearing and the shirt that said TITANS SWIM. Yes, I am sure it was her. She looked around at everyone. She said, "Everybody okay?"

And then she ran out again.

EVIDENCE *P47917*

4/17/09 10:30 A.M.

Cpt. Alex Dino

Video Record 0006
Wilson, Bill

Bill Wilson, April 17, 2009.

She knocked on the door to the weight room, and everybody was running out of the school or running into rooms to hide. People were screaming. She tapped really quietly, and I saw her look both ways like she was worried the shooter would see her. I was afraid to get up and let her in, but I couldn't leave her out there, so I did it really fast. She looked terrified. She came in. She looked around. There were three of us in there, and she locked the door behind her. She put her backpack down. I remember it was brand-new. She turned around to open it—I thought she was looking for a cell phone. I said, "Thank God." None of us in there had a cell phone, 'cause we were working out and they were in our lockers. Then she turned around really fast and shot Tony and then Rick. Just one then the other. But I don't remember a gun. For a minute I almost thought the shots came through the door. Then she opened the door and ran out. I went over to Tony, and he was still alive because she had got him in the neck, not the head, like Rick. I put my sweatshirt on his neck and it got soaked in seconds. It took seconds. He bled to death. I don't know why she didn't shoot me. They said nobody else saw her do anything. It was her, though. I'm sure of it. It was a swimmer. I think it was her. When I remember it, I don't know, because all I can remember is Tony. I try to remember her face. No. I know it was her.

She had those blue eyes. There were no shots through the door, so it had to have been her. They said later that everyone who got shot died. No one was wounded. I guess Tony was wounded, but only for about a minute.

I was in that room with their bodies for most of the morning.

EVIDENCE *P47919*

4/18/09 12:00 P.M.

Cpt. Alex Dino

Video Record 0007
Murphy, Liam

Um, my name is Liam Murphy?

I was outside by the time the police and ambulance and everybody got there. I had run outside because other people were running after the shots. There were a lot of cars out front. And people didn't know who the gunman was. Suddenly, I saw this kid running out the door of the gym, and then there was a pop and he just fell forward. He just ran outside and got shot right while everybody was watching, while the police were there and the news was there. He thought he had gotten out. His chest hit the pavement and his feet kicked up behind him and then flopped back down. It was morning and the light was bright orange all around the school, and I remember his shadow on the ground while he was running. He died with everyone watching, on camera. It made me feel like crying. And I wondered why I didn't throw up. My mom wasn't there, but someone else's mom came over and was hugging me and she put her hands over my eyes and turned me away from the school and she walked me to the buses that were taking people away. Then I noticed there were police everywhere, a line of them between us and the school while they moved us to the buses. I didn't know I was crying until that woman put her arms around me.

I didn't know anyone who got shot really well. I'm a sophomore, and I know one of the kids was a sophomore, but I didn't have classes with him.

When I got on the bus, I was really confused for a minute. I didn't have a cell phone, and people said I could borrow theirs, but my dad works outside and has no phone and I couldn't remember the number of the restaurant where my mom works now because it's new. A teacher said, "Call your grandparents. People will want to know you are okay." But my papa works outside, too, and never even ever used a cell phone, and my grandma died last year.

I sat on the bus waiting to go to I don't know where, wherever the parents would meet us, and I was crying. Looking out the window. I didn't look at the other kids on the bus. I was thinking how I did not want to see that kid fall. How I could picture it again right then, just like it happened, and I did not want to have seen it.

A teacher sat beside me. His face looked gray, the wrong color. I thought, *I've got homework in a couple of classes.* But I didn't remember what I had done with my backpack—I might have left it in the parking lot or in a classroom. By the time we got to the state police place and people's parents were waiting for them, it seemed like everything had happened days ago, even though it had happened about an hour ago. I got off the bus, and my mother was there because they announced it on the news where we would be taken. I could see her through the window.

My mother stood, and I watched her put her hands on either side of her face, and she would take them down from her face and shake them, like, very quickly and stiffly and then hold her face again, press her hand hard over her mouth. I could see her trying to look into the windows. When I walked off the bus, she dropped her hands and her shoulders slumped. She took a breath and started running toward me. I could see her lips move, saying "Thank God," and she just reached out her arms.

And I ran over to her to hold her because she was so afraid. I was so sorry for how afraid she was. And I called her Mommy, which I hadn't done in probably ten or twelve years. I said, "It's all right, mommy." But she was saying "Shhhh" in my ear. I'm much bigger than her, and I was bent over to hug her. And I remember she was not crying.

EVIDENCE *P479110*

4/18/09 2:15 P.M.

Cpt. Alex Dino

Video Record 0008
Thompson, Karl

I'm Karl Thompson. I go to HHS. I remember there weren't even ten shots. And then things were really quiet, there was no more shooting or anything, and people were whispering to each other. We were in the library, and Alice came in.

She asked if everybody was okay. She was whispering, but she said the police were there and everyone was going to be fine. This is exactly what you'd expect from that girl. It was so reassuring to see her. I remember thinking I couldn't believe how she could be perfect even in this situation. I was almost in love with her right then. Like she was an angel that had come to us, and if it weren't for her, we would have been so much more scared. She was still wearing the Titans Swim stuff, but she took off the wig and was standing there talking to us, a bunch of people wearing glitter and stupid clothes while someone was trying to kill us, she looked really worried but, like, worried for *us.*

She said people can get real screwed up from shock, so if we were scared, we should elevate our feet and get close together for warmth. She must have known this stuff because she worked in the hospital. Her parents were doctors, too, I think. Just not in Haeden. Then she put down her backpack and went through it and got out some little cans of grapefruit juice and gave them to us. You almost felt like she could catch the shooter herself. Like she was afraid of absolutely nothing. Like bullets could go right through her. And then she said, "I have to see if everybody's all right." And she went back out into the hall.

Alex Dino. Shit, Stacy, you know who I am. Look, I've already talked to Albany about this, and I have already talked to the federal government. And I want you to know I wouldn't be talking to *you* at all if it weren't for the fact that Elmville and Chemung don't have their own reporters anymore. Which reminds me, before I forget, there's some hotshot wearing tassel shoes looking for you in the Alibi. Three of 'em got their laptops set up in there. Guess that's the kind of place you all feel comfortable. I told him I'm pretty surprised you're still here. No offense.

Don't even ask me again about DNA, I told you what happened, and you got copies of those reports. At this point I've got a hell of a lot more to worry about. You want a second opinion, convince those poor people to have their daughter dug up.

All right, take it easy. I'm getting to it. Everything changed after April 20, 1999. And everything is going to have to change again. Why these things keep happening in April is anybody's guess. Prior to what happened there, law enforcement focused on containment of these situations—making sure the problem stayed in the building. The reason there was so much collateral damage at Columbine is because police didn't enter the school until half an hour after the shooting began. They even failed to enter the outside door that went directly to the library. It was easier to understand why no one caught that gook at Virginia Tech. He killed some girl in her dorm room to begin with—and that was just seen as a domestic, which you would never lock down a school for.

In the dozen or so shootings that happened since Columbine, police enter the building right away. But that didn't help us in here. We entered the building and we couldn't figure out what had happened.

Everything was quiet. Kids were shut in classrooms, terrified. I mean, we had no idea. Thought someone could be hiding in there when we walked in. The natural assumption was that the shooter had got his targets and killed himself already. But looking at the boys who were dead, the way they were lying, no. And there was no gun by those scenes. There was no gun ever. The only thing we know is where it is not.

It was like the shooting had been done by a ghost. It was so quiet. We went through the whole building, the SWAT team, the state police, and there was no shooter. There was no one who could even describe a shooter. Finally, a few people said it was a swimmer—someone dressed up like a swimmer. But it was Spirit Day, and everyone, even the teachers, was dressed up.

It was awful. Those boys laid out in the hall and then the other ones in the weight room.

We had to hold nearly everyone. It was late afternoon before we got the powder display off of her and took her out to the county jail. And at that point she smiled. I'll never forget it. She looked me right in the eye and she smiled. Like I had done exactly what she wanted.

I mean, that's what it was that day—you were there, you know what the hell I'm talking about.

And I was right that they're affiliated with terrorists, like I told you. The Environmental Liberation Front, for one. They call themselves ELF, which sounds real innocent but is really one of the worst groups in the country.

It turns out her parents were never married. Piper is not even a family name. They made it up when they were living in New York City. I thought it was a joke when the federal officer told me these groups call themselves anti-civilization. Like there's nobody on earth stupid enough to believe you're going to be alive yourself if you believe in anti-civilization. They just want chaos and murder, which is what they brought to this town. They're out to destroy everything. Doctors gone wrong, like that Kaczynski guy was a scientist gone wrong.

They come in here and infiltrate a nice little town—they think because nobody knows what they are, they can get away with it. Well, they got more government and civilization now than they ever believed possible, I'll tell you right now. We'll see all of them in jail. We'll see the girl and her parents and the rest of those freaks like the Manson family in jail. The father and that big dark guy who comes to visit Ross Miller who's been a nut for thirty years, we'll see them in jail. Somebody taught that girl to shoot, somebody taught her what her targets were. Somebody got her a gun.

Judith Weiss, May 3, 2009. I can give you information about the case for background purposes and nothing more. So I expect none of this to turn up in print unless I have said to you "This is for attribution" or "This is on the record," which I assure you I will not. Is that clear? And I am maintaining my own recording of this conversation.

I met Gene and Claire through Constant Souriani, whom I had known through mutual clients in Manhattan. It was an unusual case for me to have taken, as Alice Piper was not a corporation. It turned out odder still, because currently, there is no defendant of which to speak. If things change in the future, I assume I will still be representing the Pipers and possibly Constant, and you may want to contact me again then. There may be personal suits against the Pipers from the families of the deceased, in which case I will be representing Gene and Claire, who have done absolutely nothing wrong.

I am confident the evidence will show their historical political leanings had no influence on Alice's actions. And that in their youth, they had been no different from other teenagers in liking loud music, bicycle riding, and traveling. I mean, please. This nonsense about anti-civilization.

As far as what exactly Alice's actions were on that day, I must stress we don't at all know. All we have is the paraffin test—the evidence of powder burns—but we also know Alice often went shooting in the early mornings with her uncle Ross. Because of sports and pep-rally events, there were at least fifteen girls at school who fit Alice's description that day. The only eyewitness admits he was so terrified he may have been mistaken, that the events didn't make sense even to him. That he couldn't be sure. Perhaps this will get sorted out for him in counseling, who can say?

What do we know about Alice Piper? She is technically a genius. Her IQ is 158. She got a 2300 on her SAT. She is an athlete. Now. Think what this means. Think what this means for a girl in Haeden. I want nothing about her intelligence coming from this firm. But for your own purposes, you may want to consider her intellectual background and the treatment she's been getting in this town.

A young woman from a family like Alice's, living in Haeden, her intelligence is going to be a huge problem. It doesn't matter that she was the sweetest girl on earth and everyone loved her. It doesn't matter that she was a conscientious kid. Her intelligence is already half criminal. Her intelligence has already convicted her. I'm certain you understand the cultural phenomena I am talking about.

The bottom line is this: There is absolutely no concrete evidence that Alice Piper is the Haeden High School shooter, no gun, no written material, and most significantly, no motive.

Sgt. Anthony Giles

The Life and Work of Philippe-Ignace Semmelweis
(Notes for first draft)
AP History Period 4
Biography and Discovery
Alice Piper
Grade 10
3/12/09

The mysterious death of a friend was the catalyst for a scientific breakthrough that revolutionized medical treatment in the mid–19th century, and presaged the work of Joseph Lister and Louis Pasteur.

In 1847, while dissecting a cadaver Jakob Kolletschka the friend of Obstetrician Dr. Philippe Ignace Semmelweis cut his finger. He died shortly after of Pupureal fever, a disease also known as Childbed Fever, which was very common in the "pauper's hospital" where they worked.

Prior to this accident, Pupureal Fever was thought to be caused by "bad air, unfavourable atmospheric, cosmic, or terrestrial influences, and inferior psychology." (324) It killed 20 percent of women giving birth in teaching hospitals. *Need to get other stats re: general population.

Semmelweis proposed that the actual cause was the transmission of the disease from corpses to patients by doctors who did not wash their hands after handling cadavers. The disease was transferred to the women they were treating. By making doctors disinfect their hands with chloride or lime, and clean bed sheets he decreased mortality rates by 90 percent in just a few months.

When more doctors began using his methods there was a public campaign to discredit handwashing and instrument disinfection. (Will get examples esp. slogans about not washing.)

In 1861 Semmelweis suffered a nervous breakdown from the frustration of not seeing his methods widely applied. In July 1865 he was committed to an asylum.

He is quoted as saying: "When I look back upon the past, I can only dispel the sadness which falls upon me by gazing into that happy future when the infection will be banished . . . The conviction that such a time must inevitably sooner or later arrive will cheer my dying hour." (544)

Semmelweis died in Wein Dobling from injuries due to beatings by the Asylum's staff. His life and struggles are socially instructive to those of us who would like to one day become doctors, as he made a simple discovery that enabled other doctors and scientists to better understand the nature of bacteriological diseases.

The University of Medicine in Budapest is named after him as is "The Semmelweis Reflex," a problem in which a discovery of important scientific fact is punished rather than rewarded. Semmelweis became known long after his death as the "savior of mothers."

Let's see here, it's May 4, 2009. And I'm Officer Karen Reynolds.

Right, well, like I said, she didn't look like a girl who had committed a crime. She looked like a *kid* just waiting for her parents to pick her up. She had the same bored, distracted, anxious look, like that.

She looked tired. She looked like my kid does after track practice. My boys go to school in Elmville, thank God. I know teenagers. I got four at home, and if I didn't know what she had done, I wouldn't have been able to tell her apart from any of them. She looked all flushed and sweaty, but not like a killer. To tell you the truth, and this is completely off the record, I mean it, *completely*. This tape is proof I said that, too. So you can't print it.

The thing is, there are times when I still don't believe she did it. The powder display was all there on her hands and face when we did the paraffin. But she went target shooting in the mornings with her uncle. We got that answer from all her teachers, hell, half the school. She wasn't the only kid with residual powder, either—but the others were boys, and they were hunters, it all looked different, and they were nowhere near the scene. There're many people who never believed she did it.

There were no cameras in that school then. It was the craziest possible day, with the pep rally, and Spirit Day, and they were allowed to play music over the loudspeaker between classes. That'll be the last of that.

When we booked her, she was polite, self-confident—like a mistake had been made and she knew she had to go through this process and her parents would pick her up soon. She asked when her parents would be there. She asked if anyone had been killed, or how many people, if we knew who. And looked upset when we said we couldn't tell her. She said she was worried about her friends. But she was composed, relieved. It seemed like a kid like her might react that way. She was in no way the kind of person that gets sent to the behavioral unit, I can tell you. She was the farthest thing from it. There were a lot of surprises with that girl.

The inmates believed it, though. She was here for a few weeks. Had a hotshot lawyer made sure she didn't go anywhere. She got given a real hard time 'cause she was a celebrity. She shoulda been in isolation the whole time, but we got limited facilities. There's eight women in here, and there were times when she was with them in the general population, and those were not easy times for her, I'm sure. I heard girls talking about her on the phone to their boyfriends and moms, or talking in the commissary or in their GED classes. They called her Pipe Bomb. They respected her and they hated her and I think that's 'cause most of the girls are from around here and went to HHS or Elmville at one point or another. She got close to a girl named Lorelei Ramos, which was a smart move, because if anyone was going to start something physical, it was Ramos. She was in on a parole violation, girl wasn't supposed to leave Kings County, got picked up here on a speeding ticket and possession, and now she's got to call it home. Anyway. They had a real bond, for some reason. Wasn't any two people here who looked or talked more different, but they got along.

Ramos is still here, and as you know, Piper is not. She might not have made it at all if it weren't for Ramos making such a racket. And I can tell you, I was not happy to be the first one to see what she had done. She's a child, after all.

I don't mind you talking to Lorelei, if she'll agree to it. She'd have to call you collect, and it's up to her to tell her lawyer, and she has a court-appointed, so you know . . . they got twenty, thirty clients, might not even give a crap, as far as I know.

She'd be your best bet for figuring things out if Piper told anyone what she planned. Or you could find a girl who likes to brag. And that wouldn't be Ramos. There's a lot of girls like to tell you how badass they are, but they make stuff up, too—so you have to be careful what you believe.

I just went to this training down at Elmira about this stuff, how to communicate and listen better to these girls and not let them manipulate you—'cause that's what they're all about, and you know we just want them to get their sentence done and be able to be okay back out there. We really do. Help them use this time to make some real changes.

It's all about reentry now. How they can go back into the world. I tell you, I like a lot of these girls, and I know they got friends here and they get treated right by us. A lot of them got stress like veterans get—not from being in *here*. I mean, they got that post-stress stuff in their lives. The course I took said 85 percent of incarcerated females got some kind of abuse, you know, physical, sexual abuse or rape, sometimes a whole lot of it, before they were arrested. So that's where the thing is—you help them know it doesn't *matter* what was done to them. They got to make the right choices *now* so they can be okay. It's up to them. You don't got money, you feel bad about yourself, you want to score some meth, you want to smoke some crack so you feel better—but you're gonna feel worse when you end up in jail and can't see your folks or, even worse, your own kids. It's all a mess, such a mess, I'm telling you.

Alice Piper, if she was guilty, had done something I'm sure a lot of them dreamed about. Hell, I think there's girls not even in jail who've had those feelings.

There's a lot of angry girls in here. That's just how it is. Put two and two together. You can see it in their faces. None of them were shedding tears over what happened at Haeden High.

Flynn

YOU KNOW THE rest. Or as much as anyone else does. A Glock 37 pistol registered to Ross Miller disappeared. A birthday check for $180 from Constant Souriani was cashed.

And then something that could have been called a school shooting happened. Could have been called a school shooting, was being called a plot. And if it was a plot, I was involved.

Tom Cutting and I continued to pay attention to what was in front of us. I had access to information and wasn't about to see this thing turn into some kind of obstructed mess the way the White case had. It was my story—and it sure as hell was the big-picture story. I intended to keep my head up and keep focused.

Some of the things in front of me were forensics photos taken in the hallway, in front of the cafeteria, in the weight room, in a science classroom, and in the school parking lot. Familiar settings and ugly subjects. The awful irony of school decorations hanging in the background in these photographs. The incongruity of desks and posters, chalkboards and murals and lockers paired with combat footage.

The shots of the crime scene, the so-called forensics photos, were no help in figuring out what had happened. Though I pored over them, thinking there would be one detail that would reveal everything. Reveal that it started as a rivalry between teammates or was the work of a classically unstable kid. Tom knew right away that wasn't it. His best EMT student had shown up for school that day, prepared to treat people for trauma and shock. And Tom knew better than anyone what the scene looked like. We slept at my place after it happened, and for the rest of the time we were in town, because he said he never wanted to look out of the window at the VFD again. This period of time for us was all about aversion. About the unspoken.

I saw Kyle Potter's mother in the grocery store one day after I had been looking at photographs of her son's body. Some close-ups of his head and torso, or what remained. In other photographs, his body was next to two other bodies. Shoulders touching, arms stretched over chests, a hand on a thigh, part of a head resting on the HHS logo across a blood-soaked sweatshirt. In some less explicit photos, the athletic wear, the intimacy, the languid posture could almost appear to be boys horsing around. Except for the blood. I had wondered if these boys produced an inordinate amount of blood because they were so healthy, so physically strong. There was blood covering the tile beneath them: dots of blood fanned out across the wall to their right. I was surprised by the quantity of blood at first but had looked at the pictures long enough to see other things—the color of an eye, smooth skin, pinkish-white sinew. They looked like little steer. The weight and muscle of their bodies obvious even in death.

I saw Kyle Potter's mother in line, and I did not speak to her. Not that anyone would have spoken to me. In those days right after the shooting, I was grateful to see the world as a series of concrete events, one following another. It goes like this: There is a great deal of blood in this photograph. I need cigarettes. I will go to the store. The sticker on my window says my inspection is up soon. There is Kyle's mother, buying Swiss Miss pudding. Cigarettes now cost $7.75. I need to put the windshield wipers on because it is raining. I forgot to buy toilet paper. They put up a new sign up at the Rooster. I wonder if Tom is on call.

This new way of feeling was also helpful when replacing my slashed tires, cleaning up glass from beneath the windows in my living room, and filing harassment complaints for Dino to ignore.

Around this time I told a radio news reporter about the release of forensic evidence in what I thought was an empathetic and professional tone. But when I heard my voice the next day, I realized

I had recounted these images and given information like I was reading off a very boring list. I listened to myself while drinking coffee. I had yet to eat a full meal since reviewing the HHS photographs. Even when Tom made me dinner it was nearly impossible. I didn't think I would ever be able to eat meat again.

The photos didn't help with anything, and ultimately, Dino's "evidence" provided a lot more information about himself and Haeden than it did about spring Spirit Day.

One day he called me at the paper to give me a copy of this letter taken from the Pipers' house, again totally unredacted. I read it but didn't get it. It could have been written by any one of my friends who decided to study business. I looked up the author—Constant Souriani, a businessman who had an aunt who had worked at the Haeden family clinic in the nineties. Already a known entity—a friend of the family, nothing new. It seemed a melancholic piece. The problems of working for "the man" and all. But Dino insisted it was crucial to understanding the case. That Souriani was an Arab. Showed me a box of books, a canceled check to Alice Piper from Souriani's account, and an essay Piper wrote for her English class—almost as good as anything I wrote in J-school. He thought that Alice was a new breed of suicide bomb, worse than a suicide bomb, because at this point there were still so many doubts about what had happened that day. Dino had been reading on the Homeland Security website about terrorists attacking our schools like they did in Russia.

It didn't help that the FBI had agents in town. That Dino, for the first time in his life, was working with them. I took his evidence. And I stayed close. In part because working so hard on the story prevented me from feeling it. From feeling what Alice had felt. From feeling what Wendy had felt. From feeling what these boys' mothers and fathers felt.

I knew there was nothing to be gained from Dino's research. The person who could put it all together was waiting in jail and more than happy to talk to me. She was unchanged. Her eyes, her face, her smile. She was herself. Waiting for me in the visitors' room, wearing the bright orange jumpsuit with side pockets. Could have been telling me about her latest science-fair project or fund-raiser. I thought of the butterfly garden and how, in a month, things would be blooming there again.

I would be the only person ever to interview Alice Piper. Ever to record her voice for the record. I had a story no one else could get, the thing Dino needed to close the case, and I needed to launch my career, as I had always planned, with a big-picture story from a backwater nowhere.

Alice Piper, April 29, 2009. I killed Bruce Haytes, Kyle Potter, Chris Ward, Paul Rees, Rick Tompkins, Tony Belardini, and Taylor Williams, who had actually made it outside the school. I think there are still probably three or four other people in town, adults, who need to be eliminated. But other than Bruce's brother, who I'm pretty certain about, I don't know who they are, and it doesn't look like I'll be able to do it. How are *you* doing?

Stacy?

There was something wrong with them. They knew where Wendy White was and there was no way to prove it. There still isn't, right? People who would do this would undoubtedly do other things that are ethically wrong and costly for the whole community—there's the moral obligation and then there's the logical aspect of it. I don't know that there's any other choice. It would be better for everyone, including the people with whom they were close, if they were dead.

They knew where she was. They talked about it, and I didn't do the right thing at the time. I thought they were joking.

No, I wouldn't call it an act of revenge. I would call it an act of extreme rationality. It's clearly eliminating a problem. I mean, I feel really good. I feel really really good about what I did. Probably better, more relieved, than I've ever felt. I don't like jail, I really miss being outside and swimming, and I'd like to see how the butterfly house is doing. But ultimately it's not that bad, considering I was able to have this positive outcome, remove six people who lack moral responsibility and would have likely gone on to do more violent things. You have to start somewhere. If a boy hurts you or your friends intentionally, he is going to hurt other people, you have the most intimate, accurate information you would need to act, you shouldn't expect a government that still debates the basic human rights of women in other countries or never passed the Equal Rights Amendment to take care of these things. That's not logical. You must already know this, though. You must have had to do a lot of research for the paper that came out when Wendy's body was found.

Are you okay?

The action I chose had the best return. School is for learning, correcting, and preventing mistakes. If I were to get caught, it would be better if it was for removing several problems in the most instructive way. People tend to think that girls don't or won't do things like this—but there's nothing stopping us, technology makes it so you can address these problems immediately instead of going through a system that doesn't work very well. Right?

There should be a more rational way to think about it, like: Men are generally nice people who live in the world, and it's possible to remove the ones who cause harm, or will in the future, in order to have a better society in which women getting raped and killed isn't entertaining or a cause for political discourse. That's not good for anyone. You know what I mean? It's great that you wrote the things you did. But by the time you are writing about it, it's too late. Plus, they were all there in one place, not expecting it, and not armed.

Nothing ever made me feel quite this responsible. It's okay if I don't ever get out of here. You should probably leave, though. You should probably leave Haeden.

Flynn

AFTER LEAVING HER, I drove out through the countryside with the windows rolled down. It was a warm day, golden buds of leaves crowned the top branches of the maples that lined the narrow winding lanes, and the cold of the recently frozen earth swept into the car from the ditches and gullies flanking the low-shouldered road.

She'd thanked me.

I had everything I needed now.

And nothing.

I didn't know if she would go on to tell Dino this story, if she would wait until her next appearance in court to give the same matter-of-fact explanation. Of course she gave this confession to me. I had a long history of breaking the stories of her achievements. Smiling at her inventions. And that was obviously how she saw it.

How did she know exactly who took or raped or killed Wendy White? The fact was she didn't. She couldn't. And because of mishandled DNA evidence, neither could anyone else who might have made a difference.

I drove into town and parked the car on Main Street, near my office, but didn't get out. I sat and watched the light begin to slant against the buildings. It was close to five-thirty, and I could see people walking from their trucks into the Rooster and the Alibi, musicians carrying fiddle cases, men in paint-splattered Carhart pants headed for happy hour, a group of girls wearing track uniforms walking into Sal's to get pizza, a waitress sitting and smoking on a bench outside the Laundromat.

*   *   *

I had come here wanting to save Haeden and had not been able to save even one woman.

Not until that day.

I went home that night and called my editor at *City Paper,* and she thought I was joking when I asked to be put back on beat. Called Brian and told him me and my boyfriend were coming home. Said I didn't care if Schiller Street was half abandoned again, could he help find us a place.

And then I deleted the interview.

This was how we left Haeden, Tom and I, and a trunk filled with photographs, transcripts, and depositions. I would not stop writing about this. I would not stray again so far from the source of malevolence, the catalyst for each criminal compulsion I'd set out to uncover since J-school. The big "who benefits" at the end of each story that we somehow keep missing in amassing the details. It was not about selling a piece anymore. Or a Polk or a Pulitzer. It was and still is about freedom. Hers and yours and mine.

Like the weapon she used and the lives she took, Alice Piper's confession no longer exists.

Beverly Haytes

APRIL 22, 2009

I HEARD FROM SOMEONE that Bruce threw himself in front of Kyle, and that's why he was the only one who was shot three times and shot in the chest as well as the head. He was trying to protect his friend and his teammate. He was braver than most. That was always true of both my boys.

I can't talk about Brucie. I don't think it would be right.

This is the last picture that was taken of all of them. Look at them. The little bucks. They all got their hair cut like that, the same way, for homecoming.

Jim talked to Alex Dino. He said they're going to see to it there is a full investigation. We just don't know why or how such a thing could ever happen. Alex told Jim it's something about that girl's family being a part of a terrorist cult. They're hiding out here in Haeden, who knows what they got up to in New York City. Well, you saw how the mother always wore black or those strange homemade clothes.

I really can't say a word about Brucie. I will not be able to do it. I can say I will live my life like Brucie lived his, and especially like he lived his on his football team, which was the most important thing to him. Jim read this at his funeral, and this is our family's philosophy and the one thing we know in our hearts our boys and our whole family brought to the world:

> The longer I live, the more I realize the impact of attitude on life. Attitude, to me, is more important than facts. It is more important than the past, than education, than money, than circumstances, than failures, than successes, than

what other people think or say or do. It is more important than appearance, giftedness, or skill. It will make or break a company . . . a church . . . a home. We cannot change our past. We cannot change the fact that people will act in a certain way. We cannot change the inevitable. The only thing we can do is play on the one string we have, and that is our attitude . . . I am convinced that life is 10% what happens to me, and 90% how I react to it. And so it is with you . . . we are in charge of our attitudes.

That quote came from Charles Swindoll, who wrote *Sanctity of Life*. It's such an apt quotation right now, as we are hurting in this way. We had it printed on a thousand prayer cards. I sent one to Dale, down where he's at the parent company. Poor Dale with his heart broken now all over again. It was just too much for him to come home for more grief.

It's a small comfort, at least, to know that to the very end, Brucie was in charge of his attitude, and I am sure he never thought twice about trying to protect Kyle. That's how he was. He was part of the team. And he was my baby. I am proud to have raised him, and I am proud to have had the opportunity to know him. And Jim feels the same. I won't see him dishonored by my self-pity.

You know, his life, as it turns out, was a little like Jesus' life. That's what our pastor said. We allowed the sin of that terrible family to gestate in this community, and Brucie paid for it. Brucie my son, my baby, paid for those sins.

Alice

SHE WOULD TEAR the pages from every book her mother had brought, after reading them. Tear out the pages and fold them into neat squares. Then she would fold the squares into frogs and butterflies and cranes, tossing each one onto the floor beside her bed. This was how she would clear her thoughts, sitting and folding squares and triangles by the dozen. She flicked them through the bars of her cell into Lorelei Ramos's, who unfolded them and read.

"What *is* this shit?" Ramos asked.

"It's a frog."

"No, stupid. From what book is it?"

"I think that was John Berger's *Ways of Seeing*."

"How many you got folded? Don't just dump them around, you should set them up in rows or something, super neat and orderly. That's how they do."

There was no bail set for her, so she could not go home. In Ramos's opinion, there was no getting out, but if she somehow were to do it, now would be the time, because she hadn't had the second psychiatric evaluation, she was just sitting there while whoever her parents hired did whatever they did to free her. There was always a chance of getting out during transport; Lorelei had heard of that kind of shit happening. These tiny town jails were always overcrowded, so eventually, they'd be moved around, moved over to Chemung County, maybe. Other than that, this was her best bet. Lorelei, like Alice, was a strategist. But as she'd explained to Alice, even strategists can make some dumb fucking mistakes if they didn't know what to anticipate.

And Alice might possibly be the stupidest smart person Lorelei had ever known.

"I just don't think there's any evidence that I'm mentally ill," Alice told her.

"No?" Lorelei asked, and sucked her teeth. "You don't think so?"

Alice shook her head. But there was no one to see her do it.

Soon it would be May 1. She wished that there was a table in her cell with a bottle on top that said DRINK ME, like in *Alice in Wonderland*, and then she could drink and fold up like a telescope and walk through the bars, tiny as a mouse. She had not talked to Theo in a week, and any letters they might send would be read. There were things she needed him to bring her. She did a handstand and walked in a circle around her cell. Then leaned on the wall, still upside down, with her heels against the cool cement. She had to do something with her hands soon. She wanted to sew.

She did some push-ups and then rolled herself down slowly into a ball and lay on the floor. Then she did what Lorelei said and began arranging her origami animals around the bars as if they were an audience.

"You'll call them?"

Ramos said, "I'll call them. I'll call them fast, you just make sure you don't make no mistakes. There's a camera anyway, but no guarantee they see it. You really gotta talk gibberish. Not like the way you already do. I mean really fucking crazy. Words that just don't go together at all. But make sure they know you're serious, they got to think you're really going to do it."

"Okay," Alice said. "Thank you."

"Don't fuck up," Lorelei said. "You fuck up, you don't *get* no other chance with this kind of shit."

Alice held on to the bars of her cell and did fifteen pull-ups. She would do it, and then Lorelei would call the guard. And after that, everything Theo would learn would be public information, and hopefully, that would be accurate. He would have to just know her. Know what she intended. There was no other option, really. He would have to go back and replay it all for the subtext, figure out how and where and what she might have needed. He would have to remember their underground river. He would have to remember the wild wood, as she did now. Remember how he always brought her things, magnets and beeswax and army men.

They were both quiet, waiting. Then Lorelei whispered to her, "Piper."

"What?"

"I wanted to tell you before you go . . . that my mother . . ." She faltered. "My mother . . ." She began again but didn't finish the sentence, and Alice could hear in her voice that something had happened that had taken her breath. She said nothing and listened to Lorelei clear her throat a few times. Eventually, the woman said, clearly and quietly, "You did right."

There was a loud echoing buzz and their lights clicked off and they sat in silence in their separate cells. Alice waited for her eyes to adjust. The corridor in front of the cells was dimly lit by one fluorescent bulb.

Alice pulled the sheet off her bed and ripped the corner, tearing one long strip down the side.

"What are you doing?" called Ramos from her cell.

"Nothing."

Alice tore two more strips and began braiding them together. Pulled herself up again against the bars, as high as she could get, and tied the fabric tightly round.

"Pipe Bomb, what the fuck are you doing?"

Alice fashioned a loop and slipknot with the remaining length. She put her head through the noose, standing on her tiptoes.

"Alice," Lorelei whispered. "Stick with the fucking plan."

"No," she said, "I'm doing something better. Permanent." And she hopped lightly, her arms out to her sides, then swung back and down against the bars, and everything went white.

Alice

HAEDEN COUNTY MEDICAL overlooked the river, but the room she was in did not. In the first few minutes before she moved to the new bed, she looked through the blinds and saw only darkness and the lights from the parking lot below. The hospital was thirty miles from the jail, and by the time the ambulance got her there, Gene and Claire were waiting. They looked drawn and pained but seemed relieved at the chance to touch and kiss her. That was before she began to drift again. Alice smelled her home on them, the dirt and baking bread and coffee, and their own smells, something about Claire's face, like honey or apples. Another man in the room asked them to leave, and she opened her eyes to see who it was. A blue uniform but a face she hadn't seen.

She was not restrained, not that she could tell. No plastic handcuffs, nothing on her ankles that she felt, but she couldn't seem to feel anything. Everything was slowed down. Any movement at all took too much time or thought or something it never used to require. She felt like she was watching everything on a screen. She looked at the guard, and he looked tired, too. Claire stood beside Alice, holding her hand. She examined the IV, then looked down and smiled at Alice, brushed back her hair.

"Please," Gene said to the guard, "my wife and I are doctors, if we could just have a moment to see that she's all right."

Alice watched the guard look at them and raise his eyebrows; he released a short dismissive breath. Standing in their shabby clothes in the middle of the night with their criminal daughter, their faces creased from wrinkled sheets, wearing their mud boots.

"No, you know, I'm serious now," Gene said. "I am a medical doctor, and I'd like to stay until she's seen tomorrow."

"I understand that, sir," the guard said. "This is not a patient visitation, though, this is still an incarcerated person in custody. There is medical staff here looking after her, and myself or another officer will be stationed outside this door from now until she goes to the behavioral unit or gets released back to County, okay?"

Claire touched the side of Alice's neck. Alice wondered if her mother could tell how bad she was hurt. She looked at Claire's face and hoped to God that she and Gene would leave.

"I'm sorry, Mom," she said, or thought she said, and began coughing again.

"It's okay, honey," Claire said, but Alice could see the disappointment in her mother's eyes. Claire was afraid of her and afraid of what she'd done to herself, what she might do. It was the opposite of what she wanted. "You got some bruise there. You could have broken your neck."

Then she heard her father say, "I'd just like to talk to the doctor on call tonight."

"Sir, you're welcome to do that; however, I can't have you in here any longer, okay?"

"My daughter is clearly injured and under mental duress. I see no reason why we can't stay with her tonight."

Alice watched the guard give Gene a look of such contempt that she felt the air in the room shift. As if hatred could cause the very space they were in to change, the molecules to rearrange. His face was fleshy and pale, his thin lips were raised at the sides. Alice watched. Were people always like this, showing everything that went on inside them? The guard shook his head slowly, squinting at Gene's audacity. "I'm not going to argue with you, sir, okay? I am here to protect your daughter as much as to prevent her from going somewhere. That's my job, okay? You have a minute now to say your goodbyes." Then he looked away from them and turned on the television, flipping impatiently through the channels while he waited to escort them out.

When Alice turned her gaze from the guard, she realized Gene was standing beside the bed. He leaned down and kissed her on the cheek. His eyes were so blue, and his hair was unkempt—she didn't remember him ever looking like this. The lines on his forehead were deep; his hair, always the same color as hers, now had white and silver strands sticking up amid the blond. He felt the sides of her neck, kissed her again on the forehead. She saw that he was beginning to cry and reached up to touch his face, and he took her hand and held it.

Her mother and father were beautiful, she thought as they stood beside her. She was sorry for them, loved them so much. And she wanted them to leave soon, before she couldn't keep her eyes open anymore. She needed to stay awake, but even as she thought it, she felt slow and heavy in the warm bed with the white sheets.

"She's had an X ray," she heard Claire say. "We'd know if there was going to be pulmonary edema by now. It doesn't look bad. And this drip is certainly going to keep her in one place."

Gene looked at the plastic bag hanging above Alice's head. Her eyes followed his and she watched him wince, then he reached up quickly, almost involuntarily, and twisted something at the top of the clear tube that ended in her forearm. *He's turned it off,* she thought. He looked back down at her and held her gaze, nodding as if to confirm that she hadn't imagined it. She closed her eyes again.

"Listen, baby," Gene told her, tapping her cheek a couple of times and putting his face close to hers. "Listen, listen. Al? Mom and I will see you tomorrow as soon as we can. If your cough gets any worse or you feel confused or like you can't remember things, or if you feel dizzy or jittery, you call the nurse, right?" He nodded at her, squeezed her hand.

"Is there a nurse?"

"Yeah, honey," Claire said. "There's a nurse or an aide who will come. You press the button they showed you. But you're going to be fine, and you need to sleep."

"Okay."

The guard shut her parents out and then placed the remote to the television beside her without saying a word. The room was filled with a diffuse blue light. The ceiling looked far away, and she felt like she was looking down at it.

The guard sipped something from a Styrofoam cup, glanced up at the clock. He had not looked at her once, and she felt like she was a package in the room waiting to be claimed. *She* was something inside her body, and her body was being held there, but it was also holding the thing that she was. Whatever that was. She watched the guard as she began to doze. He was the same as her, a thing inside himself.

When the door shut behind him, she heard it click, and then there was the sound of something—a chair, maybe—being scraped along the floor outside. Tomorrow was May 1. She tried to read *The Wind in the Willows* in her head, remembering the sentences. Tested to see if her memory was sound.

Sometime after Gene and Claire had gone, she didn't know how long, minutes or hours, she began to feel incredible pain in her neck and shoulder, the back of her head. A bad muscle pull, a bruise. She felt the injury, but she also felt awake. Whole again, not a thing inside a thing. Her thoughts turned to what to do with herself. She clearly hadn't needed whatever was in the drip that badly, it had just made it impossible to think or move. Slowly, she tore off the clear tape that held the IV in her arm, then slid the needle out, pulled the hard blue plastic end free from the tubing and jammed it into the mattress.

Minutes, maybe an hour, went by, and she could feel the strain in her neck more intensely. She began to mentally check herself for symptoms, move her hands and feet. She turned her head to the side and felt a sharp pain move somehow from her shoulder to her sinus cavities. Maybe this was what Gene meant by jittery.

It would be very easy for someone in her position to have made a mistake or miscalculation, to have done things irrationally. So she played it back. She did not want to see human beings die. She did not want to leave her home and never come back. She had wanted to do what she was ethically obligated to do under the circumstances. Now she had to complete that obligation. Like she and Lorelei had talked about.

She sat up, swung her feet off the bed. The bathroom was just a few feet away. She walked to it slowly and did not feel dizzy. After peeing, she looked at herself in the mirror to assess the damage. Her neck, chin, and the side of her face were slightly bruised. Not good. Otherwise, she looked fine. She was wearing a blue and white hospital gown and underwear, but there were no shoes in sight, and she had no memory of dressing or undressing. The bathroom offered nothing. Liquid soap, paper towels, a garbage can. There was a drop ceiling and a fluorescent light. She moved slowly back into the dim light of her room, looking at every unhelpful object. The drip hung from a long metal pole with wheels. There was a box of rubber gloves, several locked drawers. Sheets and pillows, window blinds, windows with a small crank in the corner that she supposed could open just a crack. She looked outside and knew which side of the building she was on from all her days working there and following nurses around, thinking about what her parents must have been like when they were practicing, when they were saving lives instead of planting crops. She had wanted to save lives. But it didn't always happen in a hospital.

Alice knew that she was on the fourth floor. She had not been taken up to the behavioral unit, and it wasn't the ICU, by the look of the room, unless it was a room she had never seen—reserved for people who needed supervision outside of the general population—and she thought that was possible. She scanned. A loose floor tile, plastic tubing, the needle that she'd pulled from her arm, accessible lightbulbs, something in the drip bag that killed pain and caused sleep.

She lay back in bed. She knew where the service entrances were, and she mapped them in her head, closed her eyes, and pictured a walk through the hospital from each entrance, then a walk from each floor to every janitorial closet and to the service exit facing the river. She imagined it several times, taking a different elevator and staircase each time, until she had pictured all of them, every closet, every exit, in various combinations.

Who was outside with the guard? If no one, then a pillow and a needle might be all a person needed. A pillow, a needle, a knowledge of anatomy, the powers of invisibility. The same would hold true for calling a nurse. And that would provide her with clothes to wear.

She pictured the drop ceiling in the bathroom: high enough that it could not be reached easily by standing on the toilet. The IV pole could push the tile up and slide it over. Then jump, hang, pull, and a person could be inside the ceiling. A place that was extremely limiting because she would only be able to imagine a map of where things were, not re-create one from memory. But still, a place. Her neck and shoulder hurt, and she focused on the ceiling and breathed slowly. This kind of thinking calmed her like nothing else. Before every meet, before every trapeze trick or project or test or report, for as long as she could remember, she would do this. She would lie in bed and watch several possible futures from beginning to end, before picking one to attempt.

There was always going back. There was no murder weapon.

In a few days she'd be back in court, and things would take time. There were bullets but no weapon. Without a gun or a motive, the case would be difficult to make. There was a canceled check and a missing gun, but those things did not prove anything. She had told Stacy Flynn when she thanked her. But she had done what Lorelei said, gone even further, and could now be considered insane, unreliable. The pain of jail was boredom and confinement and the threat of violence, but that was not real pain, it was something akin to rural life on a different order of magnitude. Something people got through, poor people, real criminals, and political prisoners. Strong and weak, smart and slow, they got through it somehow, but she didn't think she could.

Outside the door, she heard the chair scrape the floor and a low rolling sound.

She heard a woman's voice, indistinct words, no accent but the flat A's and lilt of a question being asked.

"No, no, no," the guard said. "You don't got to worry about that."

The woman's voice again, and she could hear this time that she was whispering, afraid.

"She's been out cold for the last three hours," the guard said. "She won't be up until we want her up. Take your time."

Alice shut her eyes and breathed easily as the metal handle clicked. She did not hear the door shut. The hollow rolling sound passed her, and she heard the bathroom door swing and hit the rubber stop, which reverberated. She opened her eyes to see a square gray bin on wheels a few meters away. The door to her room hadn't been shut, and she could see partway into the hall through the opening and also through the narrow crack at the hinges. She saw the guard's legs and part of his back. Water was running in the bathroom, and she stood quickly and looked into the bin, thrust her hands in and found sheets, flimsy hospital gowns, their ties tangled and wound. It didn't matter who came out of the bathroom or if the guard turned around, it didn't matter anymore if anyone saw her, what could they do to her now?

She saw his legs move. He uncrossed his ankles, drew them in, and stood. It didn't matter. He could come in and it wouldn't matter; she did not have time to get back in bed. She had not picked one of her strategies—she had jumped at any little chance, and now she would pay. She stood perfectly still, peering through the crack where the door was hinged to the wall, and saw the guard walk away from his chair, away from her room. Straight into the hall. Her skin broke out in goose bumps, and she could feel the hair standing up on her body.

She dug quickly through the pile of linen and spotted at last a dirty V-neck scrub shirt. She tore off her gown and put it on. And pants—two sizes too big, at least, and covered in something orange, dye or food. Inside the bathroom, the water was still running. She had no idea what the person inside looked like or wore, but that didn't matter, either. She put the pants on and tied them, rolling the waist over a few times but not enough to expose her bare feet. Then she threw the clothing and sheets back into the bin, pulled a pair of rubber gloves out of the box near the bed, grabbed the pillow and the needle from the mattress, and pushed the bin toward the door. She stuck the needle into the top of the scrub pants. It didn't matter now. Out the door into the bright empty hall. The nurses at the round station did not look up when she went past. She held the pillow in front of her and to the side to cover her bruised neck and jaw. Pushed the bin away from the bathrooms and vending area, rounded the corner to the elevator that was closest to the emergency stairs, and jabbed the button several times. As it arrived, she heard a woman scream, frantically calling to the nurses, calling for the guard, and she pushed the bin and pillow into the elevator and sprinted to the heavy gray door that opened to the emergency stairs, knowing someone must have heard the door shut and the bell of the elevator and that she had just minutes.

She climbed over the painted metal rail, raised her arms above her head, and jumped straight down the narrow center of the stairwell. Falling fast, she caught the rail two flights down. She turned herself around so that her feet rested on the rail, then let go again. Falling another flight, catching herself on the opposite rail and then another until she heard a door open above her and voices, and she slipped back through the bars onto the concrete stairs so she would not be seen. Voices echoed above her, and she ran quickly and silently in her bare feet the last short flight that ended in the basement. She opened the door and walked slowly toward the clock-out station to the left of a service exit that led directly outside and was closest to the river. There were orderlies and cleaning staff in the glassed-in break room, and she walked past them because there was no other way, and she tried to look worn out and happy to be going home for the night. She was in physical pain and figured that couldn't hurt her impersonation of a member of the cleaning staff, and they probably had no idea she was there or who she was, or if they did, it didn't matter anymore. The risk benefit needed to be reconfigured every foot she got closer to the door. If someone tried to stop her now, she would use the needle to buy time. She didn't think the hospital would issue a general alarm. It would terrify the patients. So, calmly, naturally, she pulled a random time card from the slot and pushed it beneath the stamp for the sake of appearance, opened the door, and was hit by a wave of cold night air. She shut the heavy metal door behind her and ran across the sidewalk and down the embankment into a ditch and caught her breath. There were no stars. But the sky was paler than she had expected, and she thought it must be close to four in the morning.

She was in just a little pain. And the flood of adrenaline had cleared her head of the drugs. She was elated and terrified to be outside. She could not see the highway or parking lot from where she lay, but she could hear police sirens. She crouched and looked for the blank black space the river cut into the landscape, and finding it, she ran fast, sprinted, was in flight like in a dream, and then there was no more pain at all, just the occasional shock of a stone beneath her foot. And she ran to the river. The water was freezing, she could barely feel the smooth stones and silty bottom on her numb feet. She walked out until she was waist-deep and then put her head down and swam.

Alice and Theo

ON MAY DAY, beneath the bridge on Rabbit Run Road, Theo stood on the river bank below his car with a backpack. He had everything. Hair dye, a snorkel, an insulated bodysuit for swimming, rope, a knife, a fake driver's license with her picture, her hair Photoshopped black. He had brought a conservative-looking blouse and sweater and skirt. And a black hooded sweatshirt and black spandex pants. He had withdrawn fifteen hundred dollars from his college account, shaved his head, and was wearing colored contacts that made his eyes brown. He had driven all night from the Hudson Valley, and he would take the contacts out and drive all the way back in an hour whether he saw her or not. That was the plan, if he had read her letters right, if he understood *The Wind in the Willows*, if she had not simply lost her mind. That was the plan, and his part was small. Small enough so that he could walk away.

Whether he saw her or not, he knew she'd gotten out. Before leaving campus, he'd read online that she had been taken to the hospital the day before, and he heard it five times on the news driving there. His eyelids drooped, he squinted a little, and suddenly, he saw an eye looking at him from the reeds. Pale clear blue. She was lying in the water, and her body and face were covered with mud and sticks; he realized the thing he had thought was part of a branch was the curve of her bicep. She blinked several times when she knew he'd seen her—looked to the right to show him where to put the bag. But he didn't leave.

He picked up some rocks and threw them out into the river.

And he whistled a few bars of the Woody Guthrie song "Let's Go Riding in the Car." *Let's go riding in the car, car. I'll take you riding in the car.*

He looked down. She shook her head almost imperceptibly. He looked more closely at her. There was something wrong, not just exhaustion or cold. He felt his chest tighten like it might burst. She was waiting for him to walk away.

He threw a few more stones, whipped them hard out into the dark green water.

She was staring up at him. Her blue eye so clear, exposed. Now that he had gotten used to where she was, he was afraid she would easily be seen.

She whistled the first six bars of "Peter and the Wolf" so quietly. It was time for him to do the catch. Let go of the bar. Drop the bag. Drive away.

Her heart was pounding in terror every second he stayed, but she continued to stare at him. Looking for the place in his eye to enter, to tell him that she loved him. She received his fear, took in the way he was moving.

Then she just looked at him with pleasure, regarded his beauty. His wide shoulders and long strong arms and legs, the way his jeans fit. His chest, the curve of his jaw, his lips.

This relaxed her. They were frightened, but they were doing this. They were not too frightened to live or to live with what had happened. But they were frightened.

She whistled it again, knowing that it was dangerous now. He looked up and down the riverbank—no one around for miles. But then he hadn't seen her, either, at first. Anyone could be looking at him, at them. He experienced a moment of complete dislocation from his body, felt that he was not there. Then looked at her again, covered with mud and sticks and brush, and knew she must have been there for hours. He was glad it wasn't as cold as the week before. He set the bag down in the low honeysuckle hedges.

She blinked several times in acknowledgment. The shape of her eye arced in a smile.

And then he smiled. Stood for a moment as the first rays of sun began to shine out across the river and move, reflected red as blood on its surface. Then he walked up the embankment and back to the car to wait.

Constant

THERE WAS NO comfort in the familiarity of the house or the green of the garden or the stillness of the barn. The place rang with Alice's presence and with fear and collective ill will from the town. Days before, news helicopters had circled the property, hovering above Gene and Claire's and then Ross's compound. And last week, while still in the city, Con had seen a photograph in the *Times* of the inside of the barn—the trapeze and paintings—which meant someone had been in there without Gene and Claire knowing and found or taken God knows what.

Since Con and Michelle had arrived two days ago, Claire had not left the bedroom. She hadn't spoken to any of them, and it was unnerving. He was thankful to have something to do in helping them, because it helped combat his own shock. And though he was filled with pity, he also had to fight his baser feelings of rage at Gene. Con knew it was not rational to be hating his best friend, broken as he was, but he did at that moment. Hated him for the life he'd given Alice, brought her up to live like a colonialist, the new agrarian blind. Thinking the work to be done is in feeding your immediate family and a dozen acquaintances with artisanal food. Eating heirloom tomatoes in hell, like some kind of undead things subsisting near the River Lethe. Gene's big dream of changing what people grew was already realized in New York—the towering Whole Foods on Houston Street with the chalk sign reading ARE YOU HUNGRY? facing a park filled with homeless people. Doctors and lawyers and hipsters and losers with rooftop gardens and the Union Square farmers' market selling pork chops from rare pig breeds, two for thirty dollars.

And at the front of this movement were those who branched out to colonize the cheap fields of the hinterland. Gene and Claire and him—he bought the property, introduced them to Ross.

What had they hoped would happen? That the whole town would change? The whole town had changed now. He was trying not to be angry, but it was too much. And he could end up taking the kind of fall you read about. Him with his dark skin, him with the birthday money, the doting uncle, the summer visits.

Con had set things up with a lawyer for all of them. Left New York, left work, contacted friends in Montreal, looked into the possibility of placement for all of them with Doctors Without Borders. It was as if all the work he had done his whole life would now bankroll some soft exit or lengthy trials and civil suits. His own contradictory ideologies had come to their natural conclusion. Alice was free somewhere, he was sure of that, and he would not let them be arrested. If there was one thing he could do after all she had done, it was to make sure they were not charged with anything. Not charged with conspiracy.

Michelle was packing Alice's things, everything that hadn't been sealed in plastic bags and taken out of the house by the police. But mostly, Michelle was there to sit with Claire.

Con had gone through the house and barn, collecting books to take to the county dump: *The Revolution of Everyday Life, Endgame, Running on Emptiness, Against Civilization, The Temporary Autonomous Zone, The Betrayal of the Self, Future Primitive, Soon All This Will Be Picturesque Ruins*. He picked up Berkman's *Prison Memoirs* and threw it in the box filled with these kinds of titles, all of them comprising an awful commentary. Con had been planning to throw out the books or burn them, but it didn't matter anymore. His stomach felt hollow, and he knew that he was in shock, in a kind of controlled panic. In some ways, it didn't feel all that different from sitting in the boardroom at Pharmethik. Rage. Panic. A thing snowballing.

Con took the box of books and set it on the kitchen table.

"What are you doing, Connie?" Gene asked him softly. "Packing things up nice and neat for the feds?"

"Brother," Con said, keeping his voice low and steady, looking at his friend's face. Gene was pale, and his eyes were swollen and bloodshot. "I know we are more upset than we can even feel right now, but we can't be stupid for the next few weeks—continue to be stupid. I think our choices are very limited at this point. I've bailed out Ross, who is completely fucked, and we have now been interviewed enough by the local police to have real cause for concern. I can assure you, this is not the end. They will find things, no matter how circumstantial or academic they seem to us, and they will find reasons to have us all arrested, and very very shortly."

"Honestly," Gene told him, "the reasons aren't circumstantial. We know who we are in this place." Constant struggled to nod and stay silent, and then Gene pulled a worn paperback out of the box, opening it randomly and reading to himself for a minute before reading it out loud. "'Behind us far over the walls of the arena the vague notes of the band begin again and float like banners across the hot sky. Meat. Blood. Memory. War. We rise to greet the State, to confront the State. Smell the flowers while you can.'"

Con had nothing to say. Only his friend's grief prevented him from taking the book out of his hands and tearing it to pieces. Eating the fucking pages. None of this shit mattered one bit anymore! Meat. Blood. Memory. War. No shit. What kind of a moron was Gene Piper?

It was simply a description of their lives. Con's especially. Looking away, or maybe looking directly at all of them and at everything, every little detail for far *far* too long, until all the pain that he had understood, that he had never revealed, never acted upon, had created what felt like an inevitable moment. A moment he couldn't prevent now, no matter what—a moment he created with a fucking birthday present. It might have only hap-

pened faster if he'd been living there in the first place. Or maybe
it never would have happened at all. As he stood and looked at
Gene, his rage subsided, and he felt he might cry but didn't know
if it was from relief. It didn't matter anymore if he understood
anything or not. He was moving again in a way that required
precise thinking and acting. He knew what she had done, and he
knew how fucking brave it was, and it had set him free and might
also send him to jail.

Who, apart from Con and Alice, had been close enough to the
state to pass, to be considered a leader, considered one of them?
She may have looked exactly like Gene, but in this way, she was
Con's daughter and no one else's. And he wasn't about to let her
down, let her parents go to jail. Enough of the bullshit. They
could reflect on it when they got to Montreal.

Gene tossed the book back into the box and looked up at
Con, and when he saw his friend's eyes, so much like Alice's, his
thoughts stopped racing. A somersault in his stomach, a breath-
lessness. It came like a wave. He'd thought he was feeling rage,
but really, it was the last surge of denial before desolation, and
it was breaking, fast, to fall upon them all. The baby he and Michelle had delivered, their little girl, their friend, with her voice
and her laugh and her new questions, her drawings and ideas, her
sweetness, her incredible sweetness, was gone, and their dream
and their house and the life they'd loved was gone, too.

Michelle came out of the bedroom. Her face was drawn and
swollen from crying. "She's talking," she said. "I've written a
script for Xanax. I'm going to drive into Elmville and pick it up."

"Try to be back soon," Con told her. "I'd like to get us all out
of here by three o'clock."

She kissed him as she pulled keys from her bag, and he felt the
heat of her face and tasted salt.

"No. No," Gene said. "Fuck! If they had let us stay with her
in the hospital all night, she would still be here, and we would
know if she was okay. We'll never be able to go anywhere now!

People will think we're meeting her somewhere." His voice broke, and Con came forward to put his hands on his shoulders. "I don't want to go anywhere. What if she comes home? Oh my God oh my God," he whispered. "My God." He wept. "Please let her be safe, let her be safe. I don't care what she's done."

Flynn

FROM WHERE I sat, I could see the orange light shining on the windows and illuminating the bricks on the building across the street. People were coming and going from the art gallery next door that used to be an old slaughterhouse. Dressed up in formal strangeness, standing out front smoking. There must have been another opening. I watched a woman walk across the street wearing high boots and a poncho made entirely out of small flame-shaped white lightbulbs. My apartment is two blocks from where my old apartment was and twice as big, has a better view of the street.

From the other room, I could hear the scanner, a set of tones, and then cops talking back and forth in numbers and street names.

I shut my laptop and sat watching the pigeons, watching the fading light turning pink and bright as it fell across the buildings, cutting sharp and dark shadows into the brick. I listened to the people from the gallery talking and bringing things onto the loading dock. Someone sang the first verse of an old Velvet Underground song, and then there were kids shouting as they rode by on bikes.

"Hey! Hey! What's that?"

"It's art. You wanna come to our show? Actually, wait. You want to do us a favor? I'll give you five bucks if you ride around and give people these cards."

"Five bucks? Nigga, please."

"Were you raised by a drag queen? Because nobody says 'Nigga, please.'"

"No skinny-ass Chinese guy doesn't, maybe."

"FYI, I'm Korean. Are you guys going to do it or what? Five bucks and you can come eat at the opening, too."

"Well, FYI, you got those mini hot dogs like last time? 'Cause that shit was good."

"Yeah."

I watched the kids ride up onto the loading dock. There was a click, and the static of the scanner stopped, and I felt the icy bottle against my neck, looked up to see him smiling down at me, Cutting, wearing a T-shirt and his blue uniform pants. I took the beer from him and leaned my head on his stomach for a minute and he put his palm against my ear.

"Thanks, baby," I said.

"Dinner's ready."

I stood and linked my fingers into the belt loop of his pants and we touched the lips of our bottles together, then spilled a drop on the floor, in honor of the dead.

Epilogue

Alice

I DIDN'T HAVE THE balance I thought I did before we moved here. I was strong and my timing was good. But I did not have what Theo gives me.

The mystery of Theo is how present he is. A counterweight. He's not meant to let go or walk away. He is too slow to do what I did, too grounded to walk away. We could not be happy now if he had left me in the mud to swim some fantasy of connecting rivers, trying to slip my way here unseen and alone.

Under this beach and under this salt, there is a city, the remains of concrete, a sidewalk. Rising out of the sand and extending into the distance are partially strung telephone poles, lining streets that don't exist. This is the ghost grid. This is all the power that is left to light our trailer and to light our way down to the water.

When we have a child, we will tell her about this concrete beneath the sand. That beneath the beach, there are paving stones. We will show her that it's real. That it's part of a world that couldn't last. A world that finally got flipped right side up. We'll walk together beside the water and read together in the evenings. We will plant a new garden. And when night comes down upon us and up all around us, we will be there. Wide awake to greet it.

Acknowledgments

Thanks most of all to Eli Ben-Yaacov, whose love, intelligence, and sense of humor made it possible for me to write. Infinite solidarity and gratitude to Annia Ciezadlo, who was there when the story broke. I am very lucky to have my editor, Sarah Knight, and agent, Rebecca Friedman, two of the smartest, toughest girls I know. I'm indebted to my friends Annie and Harley Campbell for taking me in and predicting the future, to Rebecca Barry for her friendship and close reading, and to the radical saints; Joseph Schmidbauer, Rachel Pollack, Jan Clausen, Charles Hale, and Matthew Borrelli. Thanks to Daniel Stackman and Jacob Kotler for unplugging their amp, putting down their drumsticks, and leaving my apartment. Thanks to Glenn Hoffman. And to Mick Kubiak, Ann Godwin, Michelle Novak, Alexandra Underhill, Steve Friedman, Derek Owens, Jamie Newman, Mike Brutvan, Alexis Santi, Alexis Kahn, Cecelia Kristof, Ami Ben-Yaacov, John Fuchs, Jon Frankel, Jaime Bailey, Emily Goldman, Sonia Simioni, Candace Welch, Lisa Ford, Bruce Need, Cody Cook, Ellen Klein, Milagros Cartagena, Storn Cook, Spencer Sunshine, and Miranda Rice. I want to acknowledge my family, especially my mother, father, stepfather, and brother John, for always believing in my work.

HANNAH PITTARD

The Fates Will Find Their Way

Sixteen-year-old Nora Lindell is missing. And the neighbour-hood boys she's left behind are caught forever in the heady current of her absence.

As the days and years pile up, the mystery of her disappearance grows kaleidoscopically. A collection of rumours, divergent suspicions, and tantalising what-ifs, Nora Lindell's story is a shadowy projection of teenage lust, friendship, reverence, and regret, captured magically in the voice of the boys who still long for her.

Far more eager to imagine Nora's fate than to scrutinise their own, the boys sleepwalk into an adulthood of jobs, marriages, families, homes and daughters of their own, all the while pining for a girl – and a life – that no longer exists, except in the imagination.

'Forcibly reminiscent of Jeffrey Eugenides's hit The Virgin Suicides ... this deeply readable novel concerns itself with mysteries that are at once more mundane and more profound – innocence, longing, the winding journey to adulthood'
DAILY MAIL

'The tone is wistful, lustful, gossipy, guilty ... undoubtedly a writer to watch'
GUARDIAN

'A startling piece of work ... an unflinching account of the dark undercurrents of youthful sexuality'
OBSERVER

RAY ROBINSON

Forgetting Zoë

Zoë Nielsen was just like any other ten-year-old walking to school, not knowing that a chance encounter with Thurman Hayes would lead to her abduction and imprisonment in a converted nuclear bunker, 4,000 miles away, beneath a remote ranch house in Arizona. Enslaved in her underground tomb, deprived of food and light and water, the girl Zoë once was steadily begins to disappear ... But over time Thurman grows tired of the rapidly maturing Zoë, and when he decides it is time to get rid of her, Zoë must finally make her bid for freedom.

Forgetting Zoë is a moving, epic tale of courage, survival, horror and loss, that explores how a bond of affection and intimacy can develop between captive and captor.

'A novel which will be hard to forget'
OBSERVER

'So dark, so twisted but so good ... Horrified as you'll be, you won't be able to put it down'
EASY LIVING

'An uncompromising novel of alarming power ... one would have to look to Crace's Being Dead to recall a British novel as convincing and as calmly aware of its own menace'
IRISH TIMES

ANNA QUINDLEN

Every Last One

'Engrossing . . . spellbinding'
NEW YORK TIMES

The Lathams seem to have it all: health, wealth and a vibrant family life. As Mary Beth Latham contemplates a life built around home, friends and community, she has every reason to feel fulfilled and content.

Then, for one of her sons, a process of unravelling begins. Mary Beth starts to focus on him, only to find that the comfortable life she has spent years carefully constructing is shattered in a single moment. Forced to confront her own demons, Mary Beth realises how the inconsequential moments we all share – and one shameful act she has hidden from everybody – may have contributed to her fate.

Every Last One is a mesmerising and devastating portrait of family life, and a testament to the power of a mother's love and determination. It is Anna Quindlen's finest work to date.

'*A breathtaking novel. Quindlen writes superbly about families, grief and betrayal. I was completely mesmerised by this book and Mary Beth and the Latham family will stay with me for a long time to come*'
LISA JEWELL

'*Moves, in the turn of a page, from cosy, slow-burning American pastoral to the gripping stuff of nightmares*'
GUARDIAN

AIMEE BENDER

The Particular Sadness of Lemon Cake

THE NEW YORK TIMES BESTSELLER

On the eve of her ninth birthday, Rose Edelstein bites into her
mother's homemade lemon-chocolate cake and discovers she
has a magical gift: she can taste her mother's emotions in the
slice. All at once her cheerful, can-do mother tastes of despair
and desperation. Suddenly, and for the rest of her life, food
becomes perilous. Anything can be revealed at any meal.

Rose's gift forces her to confront the truth behind her family's
emotions - her mother's sadness, her father's detachment and her
brother's clash with the world. But as Rose grows up, she learns
that there are some secrets even her taste buds cannot discern.

The Particular Sadness of Lemon Cake is about the pain of loving those
whom you know too much about, and the secrets that exist
within every family. At once profound, funny, wise and sad,
this is a novel to savour.